D0122175

How to Marry Keanu Reeves in 90 Days

How to Marry Keanu Reeves in 90 Days

K.M. Jackson

FOREVER

New York Boston

Copyright © 2021 by Kwana Jackson

Cover design by Daniela Medina and Sabrina Flemming
Image references courtesy of Jasmine Martin; Shutterstock
Cover copyright © 2021 by Hachette Book Group, Inc.

Forever
Hachette Book Group
1290 Avenue of the Americas, New York, NY 10104

Forever is an imprint of Grand Central Publishing. The Forever name and logo are trademarks of Hachette Book Group, Inc.

The publisher is not responsible for websites (or their content) that are not owned by the publisher.

ISBN: 978-1-63910-157-3

Printed in the United States of America

For Will
These years with you have been the
most excellent adventure.

❧

And
for Keanu & crew:
some mentioned here, and many more in my heart,
thank you for bringing much needed smiles when at
times all we could see were our masks.

CYBER PUNKED

BETHANY LU

People always looked at me like I was half crazy. Made me feel like the odd girl out, but not True. Never True.

I guess that was why when he'd said I'd gone mad—or maybe the word he'd used was *insane*—this time I took it to heart. Sort of. Okay, fine. So I may have only briefly paused to give his reaction to my plan a smidge of consideration before continuing my full-steam-ahead charge.

But he had to understand, life was happening. The world was still spinning, even if it felt like mine had stopped. Once again.

Or maybe I wanted it to stop. I didn't know. But that part didn't matter, did it? Does it?

What mattered was that True got me. That he had

me. That he understood, that he'd still be there for me, be my friend. Bring me back from the edge. Like before. Like always.

Besides, True always knew it was Keanu or nothing for me.

CHAPTER 1

BREAK POINT

BETHANY LU

89 days ago

> **BREAKING: The sky isn't falling, but pre-
> pare for the storm! Keanu Reeves is tying
> the knot in 90 days! America's favorite
> boyfriend is a boyfriend no more...**

I heard something go *pop* in my ear, like a burst balloon, and suddenly felt dizzy. Time seemed to stop and do a weird sort of axis shift. It was almost as if I was floating— and not in the good "I don't want this buzz to wear off" way, but the "Crap! Somebody stop this ride. I'm about to throw up, so let me the hell off. Now!" way.

I could see myself in the spot where it all was happening, strangely outside my body, looking in like a spectator on the drama that was my life. There was me, Dawn and, of course, True—the three of us gathered as was usual for a Saturday in my West Harlem loft. On my worktable, lit by the sun streaming through the skylight, was my latest not-quite masterpiece, still in its rough form on canvas. Faint washes of color and fabric swatches with torn news clippings waited to be set into place. But the project was currently pushed to the side to make room for the fresh bagels True had brought in with him after his morning run.

Moments before, everything had been normal, each of us talking over one another as we stuffed our faces with carbs and cream cheesy goodness and drank enough coffee to keep a triple shift of ER interns alert.

But now here I was, clutching the edge of the worktable with one hand while holding tight to my phone with the other as I stared at the screen in disbelief. This had to be a joke. Probably a stunt or a promo tweet. I swallowed. Well, I attempted to, but the dry lump that had materialized out of nowhere wouldn't go down my throat. I scanned the nonsensical tweet again and told myself it was just that: No. Sense. Nonsense. Clickbait. It had to be. Keanu was the bait, but I wasn't going in for the click. No freaking way.

Sweat popped out along my brow, defying the comfortable air-conditioned temperature in my loft as I tried to resist the temptation of those three dots at the end of the tweet. Clicky little enticements, just messing my head up with silent little whispers of *Come on, you know you wanna know.*

My fingers practically twitched. I think maybe my hand was even slightly shaking. But I couldn't click. Clicking would only lead to doom.

If I clicked, I'd either (a) look like an ass and have my feed clogged with ads for whatever these evildoers were pushing for the next month—most likely some dating app or other such crap to highlight why I shouldn't be happy in my current perfect singledom status. Or (b) it would lead me to the supremely unlikely realization that the story was true and—horrors—Keanu was actually getting married, which also meant that life as we knew it to be would essentially cease to exist in ninety days.

Either outcome would be a disaster, and it seemed the only mentally stabilizing way out was smashing my phone to bits.

It was then I heard a clap, followed by the snap of fingers way too close to my face.

Wait. Was someone shaking me? And now they were hitting me on the back. Holy roughness! The hell?!

I blinked. True was standing in front of me.

Sweet, sweet True. My anchor and life preserver all in one.

He was wiping at my mouth. Shit, had I been drooling? Still, a napkin would have been nice in this moment because (a) germs, and (b) his thumb swiping across my bottom lip was hitting too hard on my sexual sensory buttons, even through my shocked stupor.

I scrunched up my face and pulled back a notch, still not enough to get out of his close range. Eep, his face was practically on top of mine. His big brown eyes clouded with worry. And I couldn't help noticing his full lips were drawn tight to the point of looking pained. Oddly, though, all these facial expressions made him somehow even more handsome, with the scruff on his chin extra scruffy, not hiding his dimples. It was quite unnerving, and slightly panty quivering. Not that I'd ever tell him that.

"Lu! Lu! Bethany Lu!"

Oh, damn. True was going in with my full government name. Something he only did when really riled up. He snapped his fingers again and reached out, putting his hands on my forearms, like he was about to give me another shake. Time to bring the brain back to earth. Lucky for me, Morphie did most of my heavy lifting and broke the scene apart with an ear-piercing, squeaky bark.

I glared at True as I pushed down on his hands, and he immediately backed up a step. "What are you doing?" I snapped at the same time Morphie nipped at True's worn New Balances. *Good dog.* It was so unlike my mini beagle to come off his lazy little high horse and put effort into anything that I got a swell of pride seeing those brown ears flop around on account of me.

But True being True and those old sneakers being damn near bulletproof, it seemed he'd hardly felt a thing from Morph's valiant efforts. Instead, he ignored poor Morphie and his spectacular show of chivalry and kept his focus on me. "What am I doing?" His voice mimicked the disbelief in his eyes. "That's what I should be asking you. At first, I thought you were choking on a piece of bagel, the way it looked like you lost your breath, but then you started zoning out, looking at your phone like one of the Walking Dead, mumbling about ninety days."

Well shit, I hadn't even realized I was thinking out loud. I coughed, then attempted something between a laugh and a growl. "Grrr."

True stared at me deadpan.

"You and your zombies," I said. "Don't worry, I'm not gonna eat your brain. It's probably unseasoned anyways."

His only reaction to my joke was a blink and the tiniest nostril flare letting me know the comment didn't pass his hearing.

I felt my lips twist. Bet he wouldn't have been all stoic and unreactive if I had licked his damn thumb like I'd been contemplating a moment before. Bet that would have gotten more than the flare of a nostril. I sighed, knowing I'd keep all thoughts of tongue licking to myself. I could joke and tease about a lot, but licking True's um . . . extremities . . . that was definitely off-limits. Forever.

Besides, the impulse was probably just a direct result of being cooped up in my loft too long and letting my double-A battery supply run low. "And speaking of," I said, though no one was speaking of anything of the sort, but I had to get my mind off licking and batteries. "What's with you and those old sneakers? Didn't I give you a new pair not long ago?" I pointed at his feet. "How those are still functioning I'll never know. They're so worn and dirty you could give my dog an infection. The least you could have done is changed them before you came upstairs from your apartment."

True lived in the same building, down in 4B. My father owned the property and had given us both a nice deal.

He looked down, then back at me like I'd grown another head. "So now my sneakers aren't good enough for your little penthouse, Ms. 10A? Should I have showered before I came or just dropped off your brunch at the door?"

"You know I didn't mean it like that."

True's left brow quirked. "Sure. Besides, these are fine. They still have some miles left in them."

I snorted. "Miles? They're practically running by themselves at this point."

He stared at me. I stared back. This was us. Standing off. Doing what we do.

"So you're good?" This question came from Dawn, breaking our little stare down and leaving us in a draw. "Can I take my finger off the 911 speed dial because for a minute there you had a sister damn near fretting, but since we're only talking sneakers and the Walking Dead, I'll cancel the red alert." Dawn was looking at me with a high level of impatience. She waved her phone in my direction and then across my worktable. "I don't know what gets into you, Lu. One minute you're normal"—she let a heavy pause rest here before continuing—"-ish, talking business, schedules and your work, and the next you're who knows where."

"I'm fine! It's no big deal. Well, probably no big deal," I said, looking back at my phone.

Dawn raised an eyebrow while I shot back with narrowed eyes plus a "seriously, stand down" silent gesture. This only caused her to grimace at me more intensely, in that moment flipping between her dual roles of my art agent and best friend since high school.

Actually, me, Dawn and True have been connected since high school. Not the trio we are now but more of a clunky quartet, brought together by time and circumstance.

Dawn shrugged and traded her phone for a cheese bagel with extra cream cheese. The handmade bagels from the place on Broadway and 94th were her weekly carb indulgence. Even with my near freak-out she wasn't missing out on this. Hell, I should be thankful she even slowed down. Dawn despised deprivation, so my manic panic would have to get put on hold. "You sure, you're fine?" she asked through a mouthful of dough and cream cheese. Her eyes shifting from my artwork laid out on the table then back to my face.

I nodded, then looked back at my work. The mass of color, torn paper and fabric now hardly made any sense to me.

I felt my lips go tight. I wasn't fine. Not by a long shot.

Keanu Reeves was getting married.

CHAPTER 2

SILVER SPOONS

BETHANY LU

This is fake, right? There's no way it can be true." I pushed my phone toward Dawn. She had been going on about my upcoming schedule and asking when I thought my next batch of canvases would be done.

"What?" Dawn took the phone from my hand, her touch surprisingly gentle. Not the brisk way she usually had. Not that I'm saying my friend was in any way rude or snatchy, but gentle wasn't generally her style either. Between Dawn going in with the soft touch and True with my full name, I must have put them both in a panic for a minute there.

Dawn glanced at my phone, and her eyes went wide. There was a brief flash of alarm, and I could guess exactly how she felt. Was she cold? Did her insides recoil and twist inside themselves?

"No way. And in ninety days? This is bullshit. It sounds like they are pulling from that reality show."

"Right?" I said, agreeing with her. Thank goodness for Dawn. I could always count on her when it came to seeing things my way. "That's what I thought." I laughed. It may have come out slightly hysterical. "He'd never do that. Not to us. Not to me. Not to the world. Also, that show is crazy pants."

"In the best way," Dawn interjected. She shook her head and handed me back my phone. "Nah. Definitely not. This really is bullshit. Keanu wouldn't do it, hon." She went from riled back down to soft and gentle again, amping my anxiety. It was as if she were talking to a small child or someone praying in the waiting area of an ICU surgery center. Fuck. Could it be Dawn thought there was some truth to this tweet?

I tried hard to look beyond her wall of defense. Through to the bond of our almost thirty-year friendship. We connected, she and I, in a way that no one else on the planet ever had and I suspected ever would. Well, all except True, but he was different. You know, given he had a penis and all, and the fact that he was, I don't know, just...True.

Dawn tapped at her phone, then looked at me, the placating tone now laced with an edge of anger. "Actually, I'm low-key pissed at whoever on the PR team thought it was a good idea to release this news. Ninety days my ass. Are they putting us all on some sort of fan-flail doomsday countdown clock? Just do it if you're ready, or get engaged and be quiet about it. We'll find out when they are on the cover of *People* like everybody else or when *TMZ* releases the telephoto shots. It's not like he's a royal. Damn!" She shook her head as she turned up her lip and placed her phone back on the edge of the worktable, careful not to put it where it would get paint or glue on it.

She glared at the phone. "Keanu is never getting married. He'd never settle down and make just one woman, man, person . . . ferret, that happy while ruining the lives of the rest of the world. I have a right mind to make a complaint."

"I agree with you, but where would you even start?"

She shook her head and gave me slightly overconfident "trust me" eyes, which I'd learned from all our years of near misses, whoops and almost-had-its not to trust all that much. But with the glint she had going on, I half expected her to go protesting at some PR firm in a stunning vintage '70s designer outfit, signage in hand, shouting about how someone must pay for these grievous misdeeds.

True let out a groan, as Dawn and I swiveled toward him in unison.

"Seriously? This is what your whole zone-out was about? Damned Keanu Reeves?" He took a step back. Lucky for him, just out of my arm's reach.

"Watch it with the blasphemy, mister."

He hit me with an eye roll and a sigh before rubbing his short nails over his close-cropped curls. "I can't with you, Lu," he said, before shifting to Dawn. "You either. The fact that you fall right in, entertaining her mess, makes you just as bad."

Dawn gasped. "Bad? The hell you say!" She scrunched up her nose and her mouth went wide with feigned shock. "I don't know what you're getting on me for, Truman Erickson, you giant soggy blanket."

"That part," I added. "Just because you're grown, don't think you're grown-grown."

True's eyes went back and forth between the two of us in silent irritation. I could almost see words being swallowed back down his throat, and I opened my mouth to argue against them. But this wasn't the time to fall into one of our bickering spirals. This was serious.

The fear had my stomach knotting up. I reached for my phone, then paused. True was right. As much as I hated to admit it. Dammit, True was right.

What the hell was I panicking for? And Dawn was right too. It had to be fake. Keanu would never be tied down. He was a free spirit. He was *the* free spirit.

And so was I—grown-ass, forty-plus fangirl that I was. There was no reason to be afraid. I was fine. I smiled and fought to slow my heart rate.

Quick Lu, think of something calming! But shit, the meditation app I'd sworn I'd listen to every day had lasted less than a week. The pressure of daily relaxation was too stressful. Now all I had was a monthly bill because I kept forgetting to cancel the stupid subscription in the app store. Besides, if I did cancel, that would mean giving up on meditating and therefore admitting defeat. *And Carlisles don't give up. We see things through. Till the end.*

I looked over to the far corner of the loft and sighed. I had set up the perfect tranquil space with a cool-ass altar and tufted pillow to get my meditation on. So what if Morphie had co-opted it?

"Look, you've got to relax. There is no need for you to get

all worked up over a bit of poorly placed celebrity gossip," Dawn said.

True let out a grunt as if agreeing to this as his phone buzzed low from his pocket, indicating a text.

"Hey, tell your T and Ai-meeee, you're busy. We have a crisis over here," Dawn continued.

"Is that what you're calling it?" True quipped back.

The inner twelve-year-old in me had to suppress a chuckle over Dawn's jibe as I piled on top. "Yeah, isn't the semester over, Professor Hottie McHottieson? Can't she ease up a bit now?"

True frowned at his phone, but I'm sure the face was really meant for me.

His teacher's assistant Aimee was into him big-time. Though he liked to annoyingly put on as if he didn't know it. Fact was, True acted as if he didn't know a good percentage of the students who took his economics and world studies class were into him. As if. For all his brilliance, at times the man didn't have a clue about how sexy his "I don't have the time to be concerned about mundane things like metro male grooming because I'm too busy thinking on higher pursuits" vibe made him.

"I swear you two have a combined age of twenty-four," he grit out as he tapped at his phone.

Dawn and I looked at each other and shrugged. "I would have accepted anything under fifty combined, so this is a win in my book," she said.

True shook his head as he picked up his mug. It was the one he usually used at my place, simple white on which I'd painted a bent spoon and the words THERE IS NO SPOON in block letters. He knew good and well it was a homage to a scene from *The Matrix*, and if he had trouble with my fan-girling or bouts of immaturity, he could have just as easily brought one of his own plain mugs up from his place.

True took his Matrix mug and his text convo with Ai-meee and headed to the far side of the kitchen island. I guess out of firing distance of me and Dawn for a little privacy. I didn't blame him, but still, it grated a bit. His nimble thumbs tapped along his screen before he paused, placed the phone down and picked up another bagel from the bag of leftovers on the island.

Like Dawn, he always had at least two bagels, and with all his running he didn't even have to worry about the carbs. And unlike me, True claimed his runs were a form of daily stress relief and enjoyment. The concept seemed ridiculous, no matter how many times he'd tried to explain it. He'd do better trying to get me to understand market conversions by country and rates of fluctuations. It didn't matter, though. True's tall, lanky but muscular frame could support one bagel or three.

Still, by the almost beastly way he tore into the poor everything bagel, I had a feeling that he was stuffing his mouth to clamp down on comments to Dawn and me he thought were better left unsaid. It was one of the deflection tactics he'd honed after years of being caught in the cross-fire of our mini rants. At least that was what my WHET app had taught me—aka Women's Health Empowerment Therapy—which was the app I *did* more religiously keep up with, not only for its cutting-edge sex talk and vibrator dis-counts but the fact that they had certified therapists writing pretty solid takes on their blog. But here it was again; I was going off the rails and the topic. Maybe I needed to check in on the app a little more frequently.

"Oh, let the soggy blanket sulk," Dawn said, as if she could see inside my head.

Dawn and I have been arm-in-arm BFFs since we first met as freshmen at Forresters Academy, an exclusive private high school just outside of Manhattan. Forresters was and still is a who's who of New York's second-tier rich progressives' kids. Those who were not A-listers, old money, ultra-wealthy, library donor types. We were the class of new money, the start-ups or perhaps second cousins of the A-listers who had to work management that kept the old money moving.

My father happened to be one of the new money movers. And he was so good as a private equity investor that the name Carlisle could just about open any A-list door. Money was funny like that.

But lucky us—not—we were C-list all day. Sure, on a good day we could pull off B-list, on account of being upwardly mobile and, in many folks' eyes, uppity Black and not where we belonged—a myth my mother loved to clap back on whenever she got the chance.

That myth is part of how we'd ended up at Forresters. My mother getting "mistaken" for a nanny at my old school's pickup one time too many. There were only so many straws before a camel's back broke or a Black mother had had enough with the bullshit and went off. And that was what happened at my private middle school before I was sent to Forresters.

I remember the day clearly, coming out of the exit on the quiet, tree-lined Upper East Side street just off Fifth Avenue where our school was. Right off Museum Mile. We were supposed to be the elites. Tourists even stopped to get glimpses of us looking so unbothered and upper-class New York chic in our navy, burgundy and tan uniforms. But there was my mother, blaring at Trishna Greenberg's mom, "You think I'm the nanny? What nanny wears Patrick Kelly and Chanel to a pickup?"

I was mortified. Though she had a point. Still, it didn't stop me from wanting one of the sidewalk cracks to open up and devour me whole. All the kids were staring like we were some sort of aberration, a strange wonder to behold. They always looked at her like that. The same way they looked at me when they spared me a glance. Once again, I wondered why couldn't she just blend. Why couldn't she be inconspicuous like the other moms in the latest Ralph Lauren getup? Or better yet, not pick me up at all?

God. I was a shit daughter even back then.

But it wasn't the slights to my mom or my second-hand embarrassment that got me to Forresters. It was the incident. The one where the new math teacher swore that I cheated off Felicity Mathis instead of the other way around. That was the final straw.

My mother could take a lot, explode and then move on, but my father wouldn't give a penny to an institution that questioned our honor. Even though I was never a math whiz like my brother, Dad never questioned me or asked if I'd cheated. He never asked for an explanation. He only said that my overpriced school would miss our money and be sorry when another school had it.

I was glad to be done of it, already on my four-year countdown to graduation and art school in Paris or London and all the things I dreamt about when I wasn't trying to disappear into the wall cracks.

But once I got to Forresters and after meeting Dawn, I lost that rush to fly away, and even the need to fade into the paint started to dissipate. Suddenly I wasn't so alone. Finally, I wasn't the only brown girl in my class. Of course, Forresters was still expensive (i.e., exclusive; i.e., pretty damned white), but the Forrester founders seemed to have had some sort of come-to-Jesus moment or maybe they were low-key class shaded too, so they liked to consider themselves woke before being woke was a thing. Ignore the fact that it still cost approximately $48K to give a kid their form of progressive wokeness.

Still, they were highly philanthropic and had a 15 percent diversity rate, but made sure to show at least 30 percent of the students in all their promotional brochures and literature were people of color. But I wasn't mad. I was happy to be out of my old school and even happier when I met Dawn on the first day.

"Bobby Brown is sooo cute. Right, Bethany?" Kaitlyn Smith, the upperclassman assigned to giving us our tour of the campus chirped by way of bonding with the Black girls. My Spidey sense went up immediately and I was getting Felicity Mathis (I'll use you till I abuse you) vibes out the gate with this one, but I stayed chill. Better to not rock the boat.

"And you look a little like Whitney Houston, but way prettier. I think she's great, but Madonna sings better," Kaitlyn continued. Dawn and I gave each other immediate wide eyes because (a) blasphemy on that Whitney/Madonna comment, and (b) what the hell was with this chick?

It went on from there—new school, same stupidity, but whatever. It was high school. At least now I had a friend to vibe with and one who understood when these not-so-micro aggressions came up. Dawn and I had something in common, and even better, we were equally silly in our immaturity and over-the-top love of '80s punk and '90s pop. B-boys were an obsession, and foreign romance drama heartthrobs were our ultimate crushes.

Always a little quirky, I had done my quirking in relative quiet. Dawn, who was a bit bolder and innately perceptive, picked up on my inner wild child and coaxed her out. There were SoHo shopping trips, sunbathing layouts on her West Village rooftop when we were out of school on the weekends. The best were our long sessions of Fuck, Marry, Kill—Comic Edition. The fact that thirty years later we could still pass time pretty much doing the same things, playing the same games, well, I didn't know if it was a good or a bad thing.

If Keanu was getting his shit together and settling down, then what did that mean for me and my life?

CHAPTER 3

BETWEEN TWO FERNS

BETHANY LU

It doesn't mean shit," Dawn said, surprising me by answering the question I thought I'd only asked silently. Maybe I was a touch too transparent.

"Dawn's right. Keanu getting married doesn't mean anything. And you need to stop with the overthinking," True chimed in from the kitchen. He was eyeing me with that worried expression again.

Jeez, the two of them. And they were getting on me about overthinking? Part of me was starting to feel like these Saturday get-togethers were just excuses to check up on me, but I tried not to go there and just keep us in the friend zone where I was comfortable and not feel like I was being managed.

I stuck out my tongue and True responded by taking a nonchalant sip of his coffee. Infuriating-ass man. "I'm not one of your students, True. You don't have to worry about me. Maybe you're the one who's overthinking. Or overanalyzing as is the case when it comes to you."

"I highly doubt that," he drawled out.

Sure, this little spat seemed ridiculous for fully grown New Yorkers on a beautiful Saturday afternoon, and there was probably no reason I should have put up with it, but there was also no reason in the world I could see myself not.

Dawn and True were pretty much the only constants I could count on after the world flipped and changed direction on me when I was eighteen.

When our quartet had been suddenly downgraded to a trio.

But I couldn't bear to think about that. Not now. Not in conjunction with the almost, maybe very real, possibility of Keanu getting married.

I looked back over at Dawn. She and I were opposite in many ways but statistically so similar. A couple of Black women staring down our midforties and successful-ish, thanks to being Black one-percenters with family funds to fall back on. We were both happily single and getting perhaps a little too content with being so after running over the river and through the city with dating. Still, anyone would tell us that because of our ages we should be looking for Mr. Right. Like real hard. Not blissfully binge-watching Netflix series, fangirling over our old crushes and drooling over the younger up-and-comers. We drove our parents nuts and our married friends even nuttier.

Over forty, single AF and okay with it. It didn't mesh for some.

I remember the night our friend CeCe announced she was getting married to her longtime boyfriend, Bruce, over sangrias at our favorite Mexican restaurant. Icky Bruce is what we called him, on account of us always making the ick face whenever his name came up. But CeCe had been with him since college, and we were long over accompanying her on recon missions to see who Bruce was cheating on her with at the moment. And now there she was, telling us about some fantasy she had of seeing us squeeze into mauve bridesmaid dresses and traveling to a destination wedding in Grand Rapids. As if Grand Rapids was an actual destination for a wedding. But it was what Bruce had wanted.

Of course, to hear her tell it, Bruce was no longer a philandering sonofabitch. Nope. According to CeCe, he'd transformed, or hell, was always the perfect sweep-you-off-your-feet type of boyfriend who bought flowers no less than once a week and served homemade breakfast in bed every Sunday after making you come four times and didn't even expect a hand job in return. For her, that was worth putting her friends in mauve dresses, matching shoes and then asking them to pay hotel and travel on top of that to stay at an airport-adjacent hotel.

After CeCe floated out of La Cantina, Dawn and I ordered up another pitcher of drinks and declared there was no way we were settling for a Kay Jewelers moment and revisionist history to tie us to a forever mistake.

Better to stick with flying solo and loving the perfect and perfectly unattainable guys in our heads than get tied down in the real world.

Sidebar: Bruce and CeCe were currently separated.

"Stop with that look," Dawn said. "You know I know what it means. That Gemini mind of yours is already off and running in some wayward direction. What you need to do is finish your coffee, eat your bagel and then get back to this piece, which looks like it's going to be fabulous BTW."

She uncrossed her arms and slipped out of her blazer, revealing a sundress in an abstract fruit print with a shirred top that flowed to about midcalf. Her strappy sandals had the cutest back bow. Though her outfit was cute and held a bit of whimsy, Dawn was pointing at my unfinished project and had on her "so what do you have to say about this?" serious look.

So that was that. Dawn was done with my games and now back to being a full-on adult career woman and my manager. Though she may have totally understood my immediate despair when it came to the shocking Keanu announcement, nothing came between Dawn and her business, and I had a show coming up in a few months at her gallery. Dawn liked what I had done so far, but I still wanted to add to the collection, so there'd be more options.

I looked back at the unfinished work, trying hard to focus and get into adulting mode again. I stared. Not long before, the mixed-media piece had been on its way to being a sublime postmodern representation of the missing stillness in the chaotic current domestic world, blah blah blah...Suddenly these were just words droning in my head. Yeah, I had the art speak down pat. But now the canvas—with its wash of blue and the delicate fabrics I'd painstakingly chosen and wanted to incorporate with black-

and-white prints, color photographs and ripped newspaper clippings—all looked like it came straight out of a scene from *Hoarders: HGTV Edition* dumped in my space.

I reached for my initial sketch and felt no connection there either. The two female figures now felt off, and the man in the photograph? What the hell was he representing? Nothing quite fit.

I looked at Dawn again, busily tapping on her phone, then at True over in the kitchen doing the same. Even within our usual connected space, today there was a disconnect.

Dammit. The stupid tweet kept flashing through my mind. *Ninety days.* It felt like a countdown to doom. How could Keanu—a public figure, a celebrity I'd never met— have that kind of power after all these years?

Shaking my head, I tried to force myself to think objectively. It had to be the work. That was it. I just had to finish it. But even without the beads and paint I'd planned to add, I knew this one was a lost cause. The original lightness and harmony I'd wanted wasn't there. The hope I had when I'd started it had faded away, and I knew I wouldn't be able to get it back. Gone was gone.

"This isn't working," I said. "It's not going to work."

Dawn's fingers stilled. "What? I mean, why?" she asked. "This is great. I mean I can already see it's going to be amazing. Don't give up now. You are the one who still insists on adding more pieces to the show, and your commissions are starting to line up too."

Great? Amazing? Commissions? All positive words that were giving me minor heart palpitations. Not that the idea of more work and paying customers at the ready wasn't good. It's just that I felt my potential for letting someone down in this case was disastrous.

Dawn continued, "There are big things happening for you, woman, including your dinner with Daniel Lim. You can't lose focus."

I sighed. The dinner tonight was one of the last things I wanted to think about. I wanted to focus on my art and on developing it as much as I could. Not dressing up to schmooze about it. Dawn knew this.

"Don't start," she warned, most likely picking up on my skittishness. "You agreed. Now you have to wow him." She gave me a quick up and down, taking in my loose cotton overalls and white tank. "None of your shapeless black sacks even if they are vintage. Daniel Lim is used to sitting front row at New York Fashion Week." She gave a saucy smirk. "And often leaving with the show's ending model."

I rolled my eyes. "If you're so into this dinner and who he ends up going home with, then you should go in my place," I said.

"Yes, you should go, Ms. Agent," True suddenly chimed in from by the kitchen sink.

Dawn and I pivoted his way, surprised by his sudden outburst.

"Really, Professor?" Dawn started. "Not that my business is your business, and not that I wouldn't go, but he particularly wants to meet the artist to see if they get on."

True snorted, letting loose with the uncharacteristic show of emotion. "Yeah, I bet."

Dawn sighed. "Oh, come on. I know you and Daniel

went to the same university and I know you didn't get on with him, but who do you ever get on with?"

True's brow wrinkled, but he didn't argue. Probably because Dawn had a point.

"Besides, this is business," she added with finality.

He shrugged, then went back to his phone. What the hell were T and Aimee talking about that was so interesting?

"I said my piece," True stated as he continued to tap away.

I could tell he was doing his best to hold on to his control, though. He was holding something back. But he stopped texting then and looked up at me and smiled. Not a full-on one, but still it was enough to get me. Like a mosquito bite. Unexpected and a total pain when it flared up later.

"Hey, Dawn's right, business is business," he said. "Besides, none of us are the same as when we were back in school, yeah?"

It took everything for me to crack a smile in return at that one. I gave him a weak half nod to let him know I agreed while my mind raced with stagnant thoughts of "speak for yourself."

True's phone buzzed again. "Listen, I've got to go," he said. "There are still some things I need to finish up, thanks to being a little too generous with some student extensions. I'll have to catch you two later."

I pouted. "So soon. No fair. This is supposed to be our fun day."

He shrugged.

There was no use arguing against that. I knew him, and, T and Aimee aside, he wouldn't shirk responsibility.

I sighed. "Well, before you go, take that box off the foyer table. I got you something."

True glared. "What did you do now, Lu? I don't need anything."

My gaze went to his feet. "I beg to differ. And don't let these get thrown in a corner somewhere like the rest of the things I get you. You are doing a lot of running if those sneakers are any indication. Your feet must be suffering. They're just socks, but they have moisture-wicking technology for runners."

He sauntered my way and gave me a long stare, coming oh so close to my face once again before tapping my worktable firmly three times.

"So they're cotton socks?"

I tried my best not to back up. "Just shut it and say thank you, smartass. What do you know about high-tech material?"

He grinned, and it was another of those little shots. "Thank you, smartass." He looked from me to Dawn, then back to me. "And don't forget, your agent here does have a point," he said, his voice all serious and deep.

"Don't I always?" Dawn blurted.

For a moment I forgot about True, the boy who used to gawk at me on the sly as he hung around with my brother all those years ago. That True's voice was nothing like this man's. Hell, that True barely had a voice at all.

He tapped the table again and I blinked.

"You need to focus," he said. "Don't let this Keanu crap distract you. It's you and your art. Everything else is just noise. Even investors like Lim."

"Um, that wasn't my point, Nutty Professor!" Dawn snapped.

True ignored her and continued. "But you have your meeting and make your own decision." He glanced Dawn's way, then back at me. "Hell, he may have changed from when I knew him, and you're an excellent judge of character, so don't listen to any voice but your own with this."

I frowned, and he shot me back a teasing, toothy grin. His smile was supposed to be goofy, but the joke was on him. It was fucking dazzling.

"You've got this," True added in a voice that for a moment made me feel like I could conquer the world. A spot about eight inches lower than my belly button clenched while my nipples hardened.

I overcompensated for my body's reaction by rolling my eyes. "What do you know about art?"

True shrugged. "Nothing, but I know you," he said, turning away.

He snagged another bagel and ripped off a piece for Morphie. Only as loyal as his last snack, Morphie rewarded him with a jump and a spin before True was out the door.

Traitorous dog. I don't know why I kept him around anyway.

CHAPTER 4

RABBIT RABBIT

TRUE

I will not worry about Lu. I will not worry about Lu.
I fought the urge to put the declaration in my phone's notes app. Why waste the energy? Of course, I'd worry about Lu. Worrying about Lu came second only to thinking about Lu. Shit, the amount of time I spent worrying over that woman made me no less ridiculous than her and Dawn with their fangirling over completely unobtainable men.

I swiped away from Aimee's text and put the one from the dean on the back burner too. I'd deal with the four students' pleading emails when I got back down to my apartment. For now, it was more interesting to watch whatever was going on over by Lu's worktable. I leaned back and stared at her, Little Ms. Never Grow Up. A Peter Pan in her own mind. When was enough going to be enough? Damn near having fits over men who didn't even know she existed. And Dawn was no better, feeding into her mania when she could at least, if not as her friend then as her business partner, tamp it down.

I stole another glance and caught the indecision in Lu's eyes as she looked at her work in progress. The frustration as she pushed her wild curls back and worried at her bottom lip. Fuck. I hated it and at the same time was ridiculously revved up over the fact that she still excited me, that I still thought she was just as cute now as she had been when I first caught sight of her all those years ago.

Fangirl? I was probably the ultimate fanboy at this point.

But damn, shouldn't every crush have an expiration date?

"It doesn't mean shit. You can't let a stupid tweet bother you," Dawn was saying.

I looked down at Morphie and he back up at me with eyes that clearly said "And there's your answer, dummy." I shook my head. Lu's damn dog was named after her crush of over twenty years, so obviously expiration dates varied widely by owner.

I made a move to take another sip of coffee, but it mocked me too. Dammit. I pulled my hand back. Keanu was everywhere. On dishware, figurines, she even had a freaking bedazzled pillow. No wonder the tweet freaked her out. She'd essentially been living in a Keanu shrine. I shivered, then looked back over at her.

Lu stuck her tongue out at me. *Yeah, that's mature.*

I went back to my phone and swiped on my emails, now actively looking for a distraction.

Professor Erickson: I'd like to talk with you about my grade during your office hours.

I don't think a B takes into consideration my dedication to the project. You must have missed my total commitment. Yours, Viv Henry.

Yours?

Hell no with that shit. And I was being generous with the B I'd given Viv. Very generous. It was students like Viv Henry who made my job a pain in the ass and the offer from the dean to head my department that much less appealing.

I considered quitting, but for the most part I enjoyed my job, and I didn't see going back to corporate full time as a way out. I'd lived that life and knew it wasn't for me either. Fending off eager students who felt they deserved an A over a B was a smidge easier than trying to advise the supremely rich how to invest their money. Or maybe it was that teaching just didn't bore me to tears. But now that the dean was talking about this promotion, which would take me out of the classroom and into endless budget meetings, what was the difference from being chained to a cubicle?

I heard Dawn saying something about Daniel Lim and inwardly cringed. I couldn't believe that Lu was meeting him to talk business or that Daniel even had a business to talk about. But then again, of course he did. He always had everything handed to him on a silver platter—including me bailing him out for our statistics class in college. Still, I didn't like the idea of him meeting up with Lu.

"What do I care?" Lu responded, but in a way that indicated she actually did care. "But do you think the rumors about him breaking up with that Australian model are true?" Her and Dawn's voices were suddenly lowered, and I was way less interested in my messages and more in what they were talking about.

The dean's offer was significant but not significant enough to compete with what Lim was likely offering her.

I shook my head to try to clear it. What the hell was I doing? One had nothing to do with the other. Lu, Lim and Dawn for that matter were not my business. I personally had plenty of business to keep myself very occupied. For the moment at least.

I knew a huge part of what the dean wanted was to get me locked in, thanks to my book, *Economics and Cultural Sustainability*, gaining surprising attention and a couple of morning talk show interviews. But why should I use that notoriety just for the benefit of the college? Maybe it was time to make a move for myself. I looked at Lu and Dawn once more. And it wasn't like the college was the only game in town.

But I couldn't think of my own games or the offers I had lined up. The fact that Lu was going out with Daniel Lim tonight made me prickly. I knew Daniel from back in college and doubted he'd changed all that much. There was growth and then there were total transformations. And transformations only happened on scripted dramas and makeover shows.

Daniel was about as scripted as they came and, back when I knew him, full of drama: classic entitled rich-kid frat boy basking in the glory without any of the grind. The only reason he associated with a scholarship non-frat kid like me was for my tutoring skills. He needed his MBA, and one "hard-assed"—at least in Lim's eyes—professor who insisted Daniel do his own data analysis had been blocking that. But of course, the idea of "his own" meant nothing to Lim. Not when his parents paid his college advisor to craft an entrance essay and deliver him into university on a silver platter. He had a path to CEO already cleared. The degree was just decoration and cachet.

Screw it. I should let bygones be gone at this point. At least I made good money—he paid me extra just to keep quiet about the fact that a lowerclassman was tutoring him. I looked over at Lu then, and still I couldn't help but worry as I wondered what else Daniel might have on the DL.

I flipped from my text app and went to my browser and looked up Lim's company once again. DLIG was a subsidiary of his family's multinational company, Lim International Group. They had their hands in boutique hotels, fashion and luxury goods and other assorted ventures. The DLIG division was doing so well that the business world speculated that Daniel was some sort of boy wonder, but I knew different. He'd had plenty of help from family money and influence. Lots.

I glanced at Lu again. Wanting to warn her, but then again not. If this was a good opportunity for her, me bursting her bubble could ruin our friendship. She was talented and she deserved the world. I didn't want to see her used or hurt. Besides, Lim would be lucky to partner with a rising star like her.

"Mister Er-ick-son," she said, drawing out my name in her Agent Smith voice. "Care to share what you have percolating in that little computer of a brain over there?"

"Not at all, Lu, and don't call me Mister Erickson."

She laughed and her damned eyes sparked. "You know you love it."

"I do not."

Or at least I'll never admit it to you, silly rabbit.

CHAPTER 5

DEVIL'S ADVOCATE

BETHANY LU

Crap. I already had the feeling Daniel Lim was a bit of a jerk and a lot of a show-off so...a jerkoff, I guess. We hadn't even met yet. But come on. This wasn't how a person started wooing a potential business partner.

My hackles spiked from the moment Daniel Lim's assistant insisted on sending a car to pick me up. The car wasn't the problem, though I'd prefer to handle my own travel. The issue was how suspiciously evasive she was. I had to insist she also give me the place we were meeting, and she finally rattled off the address of a restaurant on the West Side. So when the driver ended up heading east through the park, I immediately went on alert.

"Excuse me, shouldn't you be staying on the West Side,"

I'd said, quickly pulling out my phone, my emergency contact at the ready.

He gave me a knowing and reassuring glance through his rearview mirror, and something in the man's eyes told me he'd been through this game before. "Don't worry, miss. It's all fine. Mr. Lim just decided on a different restaurant. It's public, popular and you're safe. He wanted me to assure you that you'll be more than pleased with his choice."

I frowned as I leaned back against the smooth interior, still holding tightly to my phone. How did Daniel Lim know what I'd be more than pleased with? I'd be more than pleased with a hot bath, high carbs, maybe a cream sauce and a Keanu Netflix binge right now. Anything but this dress and these shoes. The hell? Who did such a thing in this day?

I let my mind wander for a moment to Keanu and the movie binge I was now looking forward to when I got home. The only question was whether I went in chronological order or by my faves, which was always dangerous since I was prone to getting stuck like an old record and tripping three or four times in a row over *A Walk in the Clouds* and *Speed* before even getting to *John Wick 2*.

"Instead, I have an interview date with the devil," I mumbled to myself, likening Daniel Lim to Al Pacino's character in *The Devil's Advocate*.

My phone buzzed with an incoming text.

Dawn: HAVE FUN. You're a star. Focus. Go get that Bag. You can think about Keanu later. Love ya. Bye.

I grimaced and stuck my tongue out at my phone. Shit. She was so in my head. Maybe I needed to break up with my best friend. She knew me too damned well.

Me: 😛 Mind your business.
Dawn: You are my business. Now go be fabulous.
Me: Fine... begrudgingly.
Dawn: I'll take it.

I let out a sigh. Dawn was right: This partnership could mean a huge boost for my career. There was only so much obscurity an artist of a certain age could endure. Shit. I wondered if that's what Keanu was thinking? Was there only so much bachelorhood an actor of a certain age could endure before falling into obscurity?

Was now my time to shine, or was this the beginning of my descent into obscurity?

Most breakouts happened for young phenoms, not forty-somethings still figuring it out. On the surface it looked like I was doing well. I had commissions, work lined up. I even lived in a Manhattan loft with amazing space and light.

But... my commissions barely kept me in coffee and canvases, and I only had my loft because my parents owned the building. I was hardly any better than the trust fund kids I balked at back in my old school days. Dawn often scoffed at my guilt, insisting I shouldn't feel bad for hitting the rare family-fund lotto when so many other Black folks had not. And I knew she was right.

Of course, it wasn't like anyone checked your bank

account when it came to racial profiling. No, there was still the extra scrutiny, all the questions and assumptions they jumped to. And then came the apologies when people found out there might be something to gain or lose from knowing you.

Still, even with all I had and the work I was doing, I felt like a disappointment at times. To myself? Maybe to my parents? Even though my father bankrolling my apartment didn't hurt his finances a bit, and he said having me in one of his buildings gave him peace of mind that was invaluable.

Focus, Lu. It was True's voice now. He always came to me when I got like this, even when he wasn't physically with me. So self-righteous. Mr. High Pride, of course he'd hate someone like Daniel Lim. It was a shock that he never looked down on me and Dawn and had stayed friends with us all these years. But I knew why. And for that reason, I'd endure.

I snorted. As much as a fancy, high-priced meal with a bachelor hot-list CEO could be considered enduring. Still, there were sacrifices, and someone had to make them.

It turned out the dinner destination for the night was Shio, an exclusive sushi place with private dining on the Upper East Side. The restaurant didn't seat more than eight parties a night, so their prices were through the roof to make up for the astronomical New York rent. By the time the driver dropped me at the front door, I already had a chip on my shoulder that was weighing like a boulder.

I was prejudging the restaurant, Daniel Lim, just the

entire evening and it hadn't even started. I'd let both the Keanu tweet and True get so deep in my head that they had permeated my spirit and ruined my whole mood. It wasn't that Lim couldn't afford the dinner—of course he could, and I doubt he'd end up paying out of pocket anyway. I knew how company dinners went. The more biggity the bigs were, the less they paid. Trickle-down was reverse psych at its finest.

And despite these theories being the very thing that got our family where we were, they still irked the crap out of me. But I'd trained myself with a tactic learned from the A-listers in middle school and the elites at Forresters. I'd perfected it so well that it had now become a part of my brand. I called it the CIU. Like the CIA, but not really except for being a kind of stealth defense mechanism. At strategic times, appear either Clueless, Ignorant or Unbothered and watch how doors open. I found the CIU particularly helpful for flipping the script on the Strong Black Woman stereotype that for too many years had us bearing an unequal amount of weight compared to our white counterparts. Sure, mental gameplay like this was exhausting, but better mentally exhausting than physically backbreaking.

I sighed, already tired thinking of the night to come. I just wanted to do my freaking art, as muddled as it was, and not deal with the rest.

I'd found lately that no matter how much I tried to keep up my CIU and play the carefree artist Lu Carlisle, there were times that the real me would seep out. The perpetually pissed Bethany Lu was constantly fidgeting to break free like The Hulk, and I had trouble keeping a rein on her.

Maybe that's what was so tiring and not the rest of the world? I'd be left exhausted and hollow.

Since I was feeling Hulky, I was glad I took Dawn's advice and dressed carefully, going for cool sophistication. I'd chosen a simple halter jumpsuit with a wraparound tie that went from my neck and crossed around my back to my waist. I'd smoothed my "you're not the boss of me!" curls as best as I could into a chignon, which showed off the back of the jumpsuit nicely. And strappy sandals completed the look.

And that's where I was now, walking into Shio all dressed up on the outside but inside, hollow. In myself, but out. Mad at a guy offering me money for my services and already sizing him up as some sort of john and feeling like a sellout. I needed to get my shit together. Still, no matter how much I tried to play the ditzy little rich girl, it felt like a betrayal.

Listen to your voice. Dammit, there was True rambling in my head again.

"Oh, shut up."

"Excuse me?"

I looked up at the man standing in front of me. Shit. It was Lim. And he looked even better in person than in the pictures on the internet. Wow. I don't know how Dawn didn't talk herself into this meeting. The man was giving off serious K-drama vibes, and I'm talking Lee Min Ho here, *Heirs* era but twenty of the best time-travel years later. Tall, dark and possibly devastating, he had almost movie-star good looks but with a slightly rugged edge. A muscular frame, broad shoulders and biceps that strained his dress shirt just enough to make you worry a bit for the threads. His skin was creamy with a slight caramel glow that spoke of good health and outdoor sports, and if he was faking it with a little tanner, then it was a good fake. Daniel's straight black hair slicked back away from his face, showing off his high cheekbones and full, full lips. Something about him made me almost want to step up my game. Hit the gym or at least take Morphie on an extra lap around the block. I blinked twice. I couldn't get unnerved by this man. Thoughts of physical fitness? I had to be out of my mind.

But then I thought of my response to True and his stupid thumb.

Daniel's eyes narrowed. "Would you care to take a seat, or would you like to tell me to shut up again?"

Fuck me and my rogue inner monologues. I tapped the side of my ear and pretended to pull out a nonexistent earpiece.

I smiled. "Sorry about that. I wasn't talking to you. Just a bee that's been buzzing around in my head all day today." *Get it together, Lu. Make this a part of your CIU and move on,* I told myself as I took the seat offered by Daniel, noticing the hostess didn't bring any menus.

Daniel smiled back, nodding as if my answer made total sense, but his gaze still held an edge of caution.

"Thanks for inviting me. It's nice to meet you," I said. I looked around at the small restaurant. The seven other tables were occupied, but it seemed that Daniel had, even with his last-minute switch, finagled us into the best one and the largest in the back corner. "Though I thought your assistant had us meeting somewhere else."

"I pulled a few strings." His tone was nonchalant. Cool, as he nodded to a waitstaff person standing at the ready off in a side corner. I purposefully didn't comment on whether I approved of his choice. I was going for the C—clueless—part of the CIU plan. When he frowned, I knew he'd expected me to gush. The tiny restaurant was nice. Lovely even, a testament to serene harmony, with its floor-to-ceiling honey-colored wood. Once you were inside the tranquil space, it was easy to almost forget the hustle of the city beyond the doors.

I bet Keanu would love it here. It was so him. Well, the him of my dreams. Not a married him. That sort of him would be happy at Ruth's Chris with the New York Strip of the night.

Suddenly my fingers itched to reach for my phone. Maybe there was an update. Something that said the news from this morning was all a joke. How could Keanu be settling down? And worse, now there were even whispers about the movie he was currently filming being one of his last. The idea of him and her walking hand in hand and toward some sort of mystic, artistic, beautiful, sex-filled, dreamlike Keanuland of retirement obscurity made me break out into a sweat. Mentally, I reached for my water, but instinctively my hand went for my phone and hovered over it.

Daniel cleared his throat, and the thinly veiled annoyance in his eyes let me know that I was probably blowing this deal. My hand pivoted from my phone to my water. I took a sip that turned into a long pull and instantly regretted it, remembering I'd chosen to wear a jumpsuit and the complications that came with it. I gave Daniel an apologetic look and traded my water for my phone. Still going in with the bad choices.

"Sorry, Daniel, please excuse me a moment. It's just that I have something I need to check. Then I'm all yours."

He nodded and smiled, but for a moment I could see a little of his facade crack as I picked up my phone. Dammit. Nothing new. Keanu's wedding was still a top trending topic.

I put my phone down and turned it upside down on the honey wood surface to avoid any further distraction. And right on time too, as just then plate after plate of little bites of food began to arrive, brought over by the most beautiful lineup of Japanese guys. And by *lineup*, I mean they literally seemed to march the plates out in line. One plate per man, eight plates total. No déclassé trays for this place. Then they silently disappeared three seconds after dropping off the plates. All eyes in the room were trained on the little curtain the drop-dead gorgeous troupe had disappeared behind.

I fought to unscrew my face and bring it back to cool and back to Daniel.

"I'm sure you know how exclusive this restaurant is. The wait is over a month to get a reservation," he said.

"And yet your assistant told me a different restaurant, and your driver said this was a last-minute change?"

His full lips thinned ever so slightly. "Like I said, I had to pull a few strings. It was short notice. I assumed you would enjoy it."

I blinked at all the little plates in front of us. Everything was beautifully presented, even the bits that appeared to still be catching a last breath. "And this. You assumed to order for me too?"

Daniel leaned back, then laughed. "The grilled eel and crab is the finest in the city. I made sure to put in our order as soon as I arrived since the chef only has limited quantities and once it's gone it's gone. I didn't want you to miss out."

I could practically hear Dawn yelling at me to stand the fuck down. Eat the eel, shut my trap and close the deal.

She was right. Well, the voice in my head was right. Why was I being so hard on this guy when all he did was preorder my dinner? I looked down at the eel, which could have used at least three more minutes of grilling for my taste, but bit my tongue against commenting. There were worse things to swallow than a bit of eel when there was money on the table.

"Come on. Please try it," Daniel said. "The eel is a little squirmy, but I swear people rave over it." His tone was milder now, and when he smiled and I let my guard down for half a second, it was really nice.

Besides, I'd chosen to accept this invite precisely because of his money and that charming smile. He could help my career get to the next level. I picked up the eel with my chopsticks and offered up a small prayer for it and my slime-feel gag reflexes. "Bottoms up!" I grimaced. "Whichever way that is."

Daniel laughed again as I downed the eel. It was cold and though not alive, you couldn't convince me it was fully dead either. It wasn't nearly as satisfying as the reviewers were gushing about. I stilled as a strange aftertaste, spice and smoke, bloomed in the back of my throat and radiated throughout my chest. This part. This part was different. I didn't like anything about the eel going down, but the way I felt now—the taste on my tongue and the tingle in my chest—I hated to admit it, but I wanted more. Crap.

Daniel raised his eyebrow and nodded, looking entirely too full of himself in that moment. I rolled my eyes and reached for the crab as he finally focused on his own meal and started in on his pitch.

I did my best at working a double focus, but the crab was tasty too. This little oasis of a restaurant was coming on strong to prove me wrong. No, it wouldn't convince me it was worth the prices or the waits I'd read about, but the food was something to remember.

I had to pace myself, though, and when it came to the shirako I drew the line. I poked at the cream-colored sacs in the translucent amber sauce and decided against it.

"It's a no on the shirako?" Daniel's voice held an edge of mirth.

I edged the dish his way. "Sorry, no. I'm pretty discerning when it comes to sperm intake. But please enjoy yourself. Don't you want it?"

"What I want is you."

I blinked. "You're joking."

"Why would I be?"

"You're talking professionally, of course?"

He paused and looked at me seriously. I could feel my blood starting to simmer, but my gut was telling me to be patient and go CIU. I could almost see his wheels turning. Daniel laughed then. "Of course professionally."

I thought of the overpriced sperm.

"I'd like to think of us starting a wonderful friendship with this dinner tonight," Daniel continued.

I stared at him for another long moment, now True and his warnings coming to mind. I thought of bringing up True but decided against it. Better to keep feeling Daniel out. So far he wasn't like the brash kid True seemed to hint at. "Fine. My new friend. Let's talk business."

Daniel grinned, then leaned back.

"Professional to professional. What is it that I can do, professionally, to help you?" I asked. "Is there a reason for you calling me that doesn't involve eel or fish sperm?"

He laughed and held up a hand. "Let's talk about your work. I think it's fantastic."

I leaned back myself, for the first time feeling like I was on better footing. "Thanks," I said, "but if it's a commission or commissions you want for your company, I'll have to be blunt and say thank you for the meal but I'm booked with works right now and pulling strings at nice restaurants won't get you to the front of my queue. Also, I have a show coming up soon at the Taylor Gallery and there are works to finish for that."

He smiled again. It felt slightly feral and this time there was a flash to his dark eyes. It was dead sexy this dangerous look. Absentmindedly, I brushed a runaway curl behind my ear, then ran my hands across my now cool shoulders.

I cleared my throat. "All that to say that now is a terribly inconvenient time for new projects."

He took a sip of his sake. Smooth and unfazed.

"Time is never convenient, Ms. Carlisle. But like I said, I want you."

My lips tightened. I'm sure he knew precisely how that sounded but had no idea how it also annoyed.

"I tell you what," Daniel said. "You're probably not used to your talent being valued in a way that it should be." He rubbed his thumb over his chin as he stared at me. My eyes, lips, shoulders, hands, suddenly it felt like every part of me was under scrutiny. Like he wasn't just assessing the value of my work but my overall value. My stomach roiled and for a moment I felt like the eel might wiggle its way back up.

"What if I commit to buying out your show now? You give me the estimated value of the pieces and you don't have to complete them. That way your time is freed up to work exclusively for DLIG."

Oh. The. Whole. Fuck. No.

Who did that? Yes, it was guaranteed money, but it was like cheating and I was not a cheat. Also, it was taking my ideas and shuttering them before they even had a chance to be born. Once again: Fuck. No.

"What?" he asked.

I looked at Daniel. "What do you mean what?"

"It sounded like you said fuck no."

I blinked at him and frowned. There I went again with my inner voice getting out. Oh well. Done was done.

I shrugged. "Sorry about that. The fuck was supposed to be silent, but it did go with the no I was going to give you. That's not how art works, or at least it's not how my art works. My art is not for one person. I am not for one person. Buying everything out before my show feels suspiciously like ownership. And besides, I don't work exclusively for anyone except myself."

I narrowed my eyes, unable to hold my mask in place, and watched as Daniel's eyes went wide.

"Oh no, of course not. Which is why we'd make a perfect partnership. My company could bring your art to so many people and make you a household name." He spoke quickly now. Like he was trying to sell me on me. Now his voice had a distinct Home Shopping Network, in-this-hour, auctioneer-time quality to it that put me on edge. I felt like the tables were turned and it was now him on the verge of losing his shit.

"Like I said, Ms. Carlisle. No, Lu. I want you. DLIG can brand you and make you a household name. Imagine your work on luxury goods sold in our shops. An exclusive collection of handbags with your artwork. Silk scarves, some of your commissioned pieces on the walls of our hotels. We can make you the star you deserve to be. All we'd need is rights to some of your works, name and likeness and—"

Once again there was that buzz and the pop. The same one I'd heard earlier that morning when I saw the Keanu tweet. They wanted my work, name, likeness and rights to it all. And though it sounded grand, it felt as if I'd be giving up so much. While making my work available to the masses, they'd be putting more limits on me and my creativity. When words like *rights* and *exclusive* were dropped, I knew to be wary. I put up my hand and stopped him midsentence. "Like I said, Daniel, it's not allowed. At least in my world."

He stared at me for a moment before he spoke again. "Since when is something not allowed in this world, Lu?"

Daniel let that hang in the air for a moment before he laughed again, as if he was filming a supervillain cameo clip. It was awkward and a little cringy and thankfully he eased up and relaxed into something that seemed like semi-normal human. "Don't worry. I'm patient. Your talent isn't going anywhere. The offer stands. For a while." Once again the pause. Shit, this guy was good at theatrics. "I do have shareholders and you are our first choice, so it will be much easier to take what we have to offer now."

"So you're looking at other artists?"

"No, you're the only artist we're considering." He lowered his tone and his eyes became somehow deeper. "The only artist *I'm* considering." He let out a sigh. "It would make things so much easier if you'd just accept."

Easy. Since when has anything been easy for someone like me? Not as a girl and not as a woman.

As he said the words, once again I felt myself zoning out. What made me so special? I blinked and tried my best to hear what he was going on about now. "You are so talented, which is why we want you. Talented, plus you have your finger on the pulse of what's going on in the urban landscape of today. We could have a multimedia showing of your work and bring it into different aspects of our conglomerate. Like I said, your artwork could be exclusively featured in our hotels and shops, and hell, we could even do a line of dinnerware."

If I balked at this, Lim didn't notice.

"The Lim name is top tier and you are beautiful, elegant

and cultured but also just urban enough to straddle both worlds." He smiled and my stomach reacted. I knew it had nothing to do with my one taste of eel either.

Just urban enough. I sucked in a breath as I wondered what DLIG's urban meter was.

Daniel pushed me a small card with an astronomical number and for a moment my breath stopped. It took another moment for me to restart it while he called over the waiter and settled the bill.

Shit. It was a good number. But was it my number? It was high, that I did know. These were the type of digits the devil dealt in.

"How about I drive you home? Or we can go back to my place and discuss things more?" Daniel's voice startled me, and looking back across the table I half expected to see the devil himself or at least Al Pacino's version. Seeing Daniel was a bit of a letdown.

I picked up my phone and hit my Uber app, then looked back at him. "No thanks, I have a car coming." I looked back at my phone. "Cherry in a Chrysler Pacifica will be outside for me in four minutes." I waved it in his face.

He looked disappointed and maybe a little angry, but that was his problem. He got a little sulky and tried to hit me with sad eyes. "But the night is still young, and the view is gorgeous from my penthouse."

I hit him with a "really?" look. "It's been a night and I think you should stop at your nice offer with all the zeros. Does bringing up your view and talk of a penthouse actually work on New Yorkers?"

He shrugged, then started to get up. "Sorry about that. I knew it was lame when it came out."

I shook my head. "Well, good for you coming in with the late self-awareness."

We made it outside. The car I'd been dropped off in earlier was still there, as was Cherry with the Chrysler. Daniel looked at me then surprised me by grabbing my wrist as I headed toward my car. "Are you sure? I can pay Cherry and you can just come with me. No more business talk. Just drinks and fun."

I looked down at his hand, then back up at him and smiled, channeling my inner Neo. I took his pinky and twisted it back just enough to make him yelp.

"Oww! You could have just said no."

"So much for your self-awareness. Besides, you could have done your research better. Didn't you know I know Kung Fu?"

CHAPTER 6

CLEARLY DARKLY

BETHANY LU

The ride across the park was quiet as I stared at Daniel's business card with the number and all the zeros behind it on the back. Oh well. I guess getting the offer was nice. But after the pinky twist, I was sure any partnership was now firmly off the table. Not that I necessarily wanted what he was offering anyway. True was right. Daniel Lim was a jerk, and my first assessment of him was spot on, despite his small glimpse of clarity.

There was no way I'd sell myself out the way he'd wanted. DLIG wanted creative ownership, plain and simple. If I allowed that, where would I be? What would they make of my brand?

Maybe I should just face the fact that I'd be an artist who only made it so far—small galleries and homes of collectors who had a taste for Black works, and that was it. That wouldn't be bad. It was more than many artists had. I was creating, and I wasn't starving. Perhaps accepting that was my life shift. Keanu was settling. I frowned, mad for even thinking that way about myself and about Keanu. He wasn't settling. He couldn't be. Maybe he was now accepting his fate, his lot, his...I don't know, destiny. My frown went deeper as I wondered if that kind of acceptance was good enough for Keanu, then maybe I should do it too.

Shit, I don't want to, get my life together. I moaned at the thought.

"You all right back there, miss?" the driver asked, catching my attention with her eyes in the rearview mirror just as my phone buzzed. I nodded and reached for the phone, knowing without looking it was Dawn and she wanted an update. She'd be thrilled with me and my pinky twist. Not.

> **Unknown:** I still want you. DLIG still wants you. We're willing to up our offer by 20%.

Holy, he likes it rough, Batman! A pinky twist and that fool was almost adding more than another zero to his offer?

Focus, Lu. Listen to your voice. True came at me again.

"How the hell can I listen to my voice when all I'm hearing is your voice?" I said out loud.

> **Me:** You may have to wait awhile. I told you I have commitments.
> **Unknown:** How long?

I thought about my works in progress, Morphie and my quiet apartment in the building my parents owned, the Jesus-looking Keanu pillow on my bed.

I let out a deep breath. Something had to give. I needed something to break up this monotony that had become my life, or at the very least some type of breakthrough. I could not settle.

Before I could stop myself, I'd hit the phone keys.

Me: 91 days and you'll have your answer.

CHAPTER 7

MUCH ADO

BETHANY LU

You know Kung Fu? Seriously?!" Dawn's voice screeched through our video chat. Then she groaned. "I should have known letting you out into the wild on your own was dangerous."

Given the incident, there wasn't much I could say to that. My carefully curated outfit from earlier was currently in a heap on the floor, and I was tucked in my bed in a pair of leggings and an oversized T-shirt with a pint of Häagen-Dazs and a bottle of prosecco. Dawn was at her place in the bathtub. I still couldn't believe she'd answered the phone.

Water sloshed dangerously while she adjusted her phone on her little bathtub ledge so it was mostly face and no nips in her camera's view. A different type of person may be wary of dropping their expensive iPhone in the tub, and at least protected it by putting it in a plastic baggie, not Dawn. Dawn liked to live on the edge.

"It was the right quote for the time. He shouldn't have put his hands on me."

"He shouldn't have *what*?" Dawn's eyes narrowed. "That motherfucker. Where does he live again? I know I had Googled it!" She was about to jump out of the tub and into action, and I was on my way to a full-frontal show.

"Hold it there, nudy booty. It's not that deep. It was just my wrist and it's all good. I handled it. How about you sit back down and suds up?"

"Big money or not, we can still beat his ass. I've got people."

I stared at her. "How do you have people?"

"How do I not?"

"What? Will we send True down there to give him a stern economics lecture?"

She laughed. "Don't knock it. True gives a killer lecture."

That did make me laugh. Suddenly imagining True in an expensive black Italian suit, shirt and tie, John Wick style, looking ready to do battle, then giving Daniel Lim a star PowerPoint. So deadly.

I shook my head. "Nah, we'll hold back the big guns. Besides, it was fine after I delivered my cool-assed line. He got the hint."

She smirked. "I don't know how cool that line was, but I'll give that win to you and Neo."

"He is The One," I said, and her face got more serious as she stared at me through the screen. "Really, I'm fine. Sure, I may have overreacted a bit with a pretty hard pinky twist."

"Oh God," Dawn moaned.

"Look, if you're worried about backlash from him, then you can cancel my show. It might flop anyway. There are plenty of other artists that would kill or"—I shrugged—"do whatever to get into your gallery."

Dawn was fine financially, but the economy had done a number on her parents and their assets, and though they were far from destitute, they were getting on her about turning a profit at the gallery that bore the family name. Then to top things off, they were also on her about settling down, getting married and having kids. If the gallery wasn't blooming, then she should be or some such shit.

When I looked at the screen again, my friend was glaring at me. "What? What did I say?" I asked.

There was clear hurt in her eyes, and I got a lump in my throat. "What are you talking like that for? I back you because you're my talented-as-hell friend and I believe in you. There is no way your show is going to flop. My gallery might not be all that, but I do know art just as much as Daniel Lim or his people, and they wouldn't have sought you out if you weren't the shit. So quit it with that talk, will you!"

I blinked. "Well shit, you don't have to go and get all sentimental. I was just trying to give you an out. I don't want you to feel saddled while I'm out here trying to find myself."

"You let me worry about that," she countered. "You're the artist, I'm the badass business boss.

"Besides," she continued, "if Lim came knocking, then that means others will too. You mark my words."

I didn't quite believe her but let her go with the fantasy

for a while. "If you say so. But hey, Lim might not be entirely off the table yet. He said he'd wait for my answer and let me set a timetable."

She nodded as she lay back on her inflatable bath pillow. "That's good. So what did you tell him for the schedule? I need to know when to start nudging and putting out more buzz on you."

I scrunched up my face and scraped out more ice cream, then took a massive spoonful before I mumbled my answer.

"What did you say?" Dawn said, coming farther forward, her right breast now fighting her lower lip for screen time. I watched as a sudsy hand picked up her phone.

"Ninety-one days," I said, loud and clear this time, before I heard Dawn groan.

"Oh, fuck me, Lu. You've gone full-on red pill. We're doomed."

CHAPTER 8

DEEP WEB

BETHANY LU

I was overpowered by the unwelcome flavor of a mouth full of pasty saliva, chocolate and nuts, all mixed with an overwhelming amount of regret. Morning afters sucked ass.

This was what I got for going full-out on my Keanu binge last night featuring terrible relationships. Which was how I was thinking of his whole ninety-day marriage. Just one more in his line of questionable scripted choices.

Like I'd never forgive Deb Messing's character from *A Walk in the Clouds*. I mean, WTF—if she'd just read the letters, she would have seen what a catch he was. Then there was *Something's Gotta Give*. Diane Keaton was out of her goddamned mind. Like really, she picked Jack. In what world? I decided to end it with *Siberia*. I know, I know. I was torturing myself for sure, wandering into a dangerous abyss of unchecked Keanu fantasy.

Morphie licked at my bare arm. Either he sniffed a last

bit of chocolate or it was because he wanted to go out. Better to err on the side of caution. I opened my eyes and looked at him. "Okay, dude. Give me a minute."

He frowned and stopped licking, his deep brown eyes going serious. His little doggie shoulders seemed to lift in a shrug before he turned and prepared to wait. But he knew I was a notorious homebody and late riser. He stood by the door to my patio, where I had a patch of faux grass installed, plus wee-wee pads. It may not have been Central Park, but Morphie and me didn't have a bad setup with his fake grass, little covered doghouse and our two matching lounge chairs. His mini matching my full one. We could see a bit of the Hudson, and the downtown view was incredible.

I rolled out of bed and unlocked the door, then slid open the screen and outer door, catching a bit of the morning breeze before the humidity started to amp up. Taking a deep breath, I caught a whiff of bacon, sausages, bread, the heavy smell of grease and the rich aroma of coffee all mixed in with the exhaust of thousands of cars already humming on the city streets.

As Morphie did his business, I became acutely aware of my own needs and headed to the bathroom. My stomach growled, then did a gurgle, and Morphie scratched at the bathroom door. "Okay, boy. You'll eat in a minute." I could still taste the aftereffects of last night's eel. The ice cream and prosecco didn't help it.

Coming back into the loft with a freshly washed face, I now got a clear look at the havoc I'd wrought the night before. My bed was a mass of tangled sheets. On the nightstand was the empty ice cream carton, big fat tablespoon still inside from where I scraped out every last bit. The prosecco bottle on the floor had maybe one glass left. But it'd be flat by now. What a waste! I took in the rest of the carnage and shook my head.

Jesus, Lu. This place looks like you had a wild night with the Keanu himself instead of a party for one.

I turned away from the scene of my mess. It would look better after coffee. Almost everything did.

Thirty seconds of drawer slamming, though, and things were looking a whole lot worse. "Fuck all!" I was out of pods. I'd searched every drawer and little canister on my countertop only to come up with way too many soy sauce and ketchup packets, plus enough cheap chopsticks in paper wrappers to throw an ultra-cool dinner party if I was into that sort of thing, which I'm not.

Pissed, I checked my cell, thinking of the notes app where I'd specifically typed order more coffee pods as a reminder and then specifically forgot to ever open that notes page again. Why was that blasted thing failing me so miserably lately?

Shit. Now I'd have to go to the store.

I went to the fridge. Jeez, I was low on everything. There was hard salami, an egg from the Stone Age, a leftover hunk from a block of cheese that almost made me pass out with just one sniff. I threw it away and grabbed the jug of Cran-Apple juice.

Oh well. At least Morphie was covered thanks to auto refill on his organic food. "As long as one of us won't starve."

I dished out some food for him and put it down.

Keanu help me, I needed to do more than work on

my pieces, have movie marathons and live in my fantasy worlds, if I expected to live on more than ketchup and soy sauce packets. Swallowing the last of the Cran-Apple juice and still feeling groggy, I did a mental recap of last night's antics once I'd hung up with Dawn.

The rewatches. The ice cream, the drinking, the YouTube surfing for Keanu behavioral cues. I glanced at Morphie as images of a dance session with me and Keanu to '80s music came to mind. Morphie looked rightly ashamed. "Sorry, Morph. You deserve better in a mama but sadly I'm all you got, kid."

My gaze went to my white task board. I usually kept my schedules and ideas there, but it now looked like part of some crime scene investigation show. There were lines and squares and lists and boxes.

I had Keanu's movie discography, music history, play history and publishing facts. But still facts were frustratingly thin when it came to his current girlfriend. Secretive bastard. I suppose that was part of what kept him so popular.

At least his film schedule was a little easier to find more info on. More but not much. My manic Googling gave me a few ideas of places where there could be a potential spotting. Unfortunately, they were all over the globe, making him an international Where's Waldo?

In the center of all this chaos was a box with my own drawing of Keanu—since I hadn't remembered to order printer ink and of course, last night realized I needed a refill—and underneath, the title:

The K-90 Plan.

Okay, so not the best name for a life journey when I

looked on it with a bit of distance and sans coffee, but it worked well enough for now despite sounding more like a 1990s kick-ass workout than a mastermind's plot to (a) win the heart of Keanu Reeves, (b) convince him to call off the wedding so the world would still have hope and a fantasy boyfriend, or (c) at the very least, take ninety days to get my shit together and finally grow up once and for all.

The name of the plan didn't matter; what mattered was the execution.

I leaned back and stared at my five points.

1. Locate—Tricky, yes. Keanu was a cagey bugger.

2. Meet—Trickier. Bodyguards would no doubt be a problem, but I'd figure something out.

3. Charm—I'd been playing the game my whole life. Number one code switcher. I'd charm Keanu and…

4. Convince—This is where it got sticky. I wasn't quite sure how I was going to persuade Keanu to call off his marriage. I mean, I'm sure his fiancée was perfectly fine and all, but was Keanu really *completely* devoted? Did he fully understand the consequences? At the very least we could come to the understanding that postponing indefinitely would be for the best. And finally…

5. Marry—Me. Okay, so this was a long shot, but hell, I wasn't throwing it away. While I was there, I might as well take it. I thought Keanu would approve. Or have me arrested.

By the time I'd executed the plan, I was sure I'd overcome my creative block and figure out my life. Everything would work out. It had to. I let out a breath just as my buzzer rang.

CHAPTER 9

THUMB SUCKER

TRUE

Mister Er-ick-son." Even clearly still full of morning tiredness she had the crank to give me shit with an Agent Smith impersonation.

"Are we still doing that?"

"Is it still your name?" Lu quipped back.

"You know it's not."

Lu looked like she'd done a quick half marathon through hell last night, but it didn't matter. Hell or not, she wouldn't drop her shield and she'd always find time to tease me. Keep me at a distance.

She folded her arms across her chest, pushing her breasts up and close together in her sleep tank. I forced myself to look past her at Morphie. The look he gave me was pure "who you fooling, man?"

"What are you doing here at this hour?" Lu asked, bringing my attention back her way. "Some people like to sleep."

I sucked in a breath and told myself to focus. This was good, actually. Seeing that she was her usual morning ray of light gave me a clue as to how the dinner went with Sir Suave, "D. Lim in da house!" according to his last annoying-ass IG story. And seriously, pick a fucking lane, dude. Either you're a smooth corporate raider or you're a shit-faced frat boy/man. But not both.

There were no darts of love shooting from her eyes and not a hint of smug "ha, you were wrong, and Daniel Lim was perfect and we're now in business together" either. I should have felt a smidge guiltier about the glee that washed over me, but I didn't.

"And good morning to you too, sunshine," I said, walking past Lu and into the loft. "Maybe I was just passing by and I'm checking on you."

"You say that like I need checking on."

"And you say that like you don't."

"Truman, dearest, respectfully I don't." She shut the door and followed me, then scurried to jump in front of me. She ran a hand through her curls, hit a knot and winced. I tried not to laugh and left it at a small chuckle. Then I looked past her to the rest of the loft.

I cleared my throat. "You need help with that situation?" I asked, pointing at her hair. "Or maybe this one?" I gestured at the mess of her apartment.

Lu looked up at me, sharp eyes and half-twisted lips. "No, I don't need help with either situation. I'm perfectly fine, thank you. Now come on, sweetling. You're moderately cute most of the time. But this is not one of those times. Care to make it quick? I have a lot of things to do today."

I looked around and put the bag I was carrying on the kitchen island. "So it would seem."

She pointed a long finger at me. "Care to go head back down to your place and judge your own mess? I'm sure you have plenty of your own."

I raised a brow. "You want to put money on it?"

Lu blew out a breath, knowing she was already beaten. Of course, I wouldn't say anything about the pile of laundry on my bedroom chair. She didn't have to know that things got out of hand at my place too at times.

"Whatever, True. I'm not in the mood." She waved her hand. "Take your eagle eye down a few floors."

I shrugged and picked up the bag. "Fine. Maybe I'll just take this coffee down there with me too."

As expected, she immediately did a 180 and her face lit to near radiant quality. It was then that little hearts did shoot from her brown eyes as she practically bounced over and snatched the box of pods out of the bag. "Hold it there, cutie! You know I was just kidding." She moaned as she held the box to her chest. "What would I do without you?"

I had to strain to keep from smiling. That was her. One minute darkness, the next light.

"It's no biggie," I said. "Thought I'd save you a trip. I know how you hate grocery trips or most outside trips in general."

Her brows quirked slightly at that, but she didn't comment further, keeping her eyes on her morning prize.

"And I noticed you were low yesterday."

It was then I caught sight of her task board. "Though

maybe getting out for air more often wouldn't be the worst thing?"

She looked from the board to me and back to the board again. Her smile this time was definitely forced. "Fresh air is totally overrated."

I frowned. "You took the red pill."

"That freaking Dawn. She's so fired. Did she call you this morning and send you with these pods? Because if so and you're just here to judge me and my plan, you can take them back."

She shoved the box toward me, then immediately pulled it back. "Well, not take them back, but you can take the money for them and head on out of here with your opinions and horrified looks because I don't need them."

I stared at her for a few beats, watching as she let her tantrum smooth out and ease down a bit.

"What are you talking about?" I finally said. "I haven't spoken to Dawn. Also, why would you fire your best friend?" I fought to keep my eyes steady as I took the pods from her hand with no small tug. "Here, let me make the coffee for you. Looks like you can definitely use it. For a little extra focus? Maybe some perspective."

She snatched the box back and ripped it open. "I can do it myself, and I don't need you telling me about my focus, True Erickson. Save that for your students. You and Dawn don't need to tell me how to run my life."

I stepped back. "Listen, I don't know what you're talking about with Dawn. I didn't speak to her, okay?"

Lu paused mid pod dispensing and stared at me again. I suddenly felt the heat of an imaginary interrogation light and could almost hear the sound of a rusty cart with an old lie detector machine being wheeled in.

"You didn't speak with her?"

"No," I said, hoping in real life my voice didn't sound like the sixteen-year-old True that echoed back to me in my ears. "So I don't know why you're being so testy. I'm just the bringer of coffee here. Now if you don't want my coffee or kindness…" I looked at the ripped box. "Well, if you don't want my kindness, I'll accept a polite thank-you and $7.99, please. I'm kinda over this ranting. I can be on my way."

Lu frowned but had the decency to look slightly embarrassed as she flipped the coffeemaker's lid down hard on the pod and pressed start. She stared at the machine a few moments as I watched her going over my words in her mind.

"Well, you did start it, True. You were the one who came in talking about how messy my place and my hair was."

Now who sounded like their younger self? My heart did a little twisty flip thing as I stared at her before forcing my gaze away.

"Well, your place is kind of a mess." I pushed a tease into my voice.

"Well, I fucking know it," she huffed. "And you made a comment about my board," she added.

I looked back at her and raised my brow, then thumbed at the board. "Come on, Lu. How can you expect me not to?" I made wide eyes and shifted them back and forth.

That brought on a slight crack of a smile, and I let out

my first really clear breath. I finally felt we were getting back on normal ground. She took the coffee and added her usual cream and sugar, then leaned back to take a sip.

"Really? I bring you gifts, and you don't even offer me a cup?"

She raised a brow. "Like you said, I need the focus, so this cup is my mental emergency. I can't go expending any extra."

"Shit. I knew that would come back to haunt me. I just didn't think it would be so fast."

"Good," she said. "Now you don't have to wait and wonder." She took a long gulp of the hot coffee and let out a contented sigh before looking back at me with a sweet smile. "Now make your own cup. There's nothing wrong with your hands."

❧

BETHANY LU

"The K-90 plan?" True was standing in front of my board, ready to go full in with the wisecracks, so I braced myself. I probably should have just paid eight bucks for the pods and gotten him to skedaddle, but for some reason I wanted to hear what he had to say.

"Oh, Lu," he started. "This sounds slightly insane. Like you were either on an all-night binge, scrolling through the infomercials, or you're pushing the next fat-burning workout plan."

Well damn, he wasn't far off on part of that, but still it stung.

"All right, smartie. So you can do better?"

He took a lazy sip of his coffee and gave me a side glance as if I'd just asked him the dumbest question ever. "I mean, if you were going for an exercise theme, then why not Insanity?"

"So you're just all in with the jokes today? Fine. If you're not taking this seriously, then go." I flipped the board to the other side and gave him a challenging stare. That was enough with the embarrassment. I was over it. Shame didn't sit right in my skin, especially not here in my own place and not in front of True.

I guess that was why I didn't flip the board and hide the plan when I first heard it was him at the buzzer. I was who I was. And I never hid with him, and though he was judgmental as all hell in his opinions, he was still accepting. I was me and he was True. This...this was just annoying. Besides, it was not like I could hide much from True. Not most things anyway. He'd always find a way to see through me. That was True's way. Probably a better name for him would've been Truth. My Truth.

He flipped my board back slowly and gently, then stared at it. Critically now. Not a hint of laughter or irony in his expression.

Though I hated to remember, still there was no way I'd ever forget how True used to look all those years ago when hanging out with my younger brother, Cole. No matter what they had going on—a movie, a heated video game— when it was time for his attention to be on something, True gave it. Fully. Stopping and focusing one hundred percent with that dead steady gaze.

I guess he realized it used to make people feel a little off, so somewhere along the way he stopped doing that pause-and-stare-and-look-right-in-the-face thing, the way he used to do when I'd walk in the kitchen while he and my brother were doing homework and I would ask some random question. "Do you want something to eat?" "No." "A drink?" "No, thank you," he'd murmur. But you put it in front of him and he'd gobble down whatever was offered. True, never asking but still silently accepting and always giving. And never one to drop his mask.

Even back then—hell, more so back then—he'd play on his phone and pretend to not be paying attention or look out the window or play with the dog while observing every seemingly meaningless detail. Detail like the fact that I was out of coffee. And then he'd come up with a plan to fix it.

Just like he was probably currently trying to fix my K-90 plan or talk me out of it.

I figured it was best for both of us if I got another cup of coffee, since the first was clearly for gulping down and becoming semi-human; the second would be better for becoming the me I needed to be. True walked up behind me, his presence blanketing me as he put his chin on top of my head.

"I'm sorry, Beth. I shouldn't have teased you."

He was so tall, and his words, as they had been for years, were ridiculously comforting. I always knew he was extra sincere when he called me Beth. I wanted to lean back into him, close my eyes and rest in the familiar feeling of safety and home. This was stupid. This was my problem right here. This reliance on True and the comfort of his safety net. So I pushed back at him. Literally and hard, with my left shoulder and then with my butt right into his crotch area. That part probably wasn't the best choice because, surprise for both of us, there was pushback to my pushback. But thankfully he didn't comment and neither did I. Instead, I spun around.

"Personal goddamn space, True. Do you mind?" I turned away from him and pretended to focus on the stream of coffee coming out of my Keurig.

"I'm sorry," he said again. His voice held a hint of anguish and it tore at me. When I looked at him again, he'd moved to the other side of the counter. His frown was so deep it looked painful. His full lips were drawn so tight his dimples were popping out, while those little crosshairs came to the center of his brow. I sighed and rubbed a hand over my face. True was a lot. I was a lot. And though to the outside world we probably looked like two of the calmest and most compatible of friends, sometimes me and True together was a little too much.

"It's fine," I said. "I mean, it's not fine-fine, but it's fine. You brought me coffee, which is perfect. But just don't go teasing my plan anymore and getting in my way and we won't have a problem."

True eyed me with a skeptical narrowing of his lids, then cleared his throat. He let out a breath and moved back before he started casually pacing in front of my board. He was doing his professorial thing that got all the coeds swoony. "Fine," he said. "Now let's look at this plan of yours seriously. What is your objective and why do you want to achieve it?"

I blinked fast and looked up at the ceiling. "I'm not doing this with you," I said at the same time my traitorous body walked forward.

"Doing what?"

"Letting you talk me out of my plan." I took a seat on the couch and shifted, pulling one of Morphie's hard chew toys out from under my behind. Morphie was into burying his favorite toys between the cushions, but why did I feel like this time it was a deliberate well-placed poke right in my ass? Sighing, I took a sip of my coffee and settled back. True wouldn't be able to talk me out of my plan, but I might as well enjoy the show anyway.

"Who said I'm trying to talk you out of anything? I'm saying we just have a conversation."

I looked at him straight on. "Nothing is ever just conversation with you, True."

"Oh, come on, humor me. Just answer a few questions."

"And what if I don't want to answer them?"

He stopped pacing and shrugged, stepping closer to me. "No problem. I guess you also don't want to get to the part where I could maybe help you with your point number one."

I jumped up, sloshing coffee all over myself and True. "You said what now?"

"Shit, Lu!" he yelled while wiping at his pants.

I reached out to help him, but realized he'd only been hit with a few droplets. My shirt, on the other hand, was soaked. I started to shake it out. Wiggling the clinging wetness away from my body.

True stilled before sighing, then stalked off toward the kitchen. He returned with both wet and dry paper towels. He wiped at his pants with the dry and came at my chest with the wet.

As he dabbed, the awkwardness of the situation suddenly hit us and we both froze for a moment. I snatched the towels and wiped at my own chest, while True went down on his knees to clean the floor with short fast swipes that radiated frustration.

"It's not my fault," I told him. "You shouldn't just blurt out stuff like that."

"Only you can find a way to blame me for your coffee spill." He sighed.

Frustrated, I yanked the towels from him and put them in the trash. "It's coffee. I don't spill coffee without good reason."

He put his hands up. I could tell he was over arguing. He turned back to the board. Fine. I was ready to be over it too. "So what were you saying about objective number one?" *Objective* sounded a lot more official.

He almost smiled. "Objective. Funny, Lu. I'll tell you after you give me your motivation for objective five."

Little shit.

He came up, leaned down a bit and stared me in the eye. Essentially knocking the *little* out of my shit comment. Still, why should I tell him? "I'll give it to you for four, not five."

I watched him. His analytical wheels were spinning.

"Fine." He crossed his arms.

I backed up. "Could you relax? I feel like I'm about to get graded. Jeez, I'm glad I never had to be in your class."

"You'd never pass it. Now stop stalling."

I took a deep breath. Last night, and even this morning when I first woke up, it seemed so clear why I wanted— no, *needed*—to go out and find Keanu Reeves to stop his wedding. But looking at True and those all-seeing, all-knowing deep brown eyes, my plan didn't seem to have the same urgency.

I forced myself to go back. Way, way back. Back to the day Keanu's smile brought me back from the brink when I didn't think there was any coming back. The smile that made my breathing full again instead of gasping and shallow like I was drowning. Yes, I knew it wasn't just for me. It was for me and the millions of others who loved *Speed*. Ironic how much I loved it. How much I clung to it given the way Cole had died, caught in a drag race with rich-ass seniors from our school barely days after I'd left for college abroad.

I never thought I'd see my way up to the light again in the grave I'd dug for myself. But that day, I'd walked out of the theater with True feeling about half my weight lighter and so much less numb. I finally heard his voice clearly for the first time as he rambled on about what he thought were the technically non-plausible parts of the film.

True had been filling the air with words for months after Cole was killed. I'll never know or remember what he talked about then, but he spoke to ease the silence of my grief. I put my fingers to his lips that day in the theater lobby and watched his eyes go wide.

"It's okay, True. I get it. You didn't like it. But I did. I really did. You know I've loved Keanu since *Point Break*, and you brought me to make me feel better. Well, it worked."

"It did?" He looked so hopeful.

I nodded at him. "It did."

He smiled so wide then you would have thought the sun shone just for him in the lobby of the Regal multiplex, and for the first time in months I smiled too. Not a false put-on smile that hurt my cheeks and made my eyes burn with unshed tears, but a true one that came easy and gently and warmed me throughout my body.

"And I love you for being my friend and bringing me here to see it and for not leaving my side and more so for being my brother's friend. There for him when I was not."

I saw something in True then. A cloud washed over his eyes and I knew how deep his grief went too. He hadn't lost a brother like me, but he did lose a best friend. I took his hand in mine and gave it a squeeze as we left to head home.

True went back to more of his normal self after that. Not as chatty but seemingly content to listen to me go on instead. So I did. And on and on.

I looked at True again, and just like it had been at the movie theater that day, it was as if his next breath depended on my answer and reassuring him was all I wanted to do.

But I couldn't. I couldn't lie. Not anymore. So I opened my mouth and this time I told the truth.

"Because I need to take a chance on joy."

True blinked and his eyes softened. "Joy?"

I nodded. "Yep. Joy."

He let out a sigh. "That's a little unlike you but…okay."

I frowned. "What do you mean, unlike and oooh-kayyy?"

His eyes shifted. "I didn't mean anything."

I raised a brow. "Oh, you sure as hell did."

"I didn't. Listen, it's great. Oooh-kayy. And I can work with it. Like I said, I may know a guy who knows some things."

I groaned. "Are you kidding me? You made me come up with joy and then you get all cagey with 'I may know a guy'? I can't believe I fell for it. Just leave it to me. Thanks for the coffee. I'll invite you to the wedding. You and Dawn will be my best man and woman. Be prepared." I started pushing him toward the door.

True turned quickly and I bumped into his chest. He tipped my chin up, then got close. I took a whiff of the air, sensing something besides the normal outside-and-coffee scent. It was nice—spicy and slightly musky.

True frowned and leaned back, sniffing under his armpits. "What are you doing? Do I stink?"

I didn't answer. Just blinked. Better to just leave it at that than explain, because I didn't even know what I was doing.

"Lu, seriously, I know a guy. And I also don't want to see you going all half-cocked and ending up in jail. Let me look into this for you."

I stared at him. Ever since Cole had left us, True had never steered me wrong. He'd become a part of my extended family and me his because of the shared tragedy of losing my younger brother and his best friend. So I knew he was only looking out for me. I also knew he probably hated with every ounce of his being the idea of me chasing off after Keanu Reeves like a damned horny salamander.

But that wasn't it. This was more and I think at True's core, he got it. All I could do at this moment was hope.

CHAPTER 10

TO THE BONE

BETHANY LU

W ait. He said what now?" Dawn couldn't keep the disbelief from her voice. "Since when did Doctor Economics become the type to 'know a guy'?"

"I know, I was kind of surprised too. But he seems serious." I took a bite of my chicken wing, the best part of trekking downtown. "True says he tutored this guy in physics and now he works in film doing something. I don't know. But True wouldn't lie."

"No, he wouldn't do that. But still. This is really not like him. Why would he go along with something so outlandish?"

"Outlandish?" I was shocked. Dawn was usually my all-in ride or die. I couldn't keep the disappointment from my voice. "This is coming from the woman who used coming to Koreatown for beauty products as an excuse to stock up on K-pop merch. What all do you have in that shopping bag? Three hydrating masks and four CDs of the same album."

She opened her mouth and I held up a hand. "I know, I know. There are different versions."

Dawn twisted her lips, extra shiny from her YSL lip gloss with sticky chicken glaze on top.

We were currently having Korean BBQ chicken and some sides on 32nd Street. My win for the trip downtown.

I continued on a bit of a self-righteous roll. "Oh, and there's a poster you won't hang in your perfectly decorated apartment and two sets of sticker cards."

"Those I'll use for my planner. But whatever," she said, sounding more like back-in-high-school Dawn than art-agent Dawn. She gave me a glare. "Your point is?"

I gave her a cold smile. "I don't have one really."

"Good." She bit into her wing.

"Except."

"Great," she mumbled out over the wing. "Here it comes. I know I went overboard today. But I was a little down, and I sold an old purse on eBay to cover for it."

"Poor baby. I know that was hard."

"Don't patronize me, Lu."

I swallowed, but my throat was dry. She was right; that wasn't fair. We all had our shit. "But my point was that I was not judging you. When have we ever done that? I just thought you, more than anyone, would be behind me on this."

Dawn was quiet and stared at her wing. When her head came back up, she looked suitably guilty.

"Why did you choose this year to jump into some ridiculous state of reality?" I asked. "Do I have to give both you and Keanu an intervention?"

She laughed. "Is that what you're calling what you want to give Keanu? An intervention?" She raised her arm high, chicken wing in hand, and mimicked a stripper-like gyration, then snorted, sending chicken spittle flying.

I threw my hand over my food. "Seriously? In front of my salad!"

Dawn burst out laughing, sending more spittle flying, and eyes in the crowded eatery turned our way.

I looked around. "Don't mind her. She always dances with her wings. Side effect of her pole days."

"Hush, you said you'd never bring that up again once we got out of Atlanta, Miss Lucille!" Dawn yelled.

I rubbed my head and went back to my food. Pretty much the same as everyone else. Seemed our little theater was de rigueur for the likes of this busy midtown bunch. "Had your fun deflecting?"

"I wish. And I'm not the one deflecting."

"Neither am I. I'm the one facing reality and life head-on. At least True sees that."

She gave me a hard and skeptical look. "Is that what True sees? I'm sure." She drawled the last word out.

"Don't start, Dawn."

"Who's starting? I didn't say a thing. That's your mind going all sorts of ways."

"My mind's going nowhere."

She snorted. "Your mind's always going somewhere. Just like True's."

"Oh, really? And where could True's mind be going? It's always on numbers."

"Sure, you go on telling yourself that if it keeps your head firmly attached and your panties in place." She shrugged and went back to concentrating on her food, though I knew she wasn't concentrating on her food at all. She was practically salivating waiting for my reaction. I shouldn't say a thing and just let her stew.

Yeah, that would've happened if I had an inch of willpower. I didn't.

"My panties are perfectly secure," I said.

"Not if you and True go flouncing around on a quest for Keanu."

I grinned. "Quest for Keanu? I like the sound of that."

Dawn sighed. "You really have a one-track mind. How did you focus on that when I was talking about True getting into them drawers?" She waved her chicken-free hand toward my bottom half.

"You're being ridiculous. You know True has zero interest in me and same the other way around. He's like a little brother."

She gave me that "yeah sure" skeptical look.

"Or cousin," I said.

Her eyebrows raised.

"You are reaching so far now, my friend, you might just dislocate something." Dawn sighed.

"How about older cousin's sister's friend?" I said.

Dawn shook her head. "Yeah. That one she brings to the cookout who you only see once a year and you've been looking forward to seeing because you've had the biggest crush on her and you can't wait for her to see how much you've grown since last summer. That one? The one you're not even related to but since their kin lived next door to each other, somehow it turned into 'cousins'? Okay then."

My chicken turned to sawdust in my mouth. "Sometimes I can't stand you, you know."

"I know. But I want to see you happy. And now that I've said it and it's off my chest, I can happily tell you to go with God and live free." She looked so proud and full of herself after her little bomb drop that if she wasn't my best friend, I'd hate her. "Please," she continued, "find Keanu and at the very least, True will ensure you stay the hell out of jail. I'm just giving you the warning that if you do find our dream boyfriend, please be careful with our little boy True's heart. It's fragile."

I held up my hand. "All right, all right. I get the picture. You act like True's been a saint, pining for me all these years. Which we both know he hasn't. Not with the number of women who have thrown themselves at him. Hell, we've even helped him get ready for dates."

Dawn frowned. "That we did. But so what? Everything needs its right time."

I sighed. "Well, there is no right time for us. Besides, very helpful TA Aimee is bouncing to pounce if she hasn't already."

"Trust and believe for all my ball busting she hasn't . . . yet."

I nodded, my focus on the heavily loaded *yet* in Dawn's sentence. There was no reason for me to care about True's TA. Her T or her A. But I did. Either way, I should be happy for him. I wanted him to be happy. He supported me for so long. Both my friends had. I owed them the same support.

I poked at my salad, wondering if taking True's help was asking too much.

"Don't look like that."

I looked up at Dawn. "Like what?"

"Like I just kicked your puppy."

"Those are fighting words. True is nobody's puppy."

Her lip quirked. "But he is your special companion. Sort of your energy. It's very John Wick of you."

I sighed and swore I felt my eyes roll back. "Oh, come on. I've got Morphie, and you are going a bit far in your analyzation today. You're lucky I'm distracted, or I'd be all up in *your* shit."

She shrugged. "Lucky me. But it's not like I've got shit to get in. I'm as clear as glass. But seriously, you're fine. Do you."

"I don't know. Maybe you were right from the start. I should just do my thing. Focus on these last pieces for the show. See what's up or not up with Daniel Lim and maybe do a few commissions. If growing up is good enough for Keanu, then maybe it's worth a try. Besides, I don't want to put True out."

Dawn frowned. "Put him out or bring him in?"

"Whatever. I don't know why I'm getting all up in arms. He probably doesn't know a guy anyway." I laughed, not convinced but trying to get there, when my phone buzzed with a text.

I continued eating my salad.

"Well, aren't you going to look?" she said.

"I'm eating."

"Girl, you know it's the pup. We talked him up. Just look."

I gave her a glare. Then wiped my hands and flipped over my phone. Of course it was the pup, um, True.

My guy came thru. First stop: Coney Island. Cyclone.

Cyclone?? My stomach dropped, like I was already riding the infamous roller coaster, and I swallowed before looking back up at Dawn.

"He knows a guy?"

I nodded. "He freaking knows a guy."

CHAPTER 11

LIAISONS DANGEREUSES

BETHANY LU

For all my outward bravado, I was pretty full of shit and I knew it. But we all had our masks. Didn't we? Without them, society would crumble. It's how we all got along. Mask on. Shit tucked. And not in constant rage-fueled cursing tirades.

But today, back in the loft after lunch with Dawn and walking Morphie, I had nothing left to fill my mind but the damned nerve-racking text from True. The man was really trying me, and my mask was slipping, no, cracking. Hell, maybe suffocating me and I just needed it off. Why Coney Island? Did he have to mention the Cyclone and leave it just dangling there? Was he testing to see how far I'd actually go for Keanu and my plan? I'd show his smart ass.

Well, hopefully, I'd show him.

I changed into a pair of loose sweats and a tank, thinking

I could paint away my high-key anxiety. Usually, it helped to lose myself in a world I had some control over.

But ever since the disastrous news about Keanu's wedding, my work felt stilted. No matter what I did, it didn't flow right. Everything seemed to be just a mass of shapes and ripped pieces of paper that didn't quite fit together. No matter what materials I tried, I couldn't get it to make sense. There was no way I could see myself showing at this rate, let alone being licensed by DLIG. A middle school art fair would laugh me out of town.

Frustrated, I pushed my two chairs up against the kitchen island and slid the coffee table to the far corner by the end tables out of the way, making space to spread out my large tarp.

Screw it. Keanu or not, I had to get past this block.

I dropped a four-by-four-foot canvas, then got to work laying down an acrylic base of pale gold and rose. I immediately hated it and washed over it with tones of deeper indigo and fern green. I added brushstrokes of brick and flecks of mahogany and corkscrews of hot cinnamon. Splatters of ivory trekked through, disrupting the order. After about five straight hours of working, exhausted and feeling pain in my upper shoulders and knees...I looked down at the image of a faceless, amorphous woman.

Well damn. That was time I'd never get back. This work looked like it was headed down the same road as all the rest. To a place called Nowhere. A whole night and a canvas wasted.

"Fuck," I groaned and looked over at Morphie, who co-signed with a groan of his own. "Is this really it, Morphie?

Have I lost it? Shit. For all of that, I could have taken a long bath or gotten a few episodes of *Love Island* in." Morphie gave me a "yeah, you could have" look, leaving me sufficiently read by a dog. I deserved it.

I stretched and ambled over to his treat container and pulled out one for him. Bending over to give it to him, I winced. "Not a word," I said as I gave him the treat and rubbed him under his chin. "I'm not in the mood."

My shoulders and the backs of my legs hurt, and I hadn't heard anything from True since I'd texted him back to ask for more info about Coney Island. Talk about hella rude. You'd think he'd give me more to go on than those scant details.

Coming up, I wiped my hands and went to pick up my phone to text him once more when the phone buzzed in my hand with a FaceTime.

"I thought you forgot about me."

"As if," he said.

He clearly had just come from the gym or running. I could tell because he was wearing one of his usual workout shirts. This was one from a startup he'd done some freelance work for about ten years ago. They may have paid him in free shirts if I recall. But True wasn't one to turn down a job back then, and hardly even now.

Though he went to school with me, Cole and Dawn at Forresters, True was legitimately one of those students the school liked to tout—an underprivileged academic able to attend the school thanks to the benevolence of the A-list saviors of Forresters, who of course didn't need any thanks for their good deeds but were definitely not going to remain anonymous or not take the tax write-off for their donation.

True had befriended Cole right away, much like Dawn had done for me, and quickly he became a part of our lives. Outside but in. Watching in the way he does.

After Cole was gone, it didn't seem right to lose True too. Not to me and I guess not to my parents or Dawn either.

And now he was watching and frowning at me from my phone screen. "You do realize that you have yellow paint precariously close to your eye, Lu?"

"And do you realize that shirt should have gone to the trash five years ago? There's a hole in the shoulder."

He looked down.

"Other side," I said.

He poked. "Oh, crap. I didn't know. I'll fix it."

"You can throw it away. You have so many of those exact same shirts."

"So nice to know you care."

"Who's saying I care? I'm just pointing it out and trying to make your life a little easier. It's not like you have to go reading anything into it."

"Who says I'm reading? It's not like you're a book."

I took in a long breath and released it, feeling a smile threatening to slip out. "I'm sure you didn't call me to talk about the paint on my face or for me to talk about the hole in your shirt. Now come on, I'm dying to hear all about this guy of yours and your plans," I groaned. "How in the world does Coney Island fit in?"

He nodded and moved through his apartment to sit on his couch. "I hear Keanu is coming to the city this weekend for location shots and a promo. There is a shoot on Coney Island Saturday."

How in the world did I not know this? Back in the day, I'd be up on where my favorite actor was shooting. "I can't believe you got this information. You're a sweetheart."

True gave a wry not-quite smile. "I'm not. I know that look and I figured you'd find this out or die trying. How about we meet Saturday at five a.m. and take the train out?"

"Five a what?"

"Five a.m., as in in the morning," he said slowly.

"We're going to Coney Island, not freaking trout fishing, True."

"Are you trying to get on the set or not? If so, we need to be there early. My guy says this is what we have to do."

"I already have a bad feeling about this guy of yours. Is he even real?"

"Have I ever lied to you?"

I looked at the screen. He wasn't being impatient or irritated. But asking straightforward.

Our eyes connected, our long history of hard truths passing in our gaze. "No." I sighed. "Not ever."

He smiled the irresistible smile that transformed his gruff appearance to all charm and light in the blink of an eye. "See you Saturday then!"

I may have whimpered.

Saturday was three days away, and my body was already rejecting the idea of the early morning hour. What did things look like in the city at five a.m.? I hadn't seen that hour since the rare couple of times Dawn and I had sleepovers at her house while her parents were out of town. Neither of us had ever been much for wild nightlife. It was dangerous and overrated. And also hard on one's feet.

I thought of Keanu. Five a.m. Was my fave really doing things like this in his everyday life? Five a.m. call times? It was hard to believe, and given both our ages I got a twinge of empathy and a moment of understanding him wanting to slow it down. But this ninety-day marriage deal? It was too much.

CHAPTER 12

THEY ARE ALL ANGELS

BETHANY LU

So maybe the idea of staying up all night was not one of my best. But to my credit I was doing well until four a.m. and then my body just said, "Enough of that." Like it just stopped. It was done, DONE.

But that night, lying in bed looking at the ceiling, tossing and turning while imagining finally meeting Keanu face-to-face... Well, by the time four o'clock came I was completely exhausted. My body felt like I had suddenly taken on a ridiculous late-night 10K run.

When my phone rang at 5:00 on the dot, followed by my door buzzer, my body was in serious revolt mode. "You've got to be freaking kidding me."

Shit, it was dark. Which my pinky toe explicitly noticed en route to my door.

Morphie didn't even budge at my painful yelp. "Oh, so I see how much you care. Thanks."

"Remind me whose idea this was?" I said as I opened the door to see True standing on the other side looking way too bright-eyed and alert for this particular hour of pitch black.

"I believe it was yours. All yours," he said as he sailed past me and came into the loft.

"Oh yeah, it was."

He looked me up and down. I could only imagine the image I was giving. My hair was in tangles, my face lined with sheet marks and caked with dried drool, and I was still wearing my THIS IS WHERE THE MAGIC HAPPENS oversized nightshirt from an impromptu Disney detour when visiting Dawn's parents back in 2008. He tilted his head to the side and gave me that True judgy face. "Seriously, Lu? Since this is for your precious Keanu, I thought that maybe there was a slim chance you would get up on time."

"Oh, come on. Don't give me any crap. I literally just went to sleep an hour ago, and I didn't even mean to do that. I was actually trying to stay up until it was time to go." I started walking toward the kitchen and the coffee-pot, when Morphie got in my way, causing me to almost trip. I looked down. "Really, Morph? Right in my path?" I sidestepped him and almost bumped into True. Shit, it was early, and I needed to wake up.

True grabbed me gently by the elbow. "You, bathroom. Wash your face and get dressed. I'll get your coffee on and run Morphie out. Be right back."

I blinked and looked up at him, about to come back with something, but what was there? He tilted his head, then nodded. "Say, 'Thank you, True.'"

My lips pulled into a frown. "This is going to be a long day, huh?"

He raised an eyebrow.

"Thank you, dear True." I put on as much sweetness as I could for the hour, and that was pretty much none.

Still, he grinned, and even through my bleary eyes I caught the hint of self-satisfaction in the smug upturn of his lips. *Cute little bugger.* I did a mental freeze. Where had that come from? I didn't want to think of True as cute, no matter how cute True was. Maybe he was right, better to go and splash water on my face and get myself together. Better yet, better to dunk my whole freaking head.

"You go take Morphie so we can be that much faster, and I'll be ready when you get back. I feel bad leaving him for so long since I'm with him most of the day."

I practically pushed him back out the door with Morph and his leash. I hoped Morph would be okay today while I was gone, though I knew I didn't have to worry. My neighbor's daughter was coming to give Morphie a midday walk, and Dawn said she'd check on him tonight if I was really late.

Looking at myself in the bathroom mirror I wondered where my mini fit of panic came from, and recalling True's expression, I'm sure he was just as confused. "Come on, Bethany Lu Carlisle, get it together, woman," I mumbled to myself, exiting the bathroom and rushing to change.

My mind flipped to how True looked standing in my doorway. He *was* cute. Shit, that word again. His early morning super casual getup of loose khakis and a white tee with a chambray shirt on top was low-key Keanu in *Speed*.

Very low-key. Still, it had me reaching to the back part of my closet for a little ditzy print short floral dress. It was a little too short to wear on its own, so I belted it and put on some black leggings, my Converse shoes and grabbed my denim jacket.

By the time True was back with Morphie, I was ready with two coffees in to-go cups. Look at me. Grown up and responsible. On my way to Keanu.

"Okay, I'll admit you shocked me," True said upon seeing me dressed and ready to go.

"What?" I looked down at myself, feigning ignorance. "Oh, this? It's no big deal. Like you're the only person who can get it together in the morning."

"Oh yeah, you're quite the morning person," he said.

"I can be." I took Morphie from him and unhooked his leash. He instantly ran for his food.

"So I see," True said from behind me. "I guess given the right motivation you can. Good to know."

"What's that supposed to mean?"

He shrugged, then grabbed his cup of coffee from the countertop. "Nothing. Let's go! We're already running late."

"This guy of yours with the ridiculous time schedule wouldn't have a name, would he?"

He looked at me. "Do you plan on seeing your precious Keanu today by standing here arguing with me?"

I shook my head. "Let's go."

The sun was barely rising, but the streets were already surprisingly active when we hit the pavement to head to the crosstown bus we would take to get to the express train to Brooklyn. I shouldn't have been surprised. After all, New York was the city that never slept and all that. My stomach gave a growl that could be heard over our footsteps, and True looked down at me then looked up the street then back at me again.

"You want to grab a buttered roll? It doesn't look like the bus is coming yet, and I know if you don't get something in your stomach, you'll be complaining the whole way out to Coney Island."

I frowned. "You say that like all I do is complain, True Erickson. Listen, you're the one who volunteered to come with me. I can do this by myself. I don't need you and your judgment all the way out to Brooklyn and back, thank you very much." Just then my stomach made another noise.

He gave me another look. "See that? Food. The woman needs food. Come on and let's get you something to sop up that caffeine, my Bethany Lu."

"Now you're pushing it."

But he wasn't listening. He grabbed my free hand and pulled me into the bodega on the corner.

Since we were going through the trouble, I decided to add a pack of mini doughnuts and some oatmeal cookies to the buttered roll—the doughnuts for me and the cookies for True. Though he was acting like I was getting too much, I knew he'd be all over them.

This suddenly felt like a little adventure, even if we were only going to Brooklyn. But hell, I didn't get out much, and for an hour-plus trip that included two trains and a bus, I might as well have been going to Pennsylvania or Atlantic City at the least. But this was for Keanu. I took another sip of my coffee and reminded myself to slow down.

"Can I get a pack of tissues and a hand sanitizer too?" I asked the man behind the counter. True looked at me.

I slid him a look back. "What? Better to be prepared."

We walked out onto the street once again when True turned to me. "You are something. Always one extreme or the other."

I shrugged, then went to take a sip of coffee and froze before getting a good taste. "Shit."

True turned, his eyes going where mine were to our crosstown bus a little over half a block up, about to close and pull away. "Shit!" He pushed his coffee cup into my hand and took off.

I kept close behind for about three strides but was dusted out in a flash. Actually, I was momentarily stunned by the image of him: sun silhouetting his figure, long legs pumping, his shirt billowing behind him as he chased our bus so that we could chase Keanu Reeves. Suddenly everything stopped. Well, not everything, that bus and True kept on going ahead. And then there he was, turning back to me, waving and calling my name.

It seemed surreal and a little out of body. I almost yelled to him, "Don't get on that bus!" But no, that was all wrong. Those were words for another man. I blinked.

"Lu, come on!"

I nodded and started to run. "I'm coming! I'm coming." When I got to him, I frowned. "How did you expect me to keep up with you when you gave me everything to hold?"

The driver was staring at us as we stood on the step. "Care to come all the way in so that I can go?"

"Oh, I'm sorry," I said and went to hand True his coffee while I fumbled for my wallet. I heard two beeps, and then his hand was gently at my elbow. Leading me forward to two empty seats.

"I got it already," True said. "Come sit."

"Thanks." I looked over at him. He was quiet. Stoic as he looked forward. Calm, after having run for the bus, whereas I was still huffing and puffing. "I suppose you want to get on me now for taking too long in the deli."

He turned to me, his eyes flat at first before he blinked, and it was as if a light switched on and he was alive again. He reached for the deli bag. "No, I want an oatmeal cookie. I'm hungry."

CHAPTER 13

THE REPLACEMENTS

TRUE

I didn't know if I could pull this off or why I was even trying.

Even in her current condition—hyped on carbs, caffeine and the prospect of seeing her long-term crush—I had to be careful because if I made one false move, Lu would see right through me. She called me out on everything else. It was only a matter of time before I'd get called out on this too.

But still I had to try.

I knew what she was trying to do with this wild plan. She was distancing herself from her work, her worries, and if I was reading things right...she was trying to distance herself from me.

Chasing Keanu was just running away from what we've both been dodging for so long. And now here I was—a grown man, with responsibilities—chasing Keanu too.

But what choice did I have? What else was I supposed to do when I saw that look in her eyes? When I caught the signs of her slipping, no, *falling* further out of reach like Alice down the rabbit hole. I wouldn't lose her again. She'd already spent so many years lost. Now it felt like she was halfway back, and I'd be damned if I was going to lose her again.

There was a hard nudge at my shoulder. "So where's your guy? This place is a madhouse. It's gonna be like finding a Keanu in a haystack here."

She was something. I snorted. "Keanu in a haystack."

She was right. Coney Island wasn't how I remembered it. The traffic, noise, and early morning crowds—suddenly I was itchy. Why I'd imagined an ideal, sunny beachside adventure made me wonder whether I was sipping some of Lu's delusional juice.

I looked left and right. The landmark Cyclone and Wonder Wheel were like defiant old guards against the backdrop of the beach and the Atlantic Ocean, fighting not to be outdone by the oddly placed newer rides like the Sling Shot, Thunderbolt and a brightly painted newer looping coaster. It was as if an oversized toddler named Luna, high on Benadryl, had been playing with a couple of toy sets in a doctor's waiting room, one for a beach and one for an amusement park, and they were hobbled together with a city as a backdrop. Oh, and the toddler liked hot dogs. A lot.

I gazed at the white-and-green wraparound advertising that surrounded Nathan's Famous hot dog stand. I looked up, sure I was stalling. I didn't know where to go and wasn't ready to move from this spot. Also, there was a yellow, red and green painted sign on top of the building with a basket of fries with one of those little red plastic sporks sticking out of the fries. They shouldn't have looked as tasty as they did at this hour of the morning, especially since they were made of paint and they were hella grimy and there were seagulls swirling overhead and cars, cabs and express buses whizzing by, but still those fries looked good. I guess the cookies I'd scarfed down on the ride over had worn off pretty quick. Nerves would do that.

"So what are we doing? Where exactly is the location? Standing here isn't getting us anywhere." The impatience was heavy in Lu's voice as she slipped on a pair of shades. They were appropriate battle armor against the harsh sun, but I knew the shades and her sharp tone were doing double duty by camouflaging her fear. She wasn't one for crowds, or adventure rides for that matter. She liked to keep her thrills fairly tame, close to home and mostly on-screen.

She looked good today, like she looked every day. It was ridiculous how effortlessly sexy she was even just tossing her head back and putting on her shades. Shit, I should have been more prepared. How I don't know, but putting on some sort of Lu sexual crush mental block before I'd left the house would have helped. As if it were a thing.

No Nathan's fries for me this morning. I would have to drown my troubles in crinkly goodness later.

I looked around, for what I didn't quite know. A sparkly sign that read RABID KEANU FANS THIS WAY? "Um, I'm not exactly sure. My guy just said that the shoot was out here. I thought it would be more evident. And I didn't expect this much of a crowd so early. But you're the expert. You know your man. Where do you think he would be?"

She perked up with that question, her lips spreading into a smile. "I like that. I'm like the Kean-oracle!"

I just stared at her as she spun around twice in a little circle, half stumbling into my side. Then she stuck her arm out and pointed toward a jumble of colored steel and lights. A demonic face with black hair parted in the middle, red-rimmed beady blue eyes and a huge joker smile welcomed us to the entrance of the aptly named Scream Zone.

"Scream Zone it is. Makes just as much sense as anything," I said.

~

BETHANY LU

My nerves were rattled, fried and frazzled. What would I do if I actually came face-to-face with Keanu? I mean, sure my plan looked good in theory (okay, maybe not good-good), but did I have actual execution to back it up? Now that I was here with True and would be seeing Keanu, the prospect of making a fool of myself in mere moments felt very real. What was I doing here?

I turned to True. Better to channel my energy and anxiety elsewhere since words for my destined meeting with disaster weren't coming to me. "So this guy of yours..." I started. "What's his name and how is he supposed to get me to Kean—"

My words hung up in my throat as I looked just past True's shoulder and saw a person who looked very much like Keanu Reeves chatting with another who looked like him too. It was dual Keanu Reeveses. I spun around, my eyes going wide and my gaze now landing on four more not-quite Keanus. Well, if this wasn't just the shit.

"You did say something about a Keanu in a haystack, didn't you?" True said from by my side.

I scanned the area. Suddenly it seemed like Keanu was everywhere. Practically taunting me. Him but not him. "What in the attack of the clones is this?"

I began to attempt a count, but it was impossible. They were by the bumper cars, coffee stand, the Wonder Wheel, the entrance to the hall of mirrors. It was quite spectacular but also almost too cruel. My heart sank lower and lower with the pop-up of each new Keanu. "There are twelve of them."

"Nah, I think fourteen," True said. "Maybe more. I thought I saw a couple head toward the Boardwalk."

I closed my eyes. It was as if Luna Park was suddenly hosting an official Keanu Reeves lookalike convention. They were everywhere with the long hair, scruffy beards, all in long Matrix-style jackets tapered at the waist and tight leather pants, some filling them out better than others.

I fought for calm, letting out a breath and shrugging out of my jacket to tie it around my waist. I looked at True. "Well."

He looked at me. "Well what?"

"Text your guy. Surely the real Keanu must be somewhere in this mess."

He looked stunned for a moment. Blinked, then reached for his phone. It was so unlike True to be this way. Lack of focus was more my thing. I watched him scroll through his contacts. He looked over me as if excited to see something. I turned. "Is that him?"

Two of the older faux Keanus and a new way-too-short one joined the mix. This was impossible. What was going on here? They seemed to be corralling en masse near the Wonder Wheel. A sizzle of excitement shot through me once again. I turned back to True just as he looked back at me. "I texted him, but it doesn't look like he's read it yet."

"Well, something's happening over there. Come on, we can't wait on this guy of yours forever."

"Gary."

"What?"

"His name is Gary."

I shrugged. "Well, we can't wait on Gary forever. Let's go find out what's happening. See about that line over there."

I started to head over toward the pack of Keanus while contemplating a name for them. Herd? Pride? Gaggle? Kaggle?

True grabbed my hand and pulled me back, his eyes now a little wary. "Gary texted," he started. "He doesn't know all the details, but his girlfriend says that there's some big stunt happening, and those people will be extras let on to ride the Wheel during filming. The first hundred people may be in the film with all the Keanus." He looked up, then back at me with a glimmer in his eyes. "The Ke-anuses."

I held back a snort and pointed a finger. "That's...well, mildly funny. But only because I know you've probably been working on it for the past ten minutes. Still, I'll have none of your Keanu slander this way, Mister Er-ick-son." He grinned, and a lightness came over me.

True tugged at my hand, pulling me toward the forming crowd. For a second I hesitated, seeing the large Ferris wheel. He tugged again and I looked at him.

"Hurry, Lu," he said. "We need to get in that line. Before it goes over a hundred. You don't want to miss your chance."

Dammit. I didn't really want to get on that ride, but he was right. This was my chance. I didn't know if the real Keanu was out here or not, but surely he had to be. I couldn't lose out. Still, my anxiety over the uncertainty of the old amusement park ride and lack of control had my heart jumping.

True squeezed my hand. "You get in the line," he said. Easy. Steady. That's how his voice sounded. "It doesn't look like it's all that long. I think this may be our best chance."

I looked. The line was long but not that long. He was right, but still there was a level of panic now that I was potentially close to seeing Keanu. What would I do if and when I saw him? What if I blew it because I blurted out something stupid, or worse, threw up? Hell, when I went to Disney with Dawn and her parents, I kept my feet on solid ground, and when not, it was It's a Small World on constant repeat for me. What would I say? How would I get close enough? Dammit, there were so many missing steps to my stupid plan. I should have made substeps!

"Don't go getting cold feet on me now," True said. "Not after you had me chasing a bus. Hurry and get in line."

I scrunched up my face and shot True a look. "Okay. I'm going."

I rushed over and lined up, telling myself everything would happen in its time and the right words would come to me. And I wouldn't die of fright today. It seemed a very Keanu thing to say. But it was then that I noticed the people in front of us all had on green wristbands.

Dammit. Holy roadblock, Batman! I was just about to turn to True and go on a ramble about the wristbands and not being allowed on the ride when I noticed that he wasn't behind me anymore. For a moment I panicked, fearing I'd lost him. He'd just been here.

I looked around again and finally spotted him. He was a few yards ahead, talking to a young guy who looked like a possible cousin to Dave Chappelle or, if you squinted and shook your head, LaKeith Stanfield. True, rather openly, went in his pocket, then palmed the guy some money and was handed two green wristbands in return. My mouth nearly dropped. He was cute as hell when he turned back my way, a smug look on his face as he walked toward me in triumph.

"Holy crap. Okay, I'm impressed. I'll definitely pay you back."

"Who says I paid him anything or that you have to pay me back?"

I narrowed my eyes. "I saw you go in your pocket and give him something."

He shrugged. "Told you I knew a guy."

"A Gary, you mean."

"A Gary." He nodded. "Who has a girl in the business."

"Well, was that your Gary, his girl or whoever?" I stared at him hard. He was being so strange today. Not his usual cool, unflappable self. It was unnerving.

"It wasn't. That was just a guy."

This was getting me nowhere. But what did it matter? I smiled. "Well, just a guy with two green bracelets who is almost as cool as you are. You all came through with the hookup." I hopped up and gave him a quick kiss on his cheek. His whiskers tickled under the faint touch of my lips. I caught the look of surprise in his eyes before my heels hit the ground. I was literally bouncing. True grabbed my wrist, pulling me back to earth and giving me a reminder that we were indeed surrounded by a bunch of less bouncy people and incoming Keanus. The real one would be here soon. Was I shimmying now? Yes, I think I'd added a shimmy to my bounce.

"Would you stop shaking so that I can get this on you before it blows away?"

I forced myself to stop vibrating and looked at True. "Shimmying," I said.

"You always have to have the last word, don't you?" Well, he wasn't wrong, and this little way-too-early trek was now turning out to be kind of fun.

He wrapped the green band around my wrist. True's touch was quick and sure. The little curls on the top of his head looked soft as he concentrated on lining up the band just right. The sun gleamed off all the beautiful shades of brown in his hair—deep cocoa, walnut and some lighter shades of auburn threaded throughout too. A woman would've happily paid hundreds of dollars for color that rich.

I stuck my hand out to touch his hair just as he was finishing. He jerked up.

"What? Did I have something on my head?"

I nodded. "Something like that."

He ran his hand quickly across his curls, then looked at me. "Well, did I get it? Did you get it?"

I scrunched up my face at him. "Of course I got it. You know I always look out for you."

True frowned as he fumbled with his own bracelet. I took it from his hand and gave his wrist a squeeze to steady it and put it on. When I was done, he was looking up, his eyes wide as he took in the soaring height of the one-hundred-year-old Ferris wheel. I attempted to do the same but stopped midway as my innards did a flip, doubling back to tell me that focusing on True was a better option in this scenario.

I let out a breath. The fact that True was going all in with me today made me feel only moderately better about my aversion to thrill rides. Not that a silly Ferris wheel was a thrill ride. Hell, they let kids on THIS HIGH. But still, it was thrilling for some, and if you got on the wrong car, this one was downright scary. And I was getting close to that zone. But I held on to the fact that I had True. He was by my side. Safe and steady as he's always been. He hadn't failed me in all these years. Not for our Saturday bagels, our weekly chats and walks, impromptu Broadway musicals when Dawn wasn't available, pretty much all my art openings, no matter when or how small they were. Hell, the man even showed to my unveiling of a piece in the basement of an East Side dive restaurant's shared restroom.

True was solid.

He wouldn't let me fall.

But this was different. This felt bigger. A little more out of control. At least for me, and he knew it. This was a big push beyond my comfort zone, and a bit of a stretch for his too. I didn't go for thrills, and True...Well, True didn't go for fun. It wasn't his brand. Not that he wasn't funny. He was. Honestly he was one of the funniest people I'd ever met. I loved his humor. But to call it dry was ultra-moisturizing it.

This whole Keanu plan and day at the amusement park/adventure thing was definitely not my stoic professor.

I looked up at the ride again, and True nudged my shoulder. "Come on, don't worry. It's going to be fine. Or would you rather just hang out down here?"

I frowned as he looked down at me. "Of course not. I'm fine. Besides, I came all this way."

He stared at me intently. "Be honest, Lu. If you're not, it's okay. I know rides aren't your thing."

I let out a breath. I could see the worry on his face, and guilt started to prick at the back of my neck. As nervous as I was, I still wanted to give this a go and I wanted to share it with True. I couldn't let my fear rule me and miss this opportunity.

I touched his chest. "I'm fine. I can do this. Now if you don't want to go, I understand. You can stay on the ground and watch for Keanu here. I know you probably think I'm being a lame fangirl."

When he didn't protest, I frowned and looked around. There was a group in front of us with two guys and two girls who didn't look like they could be broken up, and behind us was a group of four women in denim shorts and tiny tops that made me wonder if they had raided their preteen daughters' closets before heading out this morning. I turned back to True and shrugged. "It doesn't matter. I'm sure I'll find somebody else to ride with." Just then two guys who looked straight out of *Bill and Ted* jumped on the back of the line. I pointed and grinned. "See there. I could probably ride with them."

True rolled his eyes and pushed my hand down. "Have you lost it? And when did I say I wasn't getting on? I'm perfectly fine. Now let's go and start this day of fun. Just remember, though. You owe me after this."

I gulped. "Well, so we're giving threats now, Mr. Erickson?"

He shook his head. "Whatever."

As we stood silently for a moment, I could feel the energy of us each saying our own version of silent prayers.

"Okay then! Let's do this." He gave me a wink. "So what do you say? We tackle the Cyclone after?"

My eyes widened and I was about to protest, but the people in front of us started to move and True's large hands were suddenly on my shoulders and he was propelling me forward. Ready or not, we were on the move.

About ten meters away from the head of the line, the guy True paid and another woman started to count the people still in the line. I got nervous when they proceeded to talk to a couple of groups in front of us and did some rearranging. What if True and I didn't end up together? I didn't want to do it without him. A woman came over to True, and I was all ready to go in on some heavy groveling. "It's just the pair of you?"

Shit, what was the right answer here?

"Yes. It's just the two of us," True said, all stoic and no-nonsense before I could come up with anything else.

She looked at us seriously. "Come with me."

I perked up when I realized she was leading us to an open Ferris wheel car. Alone. Just us. She shook her head and gave a cheeky grin. "Sit on opposite sides of the car, please. We need to keep balance, and hands must stay inside the car at all times no matter what happens on the outside."

True and I looked at each other with wide eyes at that last comment. "No matter what happens on the outside?" True asked.

A young woman with curly hair came forward with a clipboard and asked us to sign a paper that could've been a legit waiver or something copied off the internet by an intern the night before. True and I gave quick glances at each other, shrugged, signed and got in the car.

Suddenly, the ride lurched forward, and I almost slid off the seat. I clutched the edge and as we continued our ascent, the crowd below gawking at us, I looked into True's steady eyes and, as my heart raced, for the first time wondered if even Keanu was worth this risk.

CHAPTER 14

REPLICAS

BETHANY LU

T hank you again," I said.

"It's okay."

"Yeah, but you don't really look like it's okay, though. I know this isn't any fun for you."

True shot me a glare as the Wonder Wheel came to a body-jolting stop to let on another set of passengers. "It's totally fine," he said through gritted teeth. "A real riot of a time."

"Well, you don't have to be like that, Truman Erickson," I mumbled, and turned from him and took in the scene below, hoping to get a glimpse of moviemaking. I spotted a Keanu by one of the trailers doing deep knee bends and another talking with a guy while mimicking something that could possibly be punches.

I could feel a new frisson of excitement in the air. There was definite activity, with more people and cameras being set up. Something was really happening. I looked closer, ever hopeful as we began our jerky ascent again. Hold it. Everything in me went rigid as the largest trailer's door opened. A boot? Next came a leg. And I could see the man had chin-length hair. *Look up...look up!* I silently begged the booted man. Finally, and as if in slow motion, he looked up just as our gondola moved again. Crap on raisin toast!!

"Did you see? Do you think that's him?"

True slowly angled the top of his body from where it was anchored in the middle of the car to peer over and see where I was pointing. "I don't know what you're talking about," he said with a minuscule shrug. "There are even more Keanus down there than before. It's nuts. It looks like *The Matrix* is duplicating itself on the Coney Island, Brooklyn, strip."

Hey, he might have hit on something there. *The Matrix in Brooklyn* sounded lit. It had a kind of *Escape from New York* quality that could be cool, though maybe it skewed more Tarantino than the Wachowskis.

"I can get with an East Coast *Matrix* vibe," I said to True. Unfortunately, he was right. There was no way to make out which was the right Keanu, if anyone was, in the sea of shaggy hair and leather down below.

"You could get with Keanu Reeves in any vibe," he deadpanned.

He had a point. Though coming from him, and with his delivery, I didn't even take the time to respond.

Not that I had a chance, because all of a sudden a loud voice rang out, announcing filming and to remain calm, normal, and most of all to keep our hands inside the cars at all times. Calm? Who could remain calm now? Keanu was close. Well, maybe. But still. Hands inside for a Ferris wheel? I swallowed and looked over at True. His expression was one of deep annoyance, as if saying "See what you've gotten me into, Lu," and I shrugged.

So much for reassurance. Didn't he know I was scared?

A cheer roared throughout the Ferris wheel. At least it wasn't just me being excited as hell about what was going on.

I stared at True, hoping I wasn't pushing him too far with this, even though he was the one who'd volunteered to come with me. But still, I felt guilty. "Yay?"

A horn sounded, and the voice started again. "In case of emergency there is a red card taped to the bottom of your seats."

True and I both looked toward the floor of the car. I couldn't help my legs jiggling with nervousness. *Chill, Lu. Just chill. WWKD. What would Keanu do?* He would one hundred percent enjoy this experience in the moment and have fun.

I took in the view of the ocean to my right and the Brooklyn view to my left. It was a gorgeous day.

I gave True a hesitant smile. "Don't worry, it's gonna be fine," I said more to myself. "I promise to treat you to all the fries you want after this is over."

"Ah, you're gonna owe me a lot more than fries once this is over, Lu. That's for sure."

I nodded. "Whatever you want. You got it." Then I looked out just as a buzzer sounded and the director called, "Action!"

Suddenly, a herd of Keanus came rushing toward the

Ferris wheel and we began to slowly circle then start to speed up. My heart started to set a galloping pace along with it. There was a loud thump as a car swayed far forward. I was out of my seat grabbing the pole in the center and swung around to the other side of the car only to be caught by True and land hard into his shoulder.

"Oomph! Sorry, I didn't expect that."

"Neither did I," True said as he sat me firmly down on the seat beside him. "What the hell? I don't know about this, Lu."

I reached out and patted the top of his hand. He looked at me with tight lips and eased my hand away as he reached out for the pole in the center and pulled himself up and over to the other side of the car where I had been sitting previously.

"Why you moving?"

"They told us we had to keep the car evenly balanced. I'm balancing it back out."

"Yeah, okay, you're right. Good on you," I said. Though I wouldn't tell him it did feel better with him sitting on the same side as me.

There was another bump as the car swayed violently once again and the speed picked up even more. I may have shrieked. I'm pretty sure I did from True's wide-eyed reaction. But next we hit a downward slope and the car did a full-on dip and roller-coaster dive forward and swung out into the atmosphere before coming to a surprise halt and lurching us back. Once again, I was on the other side of the car. This time not at True's side but in his lap. His arms around me. My head buried in his neck as I held on tight.

"It's okay. We stopped," he said. "You don't have to worry. It's fine, I got you."

My heart was racing and my eyes were tightly shut as I fought to push away the fear in all my nerve endings. That fear knocked out the sounds of screams and laughter of the other riders along with the banging and squealing of the Wonder Wheel as it jerked to another stop.

I tried to focus on True and his voice. He had me, it was okay, so it would be okay.

I forced a smile and pulled my head up, opening my eyes and taking in the view of the bright and sunny day. Pairs of not-quite Keanus were on top of the cars play fighting, doing pretty cool twists, kicks and bends while going around the wheel. It was amazing!

"Hey, you think you're all right now?" True asked. "Maybe I can have my lap back. Not to mention, you're about to snap my neck if you pull it any harder."

I looked at True, suddenly realizing my position and what I was doing. "Oh, I'm sorry," I said, quickly loosening myself. I grabbed the middle bar and swung back to the other side of our gondola. I felt the heat of embarrassment wash over my face. "And there I was thinking you'd be the one having a problem up here. As if you'd be bored or something. Who knew there would be this much shaking going on? I swear, you'd think they'd warn people about the whole swinging cars and folks fighting up top." I cleared my throat. I was rambling like a teen on the train home with her crush. *Shut it up, Lu!*

But of course, I didn't shut a thing. Why would I when rambling was so much easier than actual feelings?

"I wish I could see who was on top of our car and what they're doing. Maybe we should act a little bit while we're in here," I said. "We could have a chance to make it on the screen."

"They probably have actors in other cars for that, but who knows," he said.

"Come on. Let's give it a try." I put on my best 1950s B-movie fright-night face and looked up at the top of the car in shock, playing with different expressions and hoping to get my moment of fame so that I could at least be Keanu adjacent whenever the blooper highlights came out.

When I glanced back at True again, he was sitting back, his earlier shock over my lap dance gone and his arms crossed. He stared at me with that half-smokey half-judgy and way-too-wicked look on his face.

"Can't you get into it?" I whined. "You'll end up ruining the shot. This will never work with me doing all this fine acting over here and you sitting there like a statue. Come on, True, get into it, please."

He let out a small smile. "Looks like you're into it enough for the both of us."

I looked around. He was right. I was. For a moment I'd forgotten my fear and just let go and enjoyed the experience.

True uncrossed his arms and proceeded to start miming along with me. I laughed, getting a glimpse of what I must've looked like as True did his part, overacting, pointing up, looking horrified, gasping, then laughing and smiling.

The ride slowed down to let some Keanus off the tops of the cars while the passengers stayed inside.

I heard one of our guys do a helluva good Keanu impersonation as we neared the bottom. "Very cool," he said. "Great job," came from the top of our car.

"It must be almost over," I said to True, feeling kind of sad. "It was fun. Too bad we didn't get to see You Know Who. But at least we got to see a bunch of close versions. Thanks for your help today."

"Hey, the day is not over yet. You still owe me fries, and I'm thinking that you riding the Whipper will be a good start for paying me back for this."

I made a face. The idea of being thrown about and out of my control that far was too much.

But I couldn't argue. He'd gotten me here, fake Keanus or not. "Whatever you say. You're in charge."

Our car made it to the bottom where it was now our Keanus' turn to get off. The first guy who lightly jumped off the top of our car was a really close lookalike, though he was more muscular than the real Keanu, slightly broader in the shoulders and slimmer in the waist.

But then the next faux Keanu jumped down.

"Thank you for your service," I said to his back. Stupid, I know, but in the moment I couldn't think of anything else.

He turned my way, and a bolt of lightning slammed me in the chest. "No, thank *you*."

Wait…that voice. I snapped my head forward, so fast I heard my neck crack. *Cripes!*

He smiled. There may have been music. A harp? It was definitely a harp.

I blinked and blinked, my mouth and eyes going

wide, and there was a cheer from the crowd. Our gondola went up again, and I watched as The Keanu walked through the parting throng below. He talked to the woman who'd handed us the clipboard earlier, then put on a motorcycle helmet and rode out of the park and down Surf Avenue until my eyes could no longer follow him.

I looked at True. "That didn't just happen, did it?"

He looked back at me from across the gondola. "Will you feel better if I tell you it didn't or it did?"

I stared at him. "What do you think?"

He was slow to reply, and we were once again on our descent. Our gondola door opened, and an impatient attendant motioned us with a sour expression to get out of the car. True stood first, grabbing the pole, his feet unsteady. He reached out and clasped my hand, pulling me up. I took a moment and inhaled, his scent soothing my spirit. "Nah, that didn't just happen. That guy was a total fake Keanu. You still haven't met the real one yet."

I nodded into his shoulder, willing my mind to go with the lie True was selling me. I sighed. So that was it, all my dreams had ridden away on the back of a motorcycle, most likely never to be seen again. I stumbled off the gondola and followed True, my legs wobblier and my ass sorer than I expected. I landed hard against True's back when he suddenly stopped short.

Ms. Clipboard was there again. This time she was surrounded by cameras and for some reason they were trained our way. What the hell? The star had just ridden off—taking my heart with him. I wanted to cry. I also wanted to pee now that I had hit solid ground, but mostly I wanted to cry.

No time to think of that, though. Ms. Clipster was there looking stoic, and I wondered if we needed to leave a blood sample or if we were in some sort of trouble for our antics up on the wheel. I'd fall on my sword. I was getting my story ready and high indignation up. No way I was letting True take the heat for me. Also, I wasn't in the mood to take any crap. I'd come this close to Keanu. THIS FREAKING CLOSE!

Along with Ms. Clipster was a good-looking guy with curly dark hair, a bright smile and creamy tanned skin. I'd recognized him from one of the entertainment recap shows on TV, and he definitely appeared taller on my screen. He was pointing a very phallic-looking mic with a big shiny oversized purple head back and forth between me and True, and a camera guy stood behind him and a big light trained our way.

We both instinctively dodged back from the dodgy mic.

"You two were so funny up there." The TV guy whose name I couldn't remember startled me with a high voice that reminded me why I couldn't remember his name, because his voice irritated the hell out of me. I nodded and he gave a wink. Should I say thanks?

"You practically stole the show from our leading man."

That brought me out of my temporary shock and back to the reality at hand. I looked at what's-his-name. "Leading man? Is he still here?" I asked, hating the desperate fangirl squeak in my voice. As if I was anything else.

What's-his-name looked at Clipster and the two of them shared a smirk as if I'd asked the funniest question ever. I snorted. At least I got to glimpse Keanu. And he spoke to me. *He spoke to meeee.* "Dammit!"

I grabbed True's hand and pulled him to follow me back down the gangway. Forcing my back straight, I tried my best to hold on to a bit of dignity in my undignified stomp off but failed when I got a cramp in my upper butt cheek and my bladder jumped up and reminded me how much I needed to pee.

"Oh well," I said to True. "We tried. Let me find the bathroom, and the rest of the day is yours. Bumper cars, hot dogs, fries, you name it! Just tell me what you want to do first!"

True tilted his head to the side in a sort of nonchalant "fine by me, could care less" kind of way. My eyes rolled up toward the top of the Wonder Wheel on their own. We made about three steps when Mr. High Voice piped up again loud and clear over my shoulder. "He's not here, but we do know where he'll be next week and where you two may be too."

I stopped dead in my tracks, this time making True bump into my back.

"Did he say *but*?" I asked.

True looked at me, closed his eyes, then opened them again, staring me down with a look of "Nope, I'm done," but he spoke up. "I also heard a maybe. As in 'Maybe I'm done and you're on your own.'"

I nudged True's shoulder. He didn't budge. "Oh, come on. You know you had fun today." I put my thumb and pointer finger closer together and came near his face. "Just a little fun?"

He leaned in. "When? When you were yelling in my ear or practically choking me?"

His words brought back the moment, his feel. The closeness and security of his arms. I leaned back, quickly putting my hand down. "Yeah, just then," I said. "Now come on, True," I whined. "Let's both go back and talk to that guy and see what this is all about." I turned and headed back up the gangway toward Ms. Clipster and High Voice Guy, hoping against hope that True hadn't given up and was following behind me and my wobbly ass.

CHAPTER 15

THE GREAT WARMING

BETHANY LU

Do you know that this dog is completely and utterly spoiled?"

When I walked back into my apartment later that evening, I was greeted with judging stares from both Dawn and Morphie. I waved a hand at Morphie and looked up at Dawn. "Okay, I know what his problem is, but what are you giving me the face for?"

Upon hearing the word *spoiled*, Morphie stopped giving me the judy face and looked over at Dawn, shooting her a quick "I know you're not talking about me" glance.

She pointed down at him. "Look at how he turns on a person," she said as Morphie, now over her and ready to warm up to me, came jumping up and scrambling against my thighs as best he could.

Dawn looked behind me. "I thought True would be

heading back with you. I ordered extra wings when you said you guys were heading home on the train."

I was barely into the apartment, kicking off my shoes and shrugging out of my jacket to throw it over one of the island chairs. But first I had to find a spot for the oversized plush John Wick doll True had won for me in a Boardwalk carnival game, along with the little stuffed dog that came with him. I placed them on the kitchen island for now, not trusting that Morphie wouldn't rip either to shreds by morning. I'd be furious after trekking them all the way back from Brooklyn. Not to mention the buggers cost True about sixty bucks in carnival tickets and tries. A master of the hoops he was not.

"He's probably worn out from all the Keanus, not to mention the Sling Shot, Steeplechase, the Brooklyn Flyer and the bumper cars."

"And traveling home with all that," Dawn said, pointing to my stuffed toys.

I gave her a side-eye. "Oh, hush. But you're right, it was a full day for our boy, so he said he was heading home." I started off to the bathroom but yelled back toward Dawn. "But I'm so glad to hear you got extra wings. I hope you can stay awhile. You've got to help me figure out what I'm going to wear to the Tribeca Festival party next week."

I was shutting the bathroom door when Dawn's voice held me up.

"Wait, what?" she said. "All the Keanus? You can slow down and explain, and what is this about the Tribeca Festival party next week?"

I looked back at her. "Listen, I really gotta pee. I forgot

how far Brooklyn actually is. Get comfortable, let's get the wine out, and I'll take it one step at a time. It's been a really long day and this is not going to be a short story."

When I came out of the bathroom, Dawn handed me a glass of wine and a wing. "You lucky duck. I can't believe that you actually got to see him today. I also can't believe you got on all those rides. That is complete madness!"

I looked around. "Wait, I was in there like five minutes while I washed my face and changed my top. What, are you telepathic?"

She held up her phone. "No, I'm tele-textic, you madwoman. And dammit! I totally should've gone with you. What does True care about Keanu? Or amusement parks even. It was a waste, you going with him."

"Not a total waste. We had a good day, and turns out he doesn't mind a thrill. Who knew?" I shrugged. "Though it's definitely not my thing. You know I like to keep my pace slow. I was able to draw the line at the Cyclone by buying him extra fries and Nathan's hot dogs. So thank goodness I got out of that. Still, he vowed that we'd go back. As if. And you know he had safety stats on everything."

Dawn sighed. "Leave it to True to have the stats, and leave it to you to be his defender."

"I wasn't defending him. I was just pointing out some facts is all. What he likes and doesn't, which includes Ferris wheels, by the way. But he paid a guy off so we could get on the ride and he rode with me."

Dawn gasped. "He paid a guy off? As in under the table?"

I nodded.

"That's it then."

I frowned. "That's what?"

"You have to fuck him now."

I choked on my chicken wing. "Shut up. That's not funny. True is like a sibling."

Dawn rolled her eyes. "We've been over this. Not even close and you know it."

"Well, I'm sure that's how he thinks of me."

"You keep telling yourself that if it makes you feel safer."

"Why would I need to tell myself that to make myself feel safer?"

"I don't know. Why would you?" she countered.

"Dammit, Dawn, this is not what I need after such a long day. I just missed my chance with Keanu and now you're throwing this ridiculousness at me."

Dawn put up a hand, then wrapped her arms around me. "Okay, okay, hon. I'm sorry. I know that's a lot. I'll keep my eyes on your prize. I'm sorry you missed Keanu. But maybe you'll get to meet him next week."

"You think I will?"

She nodded. "I do."

I narrowed my eyes at her. "And you're going to drop this crap with True. I don't need you making him all twitchy while he's helping me with my plan."

She stared at me and I glared at her. Finally, she nodded at that too and gestured as if crossing her heart. "Still, I'm mad. So close to Keanu and potential side dick just waiting while you work. I don't know what's wrong with you?"

"Daaaawnn," I warned, and she poked her bottom lip out before laughing.

"It's a joke. Lighten up. If I can't come with you to this party next week, you have to at least let me have fun preparing you for it."

I let out a long breath. She was right. I needed to lighten up. Me being all weighed down was what had me in this rut in the first place. "You're right. Sorry. I know you're just trying to help. And I really wish you could come with me to the party."

She waved a "no worries" hand. "You go and have a blast. I'll be in Boca anyway for a fundraiser my parents are co-chairing. I'd skip it, but I need to put on a good show if I want to keep the two of them down there and out of my hair with what's going on with the gallery."

I sighed, once again feeling the weight of the upcoming show.

Dawn gave me a hard nudge. "What's that about? You're acting like my gallery is your responsibility. It's not, so just chill. I've got this. It's not like I'm destitute. I just need to make it hot so that my parents get off this whole marriage thing. They'll lighten up. I'm not too pressed."

She mimed flipping her hair, then lowered her voice to a croaky register to emit the annoying vocal cry that had been perfected by millennials and housewives everywhere thanks to the Kardashians. "Yeah," she started, "I really don't want to go, but I have to convince my parents that this is my calling and not just my passion. You know, so that they finally take me seriously and don't (a) drag me into the family business, or (b) worse, marry me off all handmaidlike."

I snorted. Her voicing was spot on, as was her absurdity with the non-differences of calling and passion.

"You're too much."

"Too much and just enough. And I'd much rather be going to the party with you." Her voice was back to normal now.

"I know. Me too. You and I would have so much fun. True is probably going to be a pill. I know he hates this type of thing and is only tolerating me."

She shook her head and flopped back on the couch, giving me a long look.

I stared back at her, but she just took another sip of her wine and spoke no further.

"I don't know which I like better," I said, "you giving your opinion freely or you not saying a word but still making your opinion more than clear."

She shrugged at that and leaned forward to the coffee table and snagged a drumstick, then took a healthy bite.

CHAPTER 16

BABES IN TOYLAND

BETHANY LU

SEND ME ALL THE PICS! I WANT THEM IN REAL TIME!!

I sent Dawn back a 👍 and 😊 in response to her text.

I was already missing my ride or die, which was silly because she'd flown out to see her parents only two days ago, and it wasn't like we were joined at the hip or anything. Hell, we went plenty of days without seeing each other. It wasn't a big deal. It was just that the past week had been all sorts of strange going on up in my head. Sleep wouldn't come right. At all. My brain was full of thoughts of the K-90 plan and *do I or don't I* and *why was I* and *grow the F up already, why don't you?* It just kept going around and around and . . . whatever. Way too much like that wheel True and I were on last weekend.

Insert permanent twisted lip face in my brain.

Work was rolling along. Well, *hobbling* was probably a better word for it. But even that felt off. At least I finally finished the piece I'd been working on, so there was that. Honestly, I hadn't expected it to happen, but I felt a strange surge after True and I had gone to Coney Island. Like I needed to produce something. I dismissed Dawn's teasing me about it being sexual frustration with a snort. I wouldn't give her that type of satisfaction. I also wouldn't give her the pleasure of knowing I'd half thought the same thing myself. I couldn't get the feeling of being on True's lap and in his arms on the Wonder Wheel out of my mind or the tingle out of my body.

My sketchbook for the week had been filled with all sorts of ridiculous childlike happy scenes mixed with sensual bodies. It was unnerving. True had been a part of my no-fly zone forever and needed to stay that way. He was my constant rock. I couldn't ruin that with something as unstable as a romantic relationship.

My phone vibrated again with Dawn texting.

Send HELP! My mother just introduced me to a fifty-eight-year-old divorced money manager named Ted. He has thirteen-year-old twins that he has full custody of. I'll have to live through you. Be sure to send me those pics so I remember what the real world looks like!

Dammit. My poor friend. Not that I was surprised one bit. That did sound so very Dawn's mom. For all her sign-ing checks to feminist causes and knitting of pink pussy hats, she loved the ladies-who-lunched life and desperately wanted it for Dawn. She'd even tried to set me up a time or two when Dawn would wrangle me into a visit. "It's past time, Bethany, dear," she'd say, while passing a cup of her specially blended herbal tea and wearing head-to-toe St. John, cotton, silk and closed-toed shoes in Florida heat. "I don't expect your parents to push you too hard. Goodness knows they've been through enough. But I'm sure with so much on the line, they have to be considering the future. The Carlisle name. Their legacy, I mean." She'd let the implication trail off there, her gaze going from my face to my uterus as if she could see it shriveling.

Over time—like my parents, who actually did care about the Carlisle name and legacy—she stopped asking. I guess now that I was past forty, she'd given in. Figured the old girl had gone dry. Not that I had, though according to my gyn, I was on my way. But I wasn't particularly interested in kids either. Hell, if Morphie could testify, he'd be the first to say I was not the best candidate for being a parent.

I peeped again at Dawn's message. The fact that her mom was trying to set her up with a ready-made family was pretty telling. I sent her back a thumb's-up emoji, prayer hands and a hang-in-there-girl gif.

The Uber pulled up in front of a building on 22nd Street between Eighth and Ninth Avenues that looked like it used to be a factory or a warehouse. While True got out, I hesitated, putting my phone back in my purse. I should have worn something with pockets. If I missed a good shot and only had a recap with no photo proof to give to Dawn,

I'd never hear the end of it. I looked around at the scene in front of me, taking in the unusual quiet.

There was scaffolding around the building, covered with flyers. It wasn't the swankiest place for an A-list party, but that was probably the point. The only giveaway was two bouncer-looking guys and a short red carpet runner that went toward a nondescript door and then veered off to the side where there was backdrop signage with the Tribeca Festival logo for paparazzi shots.

Sans paparazzi. It was so quiet I wouldn't have been surprised if a tumbleweed went rolling across the carpet and over to hang out by the High Line park to pick up some tourist action and at least get on the Gram.

Just great. Of course, I'd score an invite to an exclusive party where not even the paps show up. Guess Keanu won't be showing up here either.

No use worrying so much over fancy shots. And all that dressing up. Annoyed, I swiped to the camera on my phone to do a last-minute check of my makeup. I'd smoothed my curls down to within an inch of their and my life, gelled and wrapped my hair and added a long low ponytail in homage to Sade. Did minimal face makeup but a bold red lip and a smoky eye look. I think it came off quite well.

Today I'd stepped to the other side of my color spectrum and instead of my usual black wore a white maxi dress accessorized with big gold hoop earrings, a long gold chain necklace and black leather boots. If the actual Keanu were to show up, which why would he, I think he could really get into this theme. Hard but sweet.

I shoved my phone back into my bag and glanced over

at True. He'd been quiet on the ride over. Not helping my nerves at all. In fact, he'd not helped my nerves all week. After Coney Island, I'd barely heard a peep from him, which was extra suspect. Mr. Pop-in-on-a-three-way-chat-and-hang-out-too-late-sitting-around-just-because had suddenly gone ghost. Why?

Even when I'd sent him texts and called to see if he'd wanted to go in on a takeout order, he'd come back with a two-word can't. working answer in return. As if he couldn't just come upstairs to get a quick bite? As if he'd ever turned down coming upstairs for a quick bite before. It was all too odd and too unnerving and had me wondering if he'd even been staying at his place at all this past week.

Another example:

I'm so excited about the Tribeca Party. You think it will be fun? It will probably be wall to wall people. I wonder if Keanu will be there and if I'll get to meet him this time. I hope I don't screw it up. I wonder if other stars will be there. Oh well. What does it matter as long as he's there. It's going to be a BLAST!

True: Yes.

What the total hell?

He didn't even come over for bagels and coffee on Saturday, leaving me high, dry and alone since Dawn had left the day before. It was just, I don't know, not him—

even if he made the excuse that he had grading to finish before the end of the year. I was starting to feel uneasy, and I didn't like it. Like I was infringing on True's time.

He looked good tonight, all upscale casual with black slim pants and a very dark gray V-neck with a loose blazer on top. It was True but to the sexy degree. Everything fit a little too well and it made me wonder where he'd gotten it all, who'd helped him and also who'd convinced him to shell out the money. Even for his on-air appearances, he recycled the same two blazers and shirts that had been gifts from me and Dawn. Still, I tried to shrug off my admittedly cantankerous mood.

At least he put in effort. It showed he cared and wanted to put up a good front for me. It also showed what a high-level ass I was since I'd purchased a cool but now useless overpriced slub knit top for him to wear today that would have been perfect just in case the outfit he'd shown up in was too Professor Langdon from *The Da Vinci Code*. But I didn't have a chance to give the top to him since he didn't show for coffee and ended up just texting me, talking about how he'd arrange the car and meet me in front of the building.

He was currently sending a text. I peeked over at his phone and he tilted it.

"Excuse you?" he jibed.

I made a face. "Oh, well excuse me, Professor. I thought maybe it was work and Aimeeeee," I teased.

He hit another button and put the phone in his pocket, clearing his throat. "It was. But you still shouldn't make a habit of looking at other people's phones. It's rude."

I stared at him. It was Aimee. And he turned the phone away. Well then. "I didn't. I mean I don't. I mean you're not other people. Whatever." I was rambling, and I hated rambling. "Sorry, sir. I'll be sure to remember. Privacy and all." I closed my eyes and put my hands to my temples.

"What are you doing?" True asked, and even with my eyes closed I could imagine the annoyance on his face. I didn't care. I had to break this mood. Get us where we needed to be. Get us to normal so we could go into this clearly not star-studded party and be ourselves.

"This is me forgetting the code to your phone and vowing never to peep over your shoulder ever again."

I peeked one eye open and looked at him. Yep, he was making that face.

"You don't know the code to my phone."

I put my hands down. "You're right, I don't. So there's part of the problem already solved!"

I unlocked my phone and pushed it into his warm hand. "Come on. Take a couple of pics of me. Looks like nobody is using this backdrop."

"It's called a step and repeat."

I blinked. "You would know that, wouldn't you?"

He shrugged.

Just then a black SUV pulled up. Sleek and shiny with tinted windows. A driver got out and came around to open the door. I instinctively moved back, almost tripping, but thankfully True was there, his hand slipping in just in time to save my ass from a hard bumper. I turned to him as I righted myself. "Really, my booty though?"

"Should I have let it hit the dirty cab you almost fell against?"

"You're my champion. I hope it was as good for you as it was for me."

He let out a grunt as I turned toward the person coming from the SUV. He looked our way and we locked eyes. Mine to his. His glare was aloof, his lips pursed ever so slightly. But the rest of his face remained unmoved. Then he turned and hit what I now knew was called the step and repeat.

"I can't believe Ben Stiller is still doing the *Zoolander* look all these years later," I said.

"I'm sure he's just being funny," True responded.

I was about to make a whatever sign with my fingers when I caught Ben's gaze again. He flashed a grin and a wink at me before quickly morphing back into *Zoolander* mode.

Two paparazzi scurried out from nowhere, as if materializing like magic. Did they come from behind a cab or out of a manhole? It was quite the trick. True and I looked at each other wide-eyed, then back at the spectacle as Ben was ushered through the nondescript door and his car sped off.

"Okay, that was strange and kind of cool," True said. The street was once again quiet, and it was almost as if Ben's entrance had never happened. The way no other New Yorker even slowed down was a testament to how everyday an occurrence these types of things were.

"Watch, we'll get in there and he probably won't even be inside," I said. "I bet he's going in and leaving out the back.

The car is probably picking him up on Twenty-Fourth Street right now."

"Keanu? Who knows where he might be?"

I made a face. "No, Stiller. I hear he goes to just about any opening but never stays. It's a thing with him."

True looked at me like I'd grown not two but three heads. "You hear? How do you have time to hear this about the Focker guy when you're all about being obsessed with Keanu?"

I shrugged, then grinned. "As a human, there are just basic things you know. But True, I'm so proud of you for knowing that movie!"

He let out an exasperated sigh. "What do I look like to you? Not human?" He took my hand. He was casual about it, and I stayed cool. I told myself it was no big deal at all. "Come on," he said. "Let's get your photos taken and get inside. I'm ready to get out of this jacket and I know those heels are a lot for you."

I nodded, feeling a release as my shoulders dropped and I relaxed for the first time that evening. That was more like it. We were coming back to us. I let True guide me toward the step and repeat and I twirled and preened on the little red carpet for True in front of the Tribeca logo. Batting my lashes and pursing my lips as if I were truly some star that people wanted to see.

True held up his phone and frowned. "Could you stop moving around so fast? How am I supposed to get a steady shot? Also, why are you acting so cute?"

I shrugged. "Sorry, I can't help it."

The bored paps who were not wasting digital space

on me at least spared a chuckle, and True's lips quirked up. He stepped forward and grabbed my hand again— hello...territorial much, Mr. Erickson?—but I kept that comment to myself as he pulled me toward the door. "Okay, Ms. Starlette, the quicker we get this done, the quicker you are back home and out of trouble."

"Oh, you think so?"

CHAPTER 17

YEAH, I THINK I'M BACK

BETHANY LU

Once inside, it was just as I thought and there wasn't a sign of Keanu or Ben Stiller. The venue's décor could only be described as rehab chic. It was all half-exposed brick and mid-demolition walls with some current and past movie posters pasted up as if they were ads on the scaffolding. Small groups milled about, a couple with VR glasses on their heads.

The dress code ranged from ultra-ultra-casual, like the middle-aged, possibly asleep man in the folding chair in a corner wearing what could be a very expensive white tee or on the other hand could just as easily be a Hanes undershirt, with plaid and snowflake-print pajama pants. It could have been a marginal pass for fashion if it weren't seventy-six degrees out. Contrast him with the woman to his right in a couture floor-length black jersey dress with a sheer mesh cutout in back that easily cost a few grand.

A blond woman stalked up to us. She had a bright smile, flawless makeup and was wearing a red body-skimming spaghetti-strap dress that stopped right above midthigh and gladiator sandals that crisscrossed around her calves. "Glad you made it," she said. "We're hoping you have a great time tonight."

True and I blinked so hard we were practically fanning her. Holy switcharoo! It was Ms. Clipster from Coney Island with a total transformation. Who knew she was a closet shapeshifter? It made her infinitely cooler, but the use of the vague "we" was annoying as hell.

"Are we now? And who would that *we* be?" I let my question hang as I looked around at the partygoers, holding bottles of beer and tumblers of drinks. All I really wanted to know was: WHERE IS KEANU?

Ms. Clipster gave me a forced grin. "Please, relax. Have a drink, walk around and explore. You'll see we have lots of interactive visuals to partake in."

Unless that interactive was me partaking in some visuals with Keanu, I didn't want to hear about it. I was this close to dropping my mask. "Really?" I started.

"So," True broke in, his voice a decibel louder than mine. "This space is interesting. Is there a theme to the party?"

Her gaze shifted between the two of us. "It's light in the darkness. I think you two will be especially interested in our exhibits. We're heavily into bringing more awareness to diversity this year."

It was barely discernible, but I caught it. That slight straightening of True's spine at Clipster's use of the word *diversity* and how we'd be especially interested. Also, light in the dark. What kind of fuckery was that? Even my ears were hot, but I fought to set them down to a low simmer with the thought of seeing Keanu. "Especially us?" I asked, innocently letting my eyes go blank.

"Yes. You know, enthusiastic fans like you."

I needed that drink. Even for Keanu, I wasn't sure I had the mental fortitude for the Clueless act of CIU right now. Thankfully a group of YouTubers turned reality stars came in just then and saved me from responding. I recognized a young guy and girl who had been an annoying trending topic for a month straight because of their viral dances and some sort of love triangle scandal in the TikTok house they summered in. Clipster took one look at their group and immediately forgot True and I were there.

True sighed. "Let's get a drink."

"Good to see you have your priorities," I said with a smile.

"Always," he countered and smiled back.

As we made our way to the bar, I gave a more careful peruse to the décor. I had to hand it to the interior designer; they did their best with what they'd been given. A huge antique mirror hung on the back wall with smaller ones flanking its sides. Candles of various heights were gathered around the room and on the bar, which was essentially a large piece of plywood. I had a strong feeling it was used by the construction workers earlier in the week for their lunch, given the noticeable grease stains. But it was now covered by a large sheet of plexiglass and held up by a couple of cinder blocks. The cinder blocks were also being used for bench seating around the perimeter of the room.

I pulled out my phone, switching to the camera to snap

off a few pics. It was kind of genius what the decorator had done with next to nothing. Dawn would eat this up. And hey, it was something to send since I didn't have any actual celebrity pics for her. I pivoted and snapped a few of the young YouTubers. At least they were having fun, looking almost real enough for TV the way they were laughing. I wondered if they were old enough to drink the cocktails they were holding. Still, I snapped.

True and I were glad to discover, thanks to hand-written details in Sharpie on scraps of paper, that the bar was blessedly an open one with signature drinks and craft beers offered.

"Any clue what the New World is?" True asked, looking down at the offerings.

I shrugged. "Nope, but I'm hoping it's a place where they would not have drinks named The Boomer. What the hell do you think that is?"

The bartender came down to our end of the plywood after handing the man in the pajama pants a tumbler full of brown liquor. "Hiya I'm Chad how are you two lovely people doing and what can I get the two of you do you have any questions about our signature drinks or perhaps I can suggest one of our craft beers?" There was a short intake of breath, but it was barely a millisecond and then Chad continued, "Tonight we're featuring a special microbrew from upstate New York 'Wet Patch' is locally sourced and organic made of delicious dry hops with a hint of herb citrus and pine." He said all this at a breakneck clip, in a high voice that did a singing musical thing at the end. I wondered if he was from the Midwest. It could have been the "hiya" but really, I needed to put my mind in the right place. Mainly on why the hell someone would name a beer Wet Patch.

I looked over at True to see if he happened to catch it, and his wide side-eyes let me know he definitely did.

True cleared his throat and looked at Chad, pointing to the menu under the plexiglass. "Just for kicks, can you tell me what this 'New World' is?"

Chad's expression suddenly changed, and it was as if a spotlight had been put on him the way his mood darkened. He looked at True and then me, lowering his voice an octave. "It's an evocative drink," he said softly. "Made slowly and meant to be savored thoughtfully." He gave me a somber look and tilted his head slightly, letting the candles give him a dramatic shadow. "At first glance it shows our differences as a people, but upon tasting, it reveals how perfectly we all blend together as one." On the "as one," he brought his hands together as if folding in prayer.

I didn't know if I should order one, clap or say amen. There was an awkward silence as the three of us stared at one another, each waiting for the other to speak up.

"And?" True finally said.

"And?" Chad asked in return.

"And what's in the drink?" True replied, his patience I could tell about done.

"Oh." Chad chuckled. "I'm sorry, I just get so moved at times. It's three parts tequila one part grenadine and a little orange juice."

I felt my lips pucker as I looked at the bartender. "So, a tequila sunrise?" I said.

Chad coughed. "Yeah, pretty much." He pointed to the

cocktail menu and The Boomer. "And this one is just an old-fashioned renamed. Listen, I've got some pretty good whiskey, the tequila is okay and there is a decent red wine and an even better white. And we have Sam Adams Pale Ale." All the sing and the song had dropped from his voice, but his smile was a little more genuine. "What would you like?" he asked.

"I'll take the white wine. And he'll have the Sam Adams."

Chad nodded, then handed me a generous pour. He gave True his bottle of beer. We clinked glass to bottle, then each took a sip.

True stifled a yawn.

"Tired already, hon?" I said teasingly and reached out, touching his neck.

"Yes, dear. Sorry to be a bore. Year-end paper grading has me wiped out. So, sadly, I think I'll have to turn down the wet spot tonight."

I practically spit my wine into True's face. "Why, Mr. Erickson, are you trying to be naughty? I think I like this side of you, Professor."

I took another sip of wine, wondering for a moment if he pre-boozed before me, but that was even more unlike him.

"Hey, nothing's wrong with getting a little bit naughty," True said, his voice slightly deeper and more gravelly than normal.

I blinked. What was happening? Was I already in some kind of virtual reality?

I coughed and looked around. "What's with you tonight? Or better yet, *who* are you tonight? I hardly see or hear from you for days and then you turn up all fancy dressed and full of the jokes and innuendoes. Truman Erickson barely jokes and doesn't do innuendoes." I gave him a hard stare. "What gives? As fun as this is, why do I feel like there's another punch line coming and I might not like it half as much?"

True stared at me for a long moment and for a second looked like he was about to say something, but then he blinked, essentially shutting his words off. "You're being ridiculous and overthinking things, Lu. Isn't this night supposed to be about your so-called dream man? What are you doing worrying about me?"

What the hell was up with that comment?

I gave True an up and down. "You're right. What am I doing? I can't waste this night on you."

"Well damn. Tell me how you really feel. Waste? I bought a new jacket and everything. Even took the tags off."

"Is that a joke or do you want me to reimburse you? Should I add it to the bill for the coffee?"

I saw his nostrils flare and immediately wondered why I was baiting him and why we had gotten into an argument so fast anyway. "Listen, True, I'm—"

"Truman Erickson. In. The. Flesh. My goodness, you are a hard man to pin down. Even when there are boatloads of money being thrown at you, you still don't return phone calls."

The woman attached to the rather grand entrance was about my age, maybe a little older, but she wore her years with a lot more confidence. She had smooth brown skin, flawless makeup and wore a killer multicolor pinstripe pantsuit that showed off her curves to ever curvier perfection.

She gave me a dismissive glance before focusing back on True. "I thought we got along so well after dinner the other night. Well, all except that little assistant constantly interrupting you with phone calls. I guess the rumors of you being offered a deanship are true." She let out a sigh that seemed more like a breathy incantation. "Oh well," she said. "Nothing's set in stone and our offer is still highly negotiable." She looked at me again. "So is this your Aimee?"

Heffer, as if? Also "your"? Since when did T and Aimee become "your Aimee"?

I hated how desperate and panicky one line from this woman made me feel, and then she pulverized me with another as she flashed an insanely white, totally insincere grin. "You all will have to figure out how to live without Truman one day. He really is too big for your small little world."

Motherfucker! I was about ready to spit my wine yet again today. True hadn't said a thing about potential job offers or deanships or anything. No, he just let me go on and on having my own personal meltdown over Keanu while he lived a totally separate life that I knew nothing about. The betrayal hit me in the gut, as if someone had thrown one of the stupid decorative cinder blocks right at my belly.

True opened his mouth to speak at the same time another voice came into the fray. "Pilar! How could you escape me so quickly?"

I locked eyes with Daniel Lim. Just perfect. I had been dodging his emojis for the past week. And though he'd agreed to wait for my answer, it still looked like he wanted to keep the lines of communication open. He gave me a wicked "fancy meeting you here" smile.

He turned to the woman he'd called Pilar. "I see you caught up with some friends of mine. Guess this party is not as dull as I thought."

Pilar raised a perfectly arched brow as she gazed at me. "Isn't it?"

True spoke up. "Pilar, this is my..." He paused for a beat, seemingly lost on what to call me. And the "my"? When was I ever his *my* anything?

Daniel chimed in once again. "Pilar, you don't know *the* artist Lu Carlisle?"

There went Pilar's eyebrow again. It said way too much without saying a word.

"Well, if you don't yet, I'm sure you will soon," Daniel continued. "She's one of the hottest young artists out there. I've been hoping to get her signed on with DLIG, though she's playing terribly hard to get."

"I doubt it's that terrible for you, Daniel."

"So you're not Aimee?" Pilar said.

"I'm afraid not," I answered. "And you are?"

"Pilar Martinez with the Copper Goose." She notably didn't hold out her hand for me to shake. "You wouldn't be any relation to Thomas Carlisle of Forty Rise, would you?"

"She's his daughter," Daniel piped in.

"You seem to be full of helpful information, now don't you?" True practically sneered.

Daniel put his hands to his chest as if he was affronted by the whole exchange. His eyes went wide, then he smiled.

Suddenly, he looked like a younger version of the smooth operator who took me out to dinner the other week.

"Truman, chill," he snorted. "I see you're just as prickly as ever. I am shocked, though, that a woman like Lu Carlisle here would still be giving you the time of day." He laughed again, and something went sour in my stomach. "I mean, I remember how you always went on about her back in college, but I'd just assumed you were desperately latching on to the family after their"—he cleared his throat, the insincerity damn near puddling on the floor beneath his feet as he said the next word and looked at me—"tragedy."

I frowned, trying to separate the word from his clear meaning. Hating how much this man knew about me and about True, not to mention my family.

"But I'm glad to see that's not the case and you're still old friends." His eyes shifted from Pilar to True to me, and he grinned. "That we can all be friends."

My mind was full of questions, but my first instinct was to reach for True's tightly fisted hand. I was too slow. Pilar stepped in my way.

"Friends sounds fantastic. And now that I finally have my friend in front of me again," she said, "True, we should talk. I won't have you making any decisions without giving me another shot." When he looked to protest, she cut him off and shook her head firmly. "You owe me that at least for cutting my dinner short. With what we're offering you to come out to LA, you'll live like a king. And I can assure you, you'll essentially be your own boss. No more campus politics or ridiculous students to deal with. No obligations from your past." She gave me a pointed look.

An obligation? Was that why he came with me tonight? Did he somehow feel obligated to me?

I went to signal for Chad, but he was already in front of me, taking in the scene as if it was better than anything he could get from the YouTubers.

"What can I get you?" he asked.

"You got anything called the Eye Opener?"

Chad looked at me, then back at True with the curvy bombshell in the killer pinstripe pantsuit draped all over him after she'd ruined my apology.

True stepped around her and whispered in my ear. He felt so close but also way too far away. "What are you doing, Lu? I think you should stick to the white wine. You know mixing is not so good for you."

I ignored him and turned back to Chad. "You know what? I'll take that sunrise but hold the orange juice and how about you add a little pineapple instead. Thanks."

I ignored True staring at me and Daniel and Pilar whispering while they tried to figure out what me and True were doing at this party in the first place. Shit, what were we doing here? What was I doing here?

It wasn't like Keanu was here. Chad gave me my drink, and I nodded.

"Listen, you want to just head home?" True said. "Maybe we get some takeout on the way?"

Takeout? At home? I wanted to eat with him at home *yesterday*. It was on the tip of my tongue to say so, but of course I couldn't, not here. Not now. If I said it, it really would make us sound like we were dating.

"No need. You stay here and talk to Pilar. Obviously, you

have some business to discuss. I think I'll go and check out the New World exhibit and see if virtual reality can hold a candle to this one."

I circled around the two of them, trying my best to keep my drink steady, now regretting my heels. The floor had little pockmarks and divots, all perfect for a heel to get stuck in, which of course mine did.

I just barely righted myself and my drink, thanks to Daniel's steadying hand at the small of my back. True was reaching but not far enough. "Whoa there. It's rocky terrain," Daniel said. He slipped a glance at True. "How about you let me escort you? Make sure you make it to the other room over this gravel."

I looked back at True. I could feel his presence, even though he was currently half blocked by Pilar.

"Sure," I said. "A girl's gotta walk somehow."

CHAPTER 18

AWAKE OR STILL DREAMING

BETHANY LU

Finally, Keanu was in front of me, but of course, not him. Not really.

I'd let Daniel lead me to the VR New World simulation that both Clipster and Chad couldn't stop going on about earlier.

"I have to say I was surprised—pleasantly, of course—to run into you tonight. You haven't gotten back to any of my texts. I thought we were friends now."

I turned to Daniel, glad to be away from Pilar but already feeling off and not quite myself being away from True. I hated it. More than that, it scared me. Probably him going away and breaking free now was way long overdue. For both of us. "You agreed to give me three months to make my decision. This isn't a friendship. It's business. If you'd rather not wait, I'm prepared to give you my answer right this minute. But I don't think you'll like it."

Daniel cleared his throat. "No," he croaked. "I can wait." He took a sip of his drink. "So are you and Erickson *together* together?"

I felt my face scrunch up. What does that matter? I thought.

"It doesn't matter at all," Daniel said, answering my inner thought, which I'd once again let slip out. "I was just wondering what type of woman my old college buddy had gotten lucky enough to snag."

And my face screwed up further. "First of all, I am not anyone's to *snag*, and second, I don't think he'd consider you an old buddy."

Daniel nodded at that one. "You're probably right."

No wonder True told me he found this guy about as appealing as an ingrown toenail. I fought to tamp down my anger. "True is a very good friend. Has been for years. He's practically family."

Daniel smiled then. I didn't know if it was genuine or if he didn't believe me. It didn't matter, but either way I didn't quite trust that smile and all it implied.

"That's good to hear," he said. "He's a nice guy. Deserves nice, um, family." Then he looked back toward the other room. I turned and saw that he and True had locked eyes and Daniel was practically preening while True was still talking with Pilar. Or more like Pilar was saying something really close to True's lower earlobe, so much so that she had to push her breasts against his chest. But still I caught the tic of True's jaw and the mischievous grin that Daniel gave him. Daniel licked his bottom lip then looked my way. "There is nothing more important than family." He did a little head nod, signaling at someone across the room, then turned back to me.

Just then a young guy in a head-to-toe branded tracksuit came over and clamped Daniel on the shoulder. He nodded my way but didn't bother introducing himself. I'd thought I recognized him or maybe not. He whispered in Daniel's ear. "I'm sorry, can I leave you for a moment?" Daniel asked me. "You partake in"—he paused, looking at the VR attendant—"whatever this is."

Of course, he was talking about the VR experience, but the way Daniel phrased it left both me and the young attendant not sure if the half-assed slur wasn't meant for her. Goodness. It seemed like whenever this guy's offer with all those zeros started to look promising, he dicked it up.

I shooed him off and turned to the attendant with an apologetic nod. She was cute, a young African American woman with radiant deep brown skin wearing a black tee that read CREW. She'd fancied up her tee with black leggings and kick-ass pink faux lizard–print boots. Her hair was pale pink and she had the same color glasses to match, which brought a much-needed breath of light and color to this place.

She was cool, brushing off Daniel's remark with a smooth side-eye as she offered me the heavy VR glasses and took my drink from my hands. Why did I get the feeling that this young woman was already way too used to dealing with rude corporate assholes? The thought made me even more pissed.

"Hi. Thanks for coming. Please just relax," she said in a

calm, professional tone. I sent her a silent signal of strength as she went on with her work speech. "It will probably take a moment to get your bearings. Don't worry, I'm here. Just feel your feelings and enjoy the experience. If you feel immersed, then don't worry. You're doing it right." She smiled. "If you need for me to stop, just raise your hand and say so. Does that sound good to you?"

I frowned. "That actually sounds kind of frightening."

She smiled again. This time a little truer, more genuine and reassuring. "Don't worry. It will be fine."

I nodded and let out a breath to let her know I was ready.

Once the glasses were on my face they were even heavier than in my hand. "I'm sure this will leave a mark," I said, only half joking.

"I'm sorry. I can loosen it," the attendant said. Her voice was surprisingly loud and seemed to come from inside my head. I jumped and spun around.

"Sorry. I'll turn the volume down too," she said.

I shook my head and held up my hand. "It's fine—the volume and the glasses. I'd rather them not slip off."

"Okay," she said in my ear, her voice taking over my brain. "And I know they are a bit heavy, but they are well designed and shouldn't leave a mark. If you don't mind, we're going to begin. I'll count you down, okay?"

I nodded and gasped as she began to count down . . . four, three, two, one and suddenly a *whoosh* went through my ear and in front of me was darkness, then a bright light. I felt myself pull back, then forward as the brightness dimmed to a pinpoint and the VR's visual opened up before my eyes with an image through a lens like an old-time camera shutter.

My body moved forward as the camera—*wait*, I told myself, *the VR*—made it feel like I was being pushed out onto a road. Shit. I'd seen this road before.

I knew the words that would come before I heard them. "I've been on this road before."

It was the late River Phoenix's voice saying the line I'd heard many times before. And the road was so similar to the movie I loved with him and Keanu. My mind took me to a place where I was younger and just in the early stages of falling for Keanu.

I heard a motorcycle in the distance.

The hairs on the back of my neck stood on edge. I should rip these glasses right off. At least raise my hand in the gesture that said stop. I had that type of free will. I knew how to avoid pain. I was a master at it. But no, like an idiot I stood there on the road that wasn't a road and listened as the sound of the motorcycle came closer and closer. Waiting for it to bear down on me.

A sudden breeze blew across my body, and I turned to the left just as Keanu pulled up beside me on the gleaming black-and-chrome bike. He smiled at me, and I felt everything inside me go soft.

Don't be afraid. It's more about the journey than the destination.

I blinked and looked at him. He was so close to me and looked so real it was like I could practically touch his face. I reached my hand up to touch him, but instead of smiling, his eyes shifted, hardened a little and he ducked away and challenged me with darkened eyes. His voice deepened to a growl. *So are you coming?*

I blinked and he was gone. Not gone, but going. Nearly a pinprick now in the distance.

Once again came the voice. "I've been on this road before."

Shit, no! I closed my eyes. It wasn't River Phoenix's voice this time, and this road... Though similar to the one in the movie, this one wasn't that one, but the one I'd been to only once and avoid like the plague ever since, taking the long way around, never that side street, avoiding that exit with my gaze when by chance on a long drive we'd just happen to pass it. This street looked eerily like the street that Cole had died on. The street he should have never been on in the first place. The street he wouldn't have been on, if only I'd been there.

It's all in your head. It's all in your head. This street couldn't be that street, though, VR or not. No designers are that good, I told myself. I blinked. Praying for the shutter to click again. Grateful to hear a click. I opened my eyes, hoping I'd see Keanu once again.

And there was that breeze. I smiled with relief. He was coming back for me. I knew he would come back for me. I waved my hand. Ready to flag him down. But it wasn't a bike in front of me. No, this was a car. And the person driving that car was my brother, Cole.

I gasped seeing him looking so beautiful. Young and exactly the same as when I'd said goodbye to him at the airport. This time the pain was fresh and unbearable as my words to him were echoed back to me. "I wish you could come with me, but not yet." He grinned. "I'll finish this race, then come back for you."

Suddenly he revved the engine, and then there was another roar drowning his out, as Keanu on his bike pulled up again with that smile, nodded at us both then sped past Cole. Cole gave me a knowing wink and shot off behind him. *Wait!*

Suddenly there was darkness, and I was alone. No Cole, no Keanu. Just the road and me. I looked out. True! There was True. A breeze and the old camera shutter clicked again. The bright sky, then sudden darkness. I was alone again. Until I heard it. That rev, then his voice. Keanu. *So are you coming? Will I see you down the road?* Then silence.

When the attendant touched me, I practically jumped out of my skin.

"Miss, are you all right?"

I ripped off the glasses. "I'm fine." I'm sure the tears and the distressed look on my face said otherwise, but I couldn't help it.

"I'm sorry, but you didn't say stop."

She was right, I didn't. I was suddenly aware of the small crowd staring at me. But no True in sight. "Where's the ladies' room?" I whispered.

"Make a left and third room down."

I rushed through the crowd as fast as my heels could take me, until I came to a door with some unfortunately graphic vector images in the act of peeing. I couldn't tell whether it was a women's room, but I needed to get out of sight before more tears fell.

There were two stalls and one was closed, so I was stuck

sobbing in a stall next to a stranger. And of course, I now had to sob and pee.

The tears flowed as I fought to keep my balance, hovering over the toilet and doing my business while snot started to leak from my nose. I couldn't believe that damn VR. Why would they make such a morbid thing? Weren't the kids into Sims and shit? What was that death memory-lane nostalgia crap?

There was no way those people could have gotten that deep into my head, though. All that stuff with Cole, that wasn't them. That was me. I brought him into that experience and meshed him with Keanu. I tightened my eyes against the thought. It was fucking official: I was going over the edge.

I let out a groan. This night sucked. No Keanu and the news that True was being wooed away by a cougar with big pockets. "Just fuck all to hell." It came out as a long wail as I finished peeing. "Fuck True, Fake Keanu, Aimee, Pilar, that fucking Lim, Zoolandering Stiller and fuck you again, Truman Erickson!"

I flushed the toilet, got up and leaned back against the side of the bathroom stall, balling up more tissues and putting them to my eyes. I probably looked like a raccoon now with my mascara all over the place, and it was all True's fault. "This is all your fault, you cold-ass sudden secret keeper. And I swear if I get an eye infection, I'm gonna make you pay and take care of meeeeee," I blubbered. "And do all of Morphie's walks. So fuck you, and deal with that too."

It was then I heard a deep snort followed by a low and very male chuckle. I froze. *Crap.* "Hello?"

"Hello," the very deep, totally male voice answered back.

"Umm…do you mind?" I asked.

"Not at all. Please continue."

What the hell? Could this get any worse? The signs on the door flashed in my mind. They were all so convoluted with figures bending this way and that, streams of pee arcing in all sorts of recreational directions, who knew whose bathroom I was currently in. With my luck tonight I could be having my meltdown in the fetish sex room of this party. *Oh, shit.* My eyes went wide as I clutched my invisible pearls. I did a quick stall scan for secret holes. I was so not prepared for what some of those signs were offering. It was late, and this night had already been enough with the revelations.

I gave my body a shake and cleared my throat while adjusting my clothes. Maybe I could quickly run out, wash my hands and flee before the person in the other stall came out. That way I'd save us both the embarrassment. Not that the guy in the next stall sounded the least bit embarrassed. I seemed to be the only person taking in that emotion today.

I put my hand on the door to leave and paused, suddenly even more nervous. What if as soon as I came out, he came out too? Any person who would stay in the stall and then laugh would surely do that. I cleared my throat again.

"I'm sorry about my outburst. It's been quite a night," I said.

Now nothing but silence from Mr. Deep Voice.

I frowned, then started again. "But I'd really like it to be over without any further embarrassment, so can we make a deal that one of us leaves here first and then the other goes a few discreet moments after?"

More silence. Did he leave already, and I didn't hear? Worse, did he leave and not wash his hands? Gross! I went to look under the stall to get a glimpse at the one next to me. I couldn't see any feet but also couldn't bend that far in the small space. *Damn me for not keeping up with my yoga app!* Yet another data drainer I should delete! I let out another breath. Fine. He was probably gone. Of course he was. Woman screaming in the stall next door would get me off the shitter right quick too.

I shook my head and reached for the stall lock, then swung it open, stepping out.

"Fuck me!"

"That was the only person you didn't have on your list."

"I thought you had left."

"I was leaving, but you sounded pretty upset so I just wanted to make sure you were okay."

I blinked. This wasn't real. I was still in virtual reality. No, I wasn't even in VR or at this party. I must be dreaming and still in bed and have not made it to the party at all, because there was no way I was in a downtown bathroom talking to the person I'm currently talking to.

Tall. Piercing green eyes. Devastating smile. Shoulders you could possibly land a small plane on. Or whatever.

I was face-to-face with Captain America!

Chris Evans smiled, then turned and washed his hands silently beside me. He glanced up at my reflection, and I snapped a mental picture so as to adequately describe it to Dawn and my fictional documentarians in my later years.

He was about to leave when I had to open my mouth and ask him the one pressing question that was killing me. "I'm sorry to bother you, but I've really got to ask," I started. Before he opened the door.

"Sure, what is it?"

"What are you doing at this party?"

He shook his head. "You know what? I really don't know. I got an Evite and heard a rumor that Keanu Reeves was going to be here, so I figured I'd come and try to get a look at him."

I stared at him. "Are you serious? But you're Captain America."

He tilted his head. "Yeah, but Keanu's The One."

CHAPTER 19

WHOA

TRUE

K eeping my face impassive and my eyes focused was turning out to be an almost impossible task. I looked over Pilar's head to try to get a glimpse of Lu. I hated the way she had run off with that look of hurt in her eyes, the way we had so quickly gotten into that stupid argument, and for what? I especially hated the way she'd taken Lim's arm.

Pilar was going on and on...and on. I mean I got it, but she needed to get it too. And back off. This hard sell was getting her nowhere. The Copper Goose hedge fund seemed like my perfect nightmare. But their rep was growing and Pilar was making it out like signing a contract with them would be akin to Aladdin getting a magic lamp with none of the strings. As if I didn't know about the semi-shady clients with their money hidden in Swiss banks, while they kept up a facade of environmentally friendly and tech portfolios. Still, there were the good parts. Like the huge expense accounts, the money, the fact that I could set Mama up with a low-stress, worry-free retirement. But at what cost?

"Pilar," I started slowly, trying to keep my cool and keep things plain and professional. "Like I told you during our last conversation, I will give your offer all due consideration. But when I say I'm quite satisfied in my current position, I mean it."

She glanced over her shoulder, gesturing toward where Lu and Lim went. "Oh, I believe that statement wholeheartedly. The way you've been keeping an eye out for Lu Carlisle, I'd say more than satisfied in your current position."

Pilar let out a sigh. "Truman. I appreciate that you and Ms. Carlisle are longtime friends. And of course, that might make you feel a bit uncomfortable, given her family is one of our biggest competitors, but believe me, Thomas Carlisle understands that this is just business." She took a sip of her drink and continued. "Now, I don't know if he's tried to woo you over the years, but if he has, then his offer was obviously not good enough. And if he hasn't, well, then it's his fault for not seeing what a diamond you are. Hell, maybe the family just doesn't know how to spot a gem when it's right in front of their eyes."

Pilar was going all out now. And yes, Lu's father, Mr. Carlisle—"call me Thomas"—had offered me a job with Forty Rise more than once. He'd been at my graduation and told me he'd seen so much of Cole in me as I walked and received my degree. He tried to recruit me then, and twice more along the way over the years. But that was none of Pilar's business. It was also not something I'd ever shared with Lu.

It was enough that I lived in one of his buildings, though he said I shouldn't feel guilty since I paid for my unit like everyone else. My only perk was being one of the first to buy while the building was still in the reconstruction stage. But living the life I was living, shadowing his daughter when I had practically snatched away his only son, was the only friends-and-family perk my conscience would allow me to take.

The whole idea of being "connected" or using the friendship I'd had with Cole and now with Lu didn't sit right with me. Thomas had said he liked the idea of me living so close to Lu after all that had happened. That he somehow owed a lot to me. If they only knew the truth. How if only I hadn't been such a shit friend, maybe Cole wouldn't have died. How if I'd stopped him from that stupid race, they would have the son they actually wanted in their life instead of his tagalong friend who they'd let stay in their orbit all these years.

Fuck, maybe it was time for a change. I looked at Pilar. Not this change but a change nonetheless.

I didn't like where this was going at all. And now that I thought about it, how much of meeting her and Lim here was really a coincidence?

"One has nothing to do with the other," I said.

She looked at me like she was either bored or didn't believe any of what I was saying. "Now, Truman, you are either playing hard to get or trying to get us to up our offer." She shrugged, then smiled. "It doesn't matter, because either way, your hard-to-get routine is working. I'm prepared to go up twenty percent on our offer right now."

I stayed steady. *All money ain't good money.* I could hear my mother's soft warning as if she were standing right next to me. If any one thing stuck from her calm lessons over the years, passed to her by my late grandmother and always delivered in that easy matter-of-fact way that let you know she was most assured in what she was saying, it was that. *All money ain't good money, and if it looked too good, that's when it was time to step back and investigate.*

An ER nurse, my mom practically worked herself to death, taking on side gigs as a home health-care aide to be sure I had what I needed to pay for books, uniforms, fees and all the other extras that my scholarship to Forresters hadn't covered. The kind of money Pilar was offering would let my mom retire in a much better lifestyle than she or I had ever imagined.

Yeah, but all money ain't good money, baby.

I knew my mother was right, and I also knew I would not be solving the Pilar/Copper Goose issue tonight. Frankly, I didn't care about it. What I did care about was figuring out whatever was going on with Lu and fixing it.

Pilar was still talking. "You would essentially be making your own hours and building your own staff in LA. What more could you possibly want?"

To not be in LA.

Where the hell had Lu and damned Lim gone off to? That shithead had better not be trying anything.

I looked at Pilar. "I said I'd think it over." Maybe my voice was a little firmer than the venue warranted.

She put her hand to her chest. "See, was that so hard?"

Very. It was all really, really hard. And instead of getting easier, it seemed to only get harder to fight these warring feelings I had for Lu. Every few years I'd put them in the lockbox in the back of my mind where my other past disappointments and things I could never have went. But the lock was failing. Age? I don't know. Maybe I should upgrade it. Make it foolproof and add an encryption to the password. Or maybe it was time to throw the whole damn thing away.

Something caught my eye, and I saw Lim was back. But not Lu. Where was she? I mean, when you escort someone you escort them.

"Listen, I've got to go," I said, interrupting Pilar mid-sentence. "We'll have to finish this conversation another time."

"I hope so."

Her voice was now at my back. I walked up behind Lim while nodding a short "excuse me" to the blonde he was sidling up to. "Where's Lu?"

"She's fine, Erickson. What are you getting all puffed up about? I cannot believe after all these years you still haven't learned to chill. Why don't you grab another drink, and we can catch up? I've busted your balls enough. If you're a friend of Lu's and Pilar is into you, you must have something. I think we need to team up."

Team up? The idea of any sort of teaming with Lim was revolting, but I didn't have time for that convo. "That's not what I asked you."

He gave me a double pat on my chest that was way too

reminiscent of school days. So much so that I felt old anger and resentment bubbling up. I pushed his hand down. "I don't have time for this."

"Come on, man. I'm not all that bad. I mean what I say about teaming up. Lu's thinking about it."

That stopped me short. I knew he was just trying to get a good reaction out of me. But shit, I couldn't give him the reaction I really wanted. It would only piss off Lu and give him the satisfaction of knowing he'd gotten to me. "Lu can think all she wants. She's a smart woman. I trust she'll come to the right decision about you," I said. "If she hasn't already."

I noticed Lim's eyes darken ever so slightly, and he shook his head quickly. "Whatever. She's over by the VR station. It looked like a bore, but I'm sure she'll be right—"

I was gone. No need to hear more of him or his voice.

But over at the VR exhibit area, there wasn't a sign of Lu. I asked the attendant and her expression immediately turned worried. "I think she went off toward the ladies' room. She seemed upset after trying out the goggles. I hope they didn't make her sick. I probably should have checked on her, but we had another person in line. I hope it isn't a problem."

I could tell she was worried about being in trouble. "I'm sure it's okay," I said. "Which way?"

"Third door on the left." She leaned out and pointed down the hall.

I pushed on the door. "Lu, you in there?"

The door pushed back, and a male voice answered. "Occupied. Just a minute."

I stood outside and looked up and down the hall. Where did she get off to? Was she so mad she left without me? I dialed her number and at the same time a phone rang inside the bathroom. I thought I heard her curse.

I stilled.

There was a man's voice and then water.

I pushed hard on the door just as some guy was coming out.

There was a standoff between me and the immobile door for a while as I pushed my weight against it. Finally and way too suddenly, the door gave way and I went flying through.

"Whoa there, tiger. Don't go hurting yourself."

I righted myself fast, ready to pounce and at the same time scouring the space for Lu. I saw a flash of the guy as he left, but all I was really looking for was her. I let out a breath when our eyes met. She was still mad and, shit, she'd been crying. "Are you okay?"

She glared. "I'm fine. Nice of you to care."

"Come on, Lu. You scared the hell out of me. I've been looking all over for you and here you are in strange bathrooms with..." I squinted a bit as the face I'd barely seen clicked. "What the Marvel? Captain America?"

Lu nodded and crossed her arms. "That's right. Captain America. So think about that when you're off to your new job."

"What are you implying?" I leaned in close to her face.

She let out a long breath. "Oh, really? Now you're concerned? After not calling me this whole week or telling me about job offers and a whole possible double life?"

"Listen, I'm sorry. Let's talk about it." I put my hand on her arm and she pulled away.

"No, I'm going home. You stay. Finish your business and sorting out your...whatever." Lu stomped past me and headed down the hall.

I listened to her steps for a moment, watching as she got farther, contemplating whether I should let her go or chase after her and share the car home. Either way would be painful. Either way would be a confrontation I wasn't ready to have and was even more not ready to lose.

Where was Captain America when I needed him?

CHAPTER 20

SIDE BY SIDE

BETHANY LU

I couldn't believe True.

The burgundy 2016 Accord that was my Uber pulled up. I glanced back just in case True had followed, but nope—just me and the bouncers. I guess True had decided to stay. Why should I blame him? It was what I'd told him to do, and if anything, True was great at following directions.

The driver turned around and looked at me. "Lu Carlisle?"

I nodded and went to the car door and slid in. The quicker I got away from here, out of these shoes, showered, the quicker I could start to wash this night from my memory. But the door was suddenly wrenched back open and there I was, looking up at True.

"Do you mind?" I said.

"Of course I mind. How are you just going to run off and leave without me?"

I tugged at the door. "I told you I was going." I pulled at the door again. It didn't budge.

"Um, do you mind?" the driver chimed in. "Either get in or don't."

I scooted over and True slid in next to me with a big sigh.

Satisfied enough, the driver pulled away from the curb with a hard left and headed up Tenth Avenue. The silence between True and me was as thick as the traffic.

"Why are you being like this, Lu?" he finally said. "I know you're disappointed not getting to see Keanu yet again. I'm sorry that didn't work out, but I'll get in touch with my guy and maybe he'll have more info."

"How's about screw you and your guy."

He looked at me, now shocked and hurt, and for a moment I felt guilty. But only a moment. I was tired and mad and couldn't get past how he was considering a whole new life on the other side of the country and hadn't even told me about it.

"Is anything you tell me the truth?"

True's mouth fell open and his brows pulled together. "What are you talking about?"

I tilted my head at him. "What the hell is with all the secrets, True? Were you ever going to tell me about LA, or would I just wake up one morning and you'd be gone?" Suddenly that awful VR experience came to mind, and my eyes welled with tears again. I just knew any moment they would overflow. Dammit! I turned away from him and looked out the window. The cars, buildings, lights of the city going by in a watery blur.

"Are you serious right now?"

Something in his tone had me turning my head back, but looking at him made me feel weak. It made me want to reach for him. To tell him I needed him. And right now I didn't want to need him. "You know what? It doesn't matter. It's not like I expected you to be all forthcoming or anything. You never were. Sharing is not what you do."

True looked down and I could see his walls coming up, being built brick by brick, and I was mixing the cement.

He let out a breath. "Okay, I know you're upset about hearing about me getting that job offer the way you did. I'm sorry. That piled on top of the Keanu disappointment must be a lot."

"That right there. That judgment thing you do. Where you act like you're better than me by psychoanalyzing me, all the while deflecting. That's the problem. You didn't have to come with me tonight. And you didn't have to come with me to Coney Island."

"You wouldn't have known about Coney Island if it wasn't for me."

I paused. "Well fine, I'll give you that, but you didn't have to come."

"You would have overslept."

I stared at him. "Well, you can be sure I won't oversleep next time. So don't worry about me while you're on the way to LA."

True sighed. "When did I say I'm going to LA?"

"When did you say you weren't or any damned thing about it at all?"

True rubbed his hands over his head. I knew he was

getting to his frustration breaking point. Good, because I was past mine.

"You're off the hook, True. You don't have to come with me on any more wild excursions or"—I searched for the most True-like words—"flights of fancy or however you think of them."

"You know you're being unfair. I never said I was going to LA. And when have I ever uttered words like 'flights of fancy'? You make me sound like someone's grandpa."

"You may not have said it, but you thought it."

He looked at me way too seriously. "You'd be surprised to know some of the things I've actually thought, Lu."

I felt a sudden tingle and a heat in my chest. "Like what?"

He looked away and I practically deflated. "I'm sure they're offering you a lot of money."

"Yeah." He sighed. "But money isn't everything."

"But it's not nothing." I shrugged. "And hell, it's not like you're the only one in demand. As you can see, your old friend is pretty keen on getting me under his employ." True stilled and his lips went firm. I knew I was being petty, but it served him right.

"Yeah, under. That sounds about like Lim."

I let out a snort. "Screw you, True. Can't you even consider that he wants me for my art and not something else?"

His brows furrowed. "Well, aren't you doing the same here? And I don't even know why. It's not like you have to keep tabs on me. I'm not a child."

"Then why were you acting like one and keeping this offer a secret?" I shot back. "And not just this one but the one from your dean. You're always full of silence and secrets. The unflappable Mr. Erickson."

True let out a frustrated moan. "I didn't say anything, Lu, because neither thing was a big deal to me."

"Come on, True. It's big. And you know it. Maybe you even dressed extra nice, knowing that Pilar would be at the party tonight. It's amazing how she would casually talk about upping her price after seeing you looking like a right snack and good enough to eat."

He laughed then. "A snack. You really have jumped the shark. I don't know what was in those drinks, but they must have been potent as hell. I don't know what you want to hear. Yes, I got a job offer. It's not a big deal. I get feelers all the time since my book came out. And yes, I got a new jacket and a new shirt. I bought them because I thought tonight was important to you. Fuck, woman, I'm even wearing designer drawers tonight to complete the image all because of you."

I sucked in a breath. "Well damn."

Hearing that was better than running into Chris Evans in the toilet. Not as good as Keanu, but it was still nice. I turned away, not knowing what to do with the feeling, and looked out the window.

"I'm sorry," I finally said. "I'm still mad, but I am sorry, I shouldn't have ridden you about the jacket. The offer, yes. You should share more. Stop keeping everything to yourself. I can't promise anything, but I'll try and not fly off the handle so much. I mean, what does it matter that that tigerish Pilar woman was pawing all over your new jacket every chance she got? I shouldn't have let it get under my skin."

True turned me toward him and tilted my head up to his face. He grinned as we pulled off the highway and onto our block.

"What are you over there grinning about?"

True wiggled his brows. "So I looked good tonight?"

I rolled my eyes and hit his knee with my own. He nodded and licked his lips, giving a wink. It was cheesy and a little gross, and dammit if I didn't clench a little where I definitely wouldn't be admitting to him.

"Yeah, I did look good," he preened. "Yeah, nope, not going for that job. Pilar won't be harassing my *fine* ass all up and down the halls. Better to keep all this *fine* here in New York where it's safe, with you."

I mimed gagging. "Okay, now you're drunk. Good thing you're home."

He looked at me, eyes going sexy. "You know I'm not drunk, but we are almost home." His voice was way too on the edge of not playing.

"Sometimes you can be frustrating as all get out," I said.

True nodded. "And I can say the exact same thing about you, right?"

He continued to stare at me, as if he knew exactly what I was thinking.

"Of course. I know I'm a lot. But this frustration is new. I don't know quite what to do with it," I said, my voice softer than I meant it to be.

True grabbed my hand. "You don't have to do anything with it, and you don't have to be frustrated. We just have to be us."

Then he leaned in and brushed his lips softly across

mine. It was sweet and seductive and sent a jolt right to the center of my thighs. I was about to lean in and tip my tongue out when we hit a pothole and our teeth and noses banged together. Hard enough to have us both pulling back and wincing.

"Fuck!"

"Shit!"

"Sorry about that! I don't know what's happened to the infrastructure of this city," said the driver.

True and I stared at each other, him holding his nose and me my mouth as we both wondered what to do next. Continue or pretend it didn't happen? For the life of me, I wanted to straddle the man.

But he spoke first. "Are you hungry? In all that drama and gabbing, we didn't even eat. Wanna get changed, order up some food and figure out the next steps on this plan of yours?"

Huh? What did that mean in True speak? I know so much about him and yet so little. On any other guy, "wanna order up food and eat" was clear for "hey, you go get ready, we grab a quick bite, and I'll see you naked in twenty." But this was True, he could be deflecting and putting me right back in my friend zone. Maybe he really wanted to eat.

Gah!!

Before I could figure out a reply, his phone rang just as we were pulling up to our building. I caught a glimpse of Aimee, phone to her ear, but True hadn't spied her yet.

"Nah," I told him. "I think I'll be ordering for one. Looks like your night is not over. Seems to me you're still in very high demand."

He looked at Aimee and then at me with an apology in his eyes that I knew was about to roll off his lips. I didn't want to hear it. "It's fine," I told him. I said goodnight to the driver and left him a great tip.

I only spared a quick wave to Aimee and tried to ignore the way her eyes shined as she looked at True as I hustled into the building.

If only she didn't look so cute. I hated myself, but I glanced back as I pulled open the door to our building. Why was she blinking so much? Jeez, was she crying? Damn, True. He was making women swoon all up and down NYC tonight. How much more could I have underestimated my dear Mr. Erickson?

I shook my head and willed the elevator to hurry so I wouldn't have to ride it with them. This was not my business. True had made it clear tonight that so much of his life was not my business, and it was probably best that way.

CHAPTER 21

SHOOT THE HOSTAGE

BETHANY LU

W ithout pics, it didn't happen," Dawn said, once I finished recapping my "In the Toilet with the Captain" story. Who could blame her? Also, maybe I should come up with a better title than "In the Toilet with the Captain"? "In the Loo"? Class it up a bit? Have Thandiwe Newton play me in the trailer in my mind.

"Let's just say it didn't, okay?" I yelled back into the speaker on my cell over the sound of my microwave. "Listen, I'm dead tired. Can I call you tomorrow?"

"You'd better," she answered. "Also, I feel like you're leaving out something really important. There are more holes in this story than a pair of distressed jeans from the nineties. But I'll let it wait...for a minute. Talk to you tomorrow, love."

When Dawn hung up, I felt like I'd dodged a huge bullet. I wasn't ready to deal with the night myself, let alone analyze it to shreds with my BFF. I couldn't handle it. Not after my near breakdown and the kiss that led to nowhere.

I thought about taking Morphie for a walk, but didn't want to risk running into True, so I went the opposite way and took him for a patio quickie before heading to bed.

I wondered if True stayed out to talk to Aimee or whether he'd invited her in. I looked back at my phone, which stayed frustratingly silent. I turned it off. "Fuck it, Morph," I said and padded over to grab some wine and popcorn and a treat for him. "You're my best company anyway."

I flipped on my DVR and queued up *Speed* once again. "Shoot the hostage, Morph. Always shoot the hostage. Get rid of all sentimental ties right out of the gate. That way, no matter which way it goes, you don't have to hurt later."

I woke the next morning to texts from Dawn, Daniel and True.

I rubbed my eyes and decided to deal with Daniel's first. The others would probably need coffee.

> **D. Lim:** Great to see you last night. But you disappeared. Just making sure you're okay. Your timetable is fine, as we're still very interested in working with you. This could be major.

There was only one emoji and that was the little bomb sign, so I guess that was an improvement for Daniel.

I responded with a quick made it home and that my agent would be in touch when there was news. The more businesslike distance I could maintain, the better with Daniel.

I let Morphie out to the patio and went to the bathroom, then came back to make my coffee. My phone buzzed and I saw a new message from Dawn stacked on others from last night.

> **Dawn:** What did you do? Why is Daniel Lim writing to me so early in the morning?
>
> **Me:** I didn't do anything. And I'm not taking his offer firmly off the table, but I just get a vibe. When you're back in New York, you can meet with him if you want and see.

...I knew she was thinking.

> **Dawn:** Okay. If you get a vibe, then that's it. We move on. Like I said. I've got your back. There are other bigtime investors in the sea.
>
> **Me:** I'm still thinking about it, but I just wanted to give you a heads-up.
>
> **Dawn:** Follow your heart. ☺

I loved her. I knew it wouldn't be easy for her to give up such a big commission if I decided not to go with Daniel or someone like him.

I looked at my work in progress, the calendar and where I stood. The days were ticking away. Keanu was getting further from me and closer to his proposed wedding date and possible retirement. And now after last night, it felt like True was getting even further than that. And not to mention I still had a couple of pieces to finish for the show at Dawn's gallery. I needed to unblock.

I had to work or at least pretend to be the artist I was supposed to be. Work, paint, sketch. Take my dog out for a walk. Do something to at least feel human.

Morphie gave me a look, then nudged at his bowl. "Fine, and you're right, priorities. That's what I love about you, Morphie. You know how to make a plan and stick with it. I don't know why I didn't consult you from the start. Dealing with True has been nothing but a disaster."

I put his food in his bowl. Morphie looked at me with silent thanks I'm sure somewhere in his rather stoic expression. "That's just what I'm going to do. Pick a thing and focus." I looked at my now not-so-white board and my K-90 plan. So what if I was still at the first step? There weren't that many. Time to just saddle up again. I could do this without True. He wasn't part of the plan when I conceived it anyway. I could find Keanu all by myself.

I flipped another pod in the brewer to get a second cup of coffee going, then grabbed my laptop.

All right, Mr. Reeves. You may have eluded me thus far, but I'll catch up with you somewhere.

My doorbell rang.

Dammit. I looked out the peephole and there was True. I opened the door and he grinned at me. It was wide, joyous and a lot. A whole lot.

All I could do for a moment was blink and stand in shock as I took in all towering six foot three inches of him encased in black spandex. All except his worn-out New Balances, which now looked like big white-and-gray flippers on his feet, and a blue pack across his body. I let my eyes roam, getting stuck over some large bumps and deep valleys. Whoa. Like I said, this was a lot.

"What in the world are you wearing? You'd better get in here before the neighbors call the cops for indecent exposure."

True's smile faded and, even though I knew I shouldn't have been looking, it seemed as if perhaps some of his earlier, um, confidence faded along with it. I looked downward again. Or perhaps not.

"You didn't read my messages?" he asked.

Oh, crap, I didn't.

I shook my head and turned to grab my phone. True followed me in. I glanced at him. He was standing in a semi-casual pose or poses. Shifting his legs and arms like he was practicing for his mix tape photo shoot or something, looking uncomfortable against my wall in that ridiculous bodysuit.

I forced my eyes away from the marvel before me and swiped my cell screen. My eyes went wide. Well, wider.

> **True:** I'm sorry. I should have been there for you. All the way.
>
> **True:** I won't let you down again.

I looked at him. "You didn't let me down, True. I was overreacting. It's over. We're fine. But now what are you wearing? I don't understand."

He looked at me confused and then stalked over, coming really close really fast. I leaned back. It was a lot with not a lot of filter between us. But he looked at my phone.

"Crap! Didn't I send the attachment and last message?"

He leaned back again, and I was shocked at the temperature change in my atmosphere of with True vs. without True.

He unhooked his bag quickly like a Black Batman and pulled out his phone. My phone buzzed.

I looked at him. "Feeling dramatic much this morning?"

He shrugged. "A little."

I sighed, then looked.

True: Are you ready to play dress up?

I almost blushed, then looked at the attachment.

NEW MEXICO Hero Fest with lots of surprise guests

Special John Wick X Matrix Panel

"Are you serious?"

He was grinning again and for some reason posing, standing tall, legs spread, hands on hips. "My guy."

"Gary?"

"Gary said he thinks Keanu might be there. So are we going?"

I shook my head and put my phone down on the counter going for my coffee. "No."

"What do you mean, no? I got into this cool-ass ninja suit for you."

I looked him up and down again, then picked up my coffee and leaned back on the counter. "Is that what that's supposed to be? I thought you were getting ready for your next big night out and you wanted me to paint a tuxedo shirt outline on it or something."

He faked laughter as he walked over to me and put his hands on the counter, surrounding me on both sides. "Very funny," he said. "You say you're not mad, but your little jokes say different. Now, why are you telling me no? You're not giving up, are you?"

I pushed lightly at his chest, noting he definitely didn't need one of those fake costume chestplate thingies. True stepped back.

"I'm not giving up. I'm just not asking you to come if I decide to go on this trip. Though I do thank you and Gary for the information."

He frowned.

"You're a busy man, True. You have work. I mean it's obvious with your TA showing up at all hours."

I watched as his lip quirked. What was that about, and now I wondered when did Aimee leave? Did she help him into the suit this morning?

"I'm not so busy. At least not right now. The semester is over and I'm free."

"What do you mean free? You're never free."

"Just that I'm free. Well, for the summer at least. Aimee was there to pick up some file keys for my office. I declined summer semester classes. I have things to do with my book and some other things to work out."

I sighed. "Aimee must be devastated."

True laughed and I had the sudden urge to kick him. "I don't know. She may be. She's got a lot on her plate with her fiancé and having to take over my classes. But that's her problem now."

I blinked, hating my sudden transparency. "Fiancé?"

"Yes." He nodded.

I looked him up and down again. He looked ridiculous but he did fill out the suit nicely. "Where did you get this silly suit?"

True did a quick turn and jazz hands. "You like it? I got it from the dance shop on 125th this morning. I was there as soon as they opened. The woman in the shop gave me a discount since it wasn't my right size." He leaned forward and down and got close to my face. "Now are you going to forgive me just a little for last night and come on and finish what the hell we started? You know how I hate having loose threads. And besides, I already bought the tickets. Nonrefundable on my miles. You can't not go with me."

"You did what?!" I yelled, slamming my cup back on the counter. "You're crazy. Why would you take that risk? What if I still say I won't go?"

He stared at me. "But you won't say that."

I stared back. "Why wouldn't I?"

He raised a brow. Then posed, one leg up, hands raised in a Kung Fu fighting stance. "Because, woman, you don't want me to have to use my special fighting powers on you."

"You look like an idiot," I said with a grin.

He smiled. And dropped his leg, toppling over in pain. "I know. An idiot with a leg cramp and a huge wedgie. Now we need to get ready to go and you have to find me another costume, because there's no way I'm going through the torture of getting in this thing again."

I shook my head. Why was he so damned cute and so off-limits?

CHAPTER 22

DESTINATION

TRUE

"What the hell, True? I thought you said you reserved a Mustang. There's no way we'll get all our luggage into this little thing." She jumped, hopping out of the way of a lizard that scurried by.

"And I thought you said we were packing light." I looked from Lu to the pile of luggage she had on the airport pushcart and back to the tiny convertible that the rental car attendant had just handed us the keys to.

"Well, what did you expect me to do?" she said. "You're the one who came to my place less than a week ago in your little unitard all full of ideas."

"It wasn't ideas my unitard was full of," I quipped back.

She stared at me. "So what, we get True the Jokester once we're out west? You should have warned me. I'd have packed a snare drum too."

"Are you sure you haven't?"

"Oh, just be quiet and call that attendant back. There's no way we can go in this car."

I looked around. "Do you see any other cars here? It's this or what?" I pointed across the lot to a tan Buick that looked like it should have been towed to the junkyard out of sheer kindness. "That?"

Lu sighed. "I don't know what you expected me to do. I had to pack us proper costumes for this. If we're getting dressed to see Keanu at a con, we should at least do it in style."

I slid her hand from the suitcase handle and pulled the bag around to the side of the car. We'd be here all day with the way she was playing around.

"Yeah, but in what style? Are we going as Mr. and Mrs. Stay Puft Marshmallow?"

"Only if it were 1984 and even then, probably not."

I took the suitcase and went to put it in the back seat.

"It's not going to fit," she said.

I shot a look her way.

"If you say it, I'll kick you," she challenged.

I shut my lips tight and mimicked the lock-and-key sign over my lips before I went around her, headed into the driver's seat, started the car and finally found the switch to take the top down. "Trust me, it will fit," I said as I got out of the car.

She let out a breath. "I should still kick you."

"Why? I know I didn't say what you were thinking. With your mind full of dirty dad jokes."

She shrugged. She looked cute and casual, though still probably too polished and put together for a dusty ride through New Mexico. Her slim jeans were designer, as was her lacy white peasant top. The same went for her stacked cork platforms, purse and the rest of the luggage. For a woman who didn't travel all that often, she did it in style.

She put her hand up. "Do you see this sun, True? It's shimmering like out of a movie. And it's practically laser beam hot. I need to find my sunglasses and get some protection. It's as if you hit the middle of the country and the shade just stops."

"Well," I said, hefting up her suitcase and after no small amount of effort wedging it into the back seat. "It's this, or the case stays. You want to leave something?"

She looked at me like I'd grown a third head. "Has the sun gotten to you already? Like I'm leaving my suitcase?"

"I guess that's the answer then." I let out a low breath. She was irritating and exasperating and, dammit, still adorable. "Now we need to get a move on. It's going to take at least two hours to get to Truth or Consequences, and I don't want to lose our room. It might not look like much, but from what I hear from my..." I paused. "From Gary, these little cons can get surprisingly big turnouts."

I got a duh look for that. "I mean it's Keanu. Of course."

I threw my backpack on top of her duffel, which was on top of her smaller carry-on tote. "Of course. Now let's hit it."

Lu got in on the passenger side, then wiggled around and leaned over to the back seat, her perfectly curved behind coming dangerously close to my lips. I moved back, fighting the temptation to do the opposite.

"What are you doing?"

"I remember now! My sunglasses are in my tote bag.

Right next to my camera case, which I definitely need for the drive. Just give me a minute."

A minute longer in this position in this tiny-ass car and I might not be able to drive.

"What?"

"Huh?"

She turned back and looked at me. "What are you mumbling about over there?"

Well shit. Was I now doing the inner monologue in an outside voice? I looked up. Booty. Then looked to the side. She was staring at me. "Nothing. Can you hurry?"

"I'm trying, but it's hard to reach." She angled up and I tried my best to think of anything besides her perfectly shaped ass. But in that moment, it was all that filled my brain. Trees, clouds, everything took the shape of her behind.

"Got 'em!" she finally yelled.

Thank God.

She flopped back into the passenger seat wearing big rectangular sunglasses that just about engulfed her face but made her lips look plumper and more kissable. I looked up. The sun shimmered. She was right. It was blazing, and the quicker I took cover the better.

"Welcome to Truth or Consequences. I'm Martina, and we're thrilled to have you at Plaza Del Sol." The older woman practically floated out of a side room, and her words of welcome came on a whisper as she greeted Lu and me.

Both Lu and I jumped, and she may have let out a yelp.

"I'm sorry," the woman said. "I do tend to step lightly.

Maybe I should put bells on." She chuckled as if it was a joke. But with her light, floaty manner, silver eyes and silver hair down her back, and her black dress, there was a definite witchy vibe about her. I'd say she needed bells and a voice amplifier. Both Lu and I leaned in to try to hear her, while still slightly leaning back in case we needed to duck spells.

"Now, how can I help you?" she said.

I cleared my throat as Lu turned around and started to take photos of the small lobby of the inn and spa. "This place is adorable. It's so, I don't know, Santa Fe. I'm starting to feel totally inspired, True."

I nodded. She'd been inspired all the way up and down I-25, and our two-and-a-half-hour drive turned into four and a half and we now already had another full shopping bag.

I looked back at Martina, hoping she could pick up on my signal of desperate exhaustion. "We have reservations for Erickson and Carlisle."

Martina's warm smile seemed to freeze for a moment and then she looked down at her ledger and then back up at me. "Erickson, you said?"

"And Carlisle."

She scratched at her head. "You see it's the time."

"The what?"

Lu stopped clicking behind me. "The time."

"You're after seven, and we had not heard from you for confirmation. I'm afraid your rooms are gone."

"Where did it go?" Lu's voice seemed calm and the question sounded sincere. Like perhaps she really thought the rooms just walked away.

Martina laughed. "Oh dear, they didn't actually *go* anywhere. They're still here of course."

Lu smiled. "That's perfect. We'll take the keys now."

Martina blinked. "They've gone too."

Lu stared at Martina. "Then I suggest you get them back." She didn't blink. Finally the older woman let out a low huff through her frozen smile. "Just a moment."

She floated away again, seemingly on the same invisible moving sidewalk she came in on, and went to another room. I turned to Lu. "You had to stop for souvenirs."

"And you had to eat," she countered.

"Well, you had to take pictures," I said. "As if the dirt changed color the farther we got down the road."

She rolled her eyes. "Actually, it did. Not that you'd understand."

"Dears." Once again Lu and I jumped at Martina's light-footed approach. "Please don't argue. That is one thing we don't do here at Plaza Del Sol."

I almost laughed out loud. Well then, we might as well head on to the next hotel—or motel, since it seemed like motels were all that this little sleepy town held.

Martina was smiling again, though. "Thankfully we have a solution to your problem."

"Our rooms have come back."

Martina's eyes shifted and for a second it looked like Lu had snatched the last of her serenity. I might just have to block a spell. "No, dear. But we do have something special for you. Not two rooms but our ultra villa accommodations. More private and still with its own private hot spring. I think you'll find it quite lovely."

"You mean we'll have to share?" I asked.

"I'm afraid it's all we have."

We'd be there two nights. The convention didn't start until tomorrow. "Would you be able to suggest another inn for us?"

Martina shook her head. "I did a quick call around and everyone is booked up with the big festival and all. Though you're welcome to check for yourself."

Lu tapped me. "Let's just take it. I'm exhausted and we've been traveling since the sun came up."

"Perfect. Just drive your car around back and to the right. I'll see you in a jiffy," Martina said.

But her jiffy was more like twenty minutes, which was literal hours in New York time. Finally, Martina came up to our car on a motorized scooter, telling us to follow her up the road. We drove past a mail office and rooms with worn pink and turquoise doors. She stopped just around a bend where there were a couple of refurbished campers with a few lawn chairs in front of them, a table setup and a hammock.

"Say this isn't it. Just keep driving, Martina," I mumbled. There was no way I could see Lu sleeping in a camper for two nights.

But Martina didn't keep driving. Instead the woman stopped, got out of her little cart and turned to us, giving her witchy smile and a wave.

"Holy hell. Spirit of Keanu. Did you really call me out to the desert to kill me?"

"I swear, Lu, if I die on your quest for Keanu Reeves you will not hear the end from me."

She turned to me, her eyes for a moment worried, but then leaned in, giving me a quick surprise kiss then pulling back with a smile. "There is no way I'm letting you die, Mr. Erickson. You know I'm the one haunting you till the very end." She hopped out of the car and for some reason that last declaration felt like a promise.

CHAPTER 23

FEELING MINNESOTA

BETHANY LU

"Oh my goodness. This is..."

"Small," True said.

"Cozy," I said at the same time. I gave him a smack on the arm. "Well sure, I guess some people would describe it that way too. And others, less bluntly."

I turned toward Martina, who was standing in the door-way, smiling like she was showing off her firstborn or a prized...I didn't know what they prized out here...prickly pear bushes? "But it's really beautiful," I said. And I wasn't lying.

Stepping into the camper was like going into some sort of mystical jewel box. It was colorful and folksy, with no surface untouched by some bright pop of color—from the hand-painted floor in a Moroccan stencil pattern to the mosaics all around the windowsills and mirrors. The pillows and quilts were all different colors and fabrics, and each looked handmade. Even the ceiling was painted with gorgeous vines and flowers that grew up from the walls.

Sure, the outside was rustic. I looked back outside, caught a glimpse—a real glimpse—of the river beyond the wall of greenery that was our view and wanted to kick myself for judging it through my jaded city lenses earlier.

Now it felt like we were really on some sort of magical adventure.

Martina gave us a quickie tour. "It's quite efficient. You have a mini fridge and a microwave here. And I had Sam run over some provisions to hold you over for now. Though here are some menus if you want something a little more substantial later. Pete's delivers until eleven p.m. Just tell him Cabana 4. And if you look right back there, you have your combo toilet and shower."

I frowned. "Combo?"

She nodded, and I wondered what that could mean. True opened a door and burst out laughing. "Well, it is efficient."

I turned to look, immediately rethinking everything about this camper's magical properties. There was adventure and then there was gross. "Hold it. You're saying we're supposed to pee, poop and shower all right there?"

Martina nodded. The fact that she kept her smile through that one was beyond me. "Sure. It's the latest technology. You'll get a kick out of it once you find your angles. Now, come on. Follow me out back. This is the best part."

I looked at the toilet in the middle of the little shower stall and then back out into the pretty jewel box, now feeling half defeated. True pinched my cheek and laughed.

"Angles. And I thought that was the best part! This is getting better and better. Come on, dear. I can't wait to see what's next!"

I growled. "I think she's a witch. If I see a bubbling cauldron, I'll throw rocks to distract her and you quickly run and start the car. All these pretty pillows and shit are clearly a distraction."

He laughed and stepped outside, getting into it way too much after seeing my horror over the bathroom setup.

I was just about ready to bolt for real. There wasn't a bubbling cauldron, but this was coming real close.

"This is one of our private hot springs," Martina said.

I stared into the dark puddle surrounded by rocks with the colorful lanterns in the trees above.

"It's what the town of Truth or Consequences is famous for," Martina continued. "Before we changed our name to Truth or Consequences in the fifties after the old TV show, we were Hot Springs, New Mexico. The water is extremely healing. Some would say, life changing. But we don't guarantee any of that." She smiled. "Relaxing, though, now, that we can guarantee. We have folks come from all over the country, and the world even, to bathe in our springs. You have troubles? Just leave them in the water."

Did she really expect people to sit in there? I shuddered to think of what else could be cooking in the water.

"A person can't boil in that water, can they?" I asked.

Martina laughed. "It hasn't happened, though what you all get up to in your private pool is your affair."

My face heated. "Oh no, there won't be any getting up to anything. We're just friends."

Martina looked at me blankly. As if I had said we're just carp or candles or some other random thing. Then she pointed. "And if you'd like to follow that trail along the river a bit, you'll see we have a spa and a couple of larger communal tubs with amazing views. They are not to be missed. If you'd like to make an appointment for an additional spa treatment or massage, just ring us up. But since you've been traveling awhile, I suggest you both rest and enjoy a restorative soak or a walk. Get to know the place. Make yourselves at home. Relax and take in the view while you get properly settled."

True and I paused and for the first time since we'd been there, really stood still with each other. Martina may or may not have been a witch, but this place was bewitching. The rocks, water, trees and quiet. It all cast a spell of tranquility that seemed to lull True and me into a stillness.

Just then a couple came into view, strolling our way. Like us, they looked relaxed. The woman was tiny and tucked under the big man's arm. He sauntered easily beside her, looking down at her adoringly. He bent and gave her the sweetest kiss on the top of her head, and I almost sighed out loud. She had a fine bone structure and long dark dreadlocks, and he was tall with broad shoulders and long— I gasped.

"Hey Lisa, Jason," Martina said. "I brought you over some new neighbors. Come to stay a spell."

Jason Momoa smiled, though the word *smile* didn't do it justice. What he did was a radiant zinging flash of Aquaman power, with a side of aw-shucks sauce. It was pure magic.

"Nice to meet you. I'm Jason and this is my wife, Lisa." He said this and put out his hand like a total normal human.

"I know," I mumbled. "Kind of hard not to." True nudged me in my side and gave me a "can you get it together?" look. As if I could. I'd try, but I didn't think I could.

He and True shook hands and then, when it came time for us to shake Lisa Bonet's hand, True blurted out, "Nice to meet you, Denise."

I let out a snort.

"Sorry about that," I broke in. "I had a feeling it would happen. He loved you on *A Different World.*"

"Hillman forever!" True squeaked, raising a fist, then coughing awkwardly as he pulled it back in the cutest way. If it wasn't so embarrassing, I would have hugged him. How the mighty have fallen.

Lisa nodded and Jason grinned as he patted True on the shoulder. "Listen, hopefully we'll see you around," he said. "You two here for the con or just to take in the springs?"

"We're here for the con. I'm hoping to see Keanu while I'm here. I loved the movie you two did together. I'm a huge fan." I tried to sound cool, even in my gushing, and hoped neither he nor Lisa minded.

"Thanks," Jason said. "I really appreciate that. Keanu's a real cool dude. And he's supposed to be here, so you may luck out."

I got a not-so-great feeling by the way he said *may* and added the *luck.* I guess it showed on my face.

"Don't worry. I'm sure luck will be with you. It's just he's a free spirit. He goes with the wind." And with that Jason looked up at a hawk that suddenly circled us overhead and did a dip before disappearing into the clouds. Okay.

Lisa laughed. "Come on, honey. I think we've bothered them enough." She gave True a wink.

True made a sound that may have been a cross between a choke and a giggle and the four of us looked at him. "Don't worry, he'll be fine in about eight minutes," Lisa said to me as she and Jason sauntered down the lane and out of sight. True giggled again and then snorted. I looked at him. His eyes were glassy. He was clearly zoning out.

I shook my head. "Seriously. This is what breaks you?" Good to know.

"Seriously, this is what breaks you?" True said, throwing my words back in my face not twenty-five minutes later.

We were back in the little camper and on our own again. True was, just like Lisa Bonet said, now pretty much back to himself and his right mind, out of the Lisa orbit.

But was I?

I was staring at him. Sure, he thought the thing that was breaking me was the idea of showering in the same space where I would be eliminating everything else. But nope. That wasn't the issue, despite being super gross.

No, what was truly breaking me was the vision of True standing in front of me. All six foot three inches of him. Naked and muscular and wet and covered in only a little flimsy floral piece of towel that barely covered his vital areas.

"Do you want to put something on?" I choked out.

"I will when you turn around," he snapped back.

"Besides, it's not like I could've gotten dressed in that little box of a bathroom slash shower. I could barely spin around to wash my ass, let alone put on a pair of drawers."

With that declaration, True started to raise one leg as if demonstrating how a person puts on underwear.

Answer: one leg at a time.

My hand shot up. "Okay, enough. I get it. I can visualize well enough on my own, thank you very much. I've put on underwear, True. I don't need you acting it out for me."

He paused with his leg still in the air and looked a little sheepish. "Oh yeah. I guess you don't." He put his leg back down and shimmied a little, trying to tighten the too-small towel.

I swallowed. Well, that didn't help the situation any at all. Nope. Not a bit.

I jumped up at the same time True stepped forward. Our chests bumped together in the small space. Instinctively my hands came up as my eyes widened. All I saw was chest. Skin and muscle and wet chest. I held my hands in the air, while my body wobbled forward and back, forward and back.

True being oh so very True grabbed my hands to keep me from falling, and we ended up tumbling back on the bed together.

And so there we were. Me, and all of him. Wet. Body to body. Curve to curve and contour to contour stuck together on the little bed, our legs hanging over the edge. The only thing that didn't quite make it in the fall was the little flowery towel. I knew this because in my panic while True was reaching for my hands, I reached out with both hands and grabbed his ass.

He gasped. "What the hell are you doing?"

I looked up at him. "What the hell are *you* doing? Why are you falling all over me?"

"Why are you falling all over?" he shot back.

We narrowed our eyes at each other.

He looked down, his eyes a little darker and a lot more smoldering than normal. Wait, when did True's eyes ever smolder? Did I have heatstroke? Or maybe he was still under the spell of Bonet. That could account for a lingering smolder.

And with just that thought I suddenly felt a distinct twitch and a rub where that towel should have been. I looked at him. "True? Would you like to get up?"

The corner of his lips quirked up along with his left eyebrow. "I don't know. Would I?"

I nodded vigorously. "Yeah, I think you would."

He let out a sigh, his mouth so close to mine that I felt his breath across my lips. Shit, were my nipples getting hard. *Don't do that. He'll definitely feel it without a shirt on. Come on, nips. Listen to your master for once in your lives!*

He grinned wider.

Traitors!

"Well then," True finally said. "I suggest you let go of my ass so that I can actually do it."

My mouth went wide, and my hands opened like I just realized I was holding hot coals. *Was I really holding his butt cheeks this whole time?*

"Yeah, you were. But I'm not complaining."

I pushed him off me. And he rolled over. I shook my head and got up, storming to the door of the trailer. But not before I got a glimpse of the front of him and my nipples zinged me once more, causing me to trip on the first step out and nearly fall flat on my face.

"Are you all right?" True yelled.

"I will be when you get some pants on!"

CHAPTER 24

BAD BATCH

TRUE

Mortified. There was no other word for what I felt. I looked down at my still ridiculously erect dick as I tried to pull up my shorts. "Do you have no shame?" The twitch I got in return for my troubles told me clearly not.

What was I going to do? I closed my eyes, and quickly opened them to erase the memory of Lu's gorgeous eyes looking up at me in wonder, her lips practically begging to be kissed, the perfect fit of her body underneath mine.

Bang, bang, bang.

"Are you done yet? How long does it take you to put on a pair of pants? Not to mention I may be getting eaten alive out here," she yelled through the door.

Shit. Come on, dick. Can't you cooperate for once?

"Honey, simmer down," I teased Lu through the door as I yanked on my shorts. "What will the neighbors think?"

I'm pretty sure I heard a growl through the door. Good.

That ought to keep her quiet for a minute. She was probably scratching that cute head of hers right now. I shut my eyes again. Not cute. Just head. And not head, not anything. Don't think about any part of her. At all.

This wasn't working. I jumped up and down. Recited some of my old chess drills in my head. Zen. Time to get Zen. *Focus.* I knew I could do it. I was used to it. Open one space in my mind and close off the other.

I looked at the little bed. The only sleeping space in the small camper. I mentally measured the floor. It was pretty but probably uncomfortable. Still, not nearly as uncomfortable as the two of us trying to make it work in that little squishy alcove. I snorted. How would we both fit anyway? How in the hell did Jason Momoa make it work in his? I frowned. Maybe they had some kind of extra back pullout?

I looked under the bed, then crawled over the top. Nothing. Just this little oasis and—I looked up—a skylight that would probably be magical once the sun fully set.

The door opened and there was Lu, peeking at me through her fingers. "What are you doing? Do you plan on leaving me stuck out here all night? I need to use that stupid pee shower."

I snorted. "You know that's not how covering your eyes works, right?"

She threw her hands down. "Just get out, so I can shower and change. I'm starting to get hungry and cranky."

I scooted off the bed. "You don't have to tell me twice. I'm getting out of your way, Hulkster. Nobody likes you when you're hangry."

She stuck out her tongue. Everything in me wanted to grab her by the shoulders and take that tongue between my teeth and give her just as good as she deserved. Capture it, suck it. Bite it. Anything and everything to just give her a fraction of the torture she was currently putting me through. I growled and her brow raised.

"Ahh, now who's the hangry one? Scoot. The quicker I get this done, the quicker we're not sniping at each other."

"Amen to that." I grabbed the basket of provisions Martina had mentioned and went out to start setting up. With full stomachs and a few moments of mindlessness, just maybe we could get back to normal.

Lu came out of the camper about twenty minutes later and I was fully prepared with jokes about the space and the pooping in a box, all the things to get us in the zone we needed to be in to get through the night. Too bad I wasn't prepared for the devastation that was her. I was never fucking prepared.

The metal door opened and when I looked up, all the things I needed for brain function seemed to drain from my upper region and rush simultaneously to two places. My chest, I guess to keep me alive, and my dick, bastard that it was, which was always at war with every other organ.

I could practically hear the both of them laughing, one on each shoulder. Heart and Hard On. *And you thought you had some jokes. Looks like the joke's on you, dummy. Close your mouth before a bug flies in.*

"Wow, what's all this?" Lu said, super casual and easy, like she hadn't come out looking like a whole pinup dream in a tiny black bikini under a sheer white cover-up that was covering nothing and stopped way above her midthigh. She had on flip-flops, a huge floppy hat and her big sunglasses. Her full lips had a glossy iridescent sheen that caught the sunlight, and I swear it called to me.

I stared.

"True? True!"

I blinked. "What?"

"What's with you? Do you want to go in? Have you had too much sun?" She tilted her shades down to the tip of her nose and stared at me hard over the top of the rims.

I frowned, more at myself than her. "It's nothing. I'm fine. Here, come and look at what we have." I tried my best to match the ease of her tone. If she could play it easy then, dammit, so could I.

Lu gave me a last hard stare and twisted her full lips. She then looked around me and smiled. "Wow! This all looks so nice! You're just full of surprises." Lu was grinning and already digging in. I'd set up the little flip-out camper table and covered it with a tablecloth, then laid out the food that Martina had left for us. Plus, Jason had come by with fish kebabs.

Lu coughed and grabbed a bottle of water off the table, taking a quick guzzle. "Wait, these are Jason Momoa's fish kebabs? He was here and you didn't get me?"

I snorted. As if I was going to. "He said he was just running them by. And what did you want me to do, go pull you out of the shower poop box?"

She made a face. "For Aquaman's fish kebabs? Hell yeah!"

"And he dropped off this bottle of wine from Lisa. I think it may be homemade."

Her jaw dropped again. "Holy shit!"

I grinned. "Amazing, right? We sure lucked out with the inn being filled."

Lu took a bite of her kebab. "Seriously. But I really have to find a way to get a picture or some sort of proof this time or Dawn will kill me. She was ready to buy me a GoPro for this trip or at the least one of those camera purses. If I don't come back with some sort of proof of Momoa she will cut me off completely. She's still pissed over me not having photographic evidence of the Chris Evans encounter."

"Oh, *she's* still pissed?" I said, feeling all over again the anger and fear of chasing Lu down in that bathroom. If she had any idea of how I felt, she wouldn't make light.

Lu narrowed her eyes. "Don't start. I don't think you want to go there. Not when it's such a nice evening." She started piling a bunch of food on a plate. "Come on. Eat. You need—"

I put my hand out to stop her.

"I've got it."

She let out a huff. "What's with you? Why are you being so cranky? Look at this place, this view. This morning we were in New York. Let's just enjoy the moment. The blasted sun is finally starting to set so it's cooling off. We have food. We might as well make the best of it."

She waved her hand in front of her face, then coughed. "Seriously, you'd think they'd do something about the bugs here."

She was right. The best of it. It's what we'd been doing all this time. Might as well continue the blissful ignorance.

If I were a logical person, which I think I've established I only pretend to be, I might actually be able to fool myself into believing that this moment eating fish kebabs with Lu, in front of a camper out on the Rio Grande, was actually real.

But that type of contentment and happiness would never be for me. The most I could ever have were moments like this. Moments of looking at the happiness from the outside and examining it while waiting for the bubble to burst.

Even now, after all these years, I knew it was time for these moments and my foolhardy pining to be over. I knew that there had to be a day that I finally stopped living on the fringe of her life and let her go. Let her live. It wasn't fair to keep holding on. I'd been pretending to be Lu's savior for all these years when in so many ways it was me who'd fully ripped her world apart.

I looked over at her. So pretty and so far out of my reach that even with a stretch I wouldn't get close. No, she'd been pretty back in high school. Then she left for college and her light "dream of me" quip cast a spell I still hadn't found a way to break. And now that pretty girl had turned into a gorgeous, radiant, accomplished and seemingly—I knew very much potentially—happy woman.

I couldn't help but wonder, as I did often, how much happier Lu would have been with a different life. How she'd look if her breathtaking smile wasn't clouded behind the pain of the loss of Cole. Without a shitty friend who, in his own selfishness and lovesickness, wasn't able to warn Cole of the wall coming up to snatch his life short.

"I can't wait to see you in the costume when the con-vention starts," Lu said. Her words brought me back to the present and the fact that we were chasing after a memory to heal the past that I'd ruined.

She pursed her lips and looked me up and down. "Though after seeing all of you earlier, I'm wondering if I ordered the right size." She smirked a bit.

"What are you trying to get at?" I said. "Too small or too big?"

She did a little back-and-forth nod, I knew trying to lighten the mood. "Eh, no matter, it will stretch where it needs to." She looked toward my waist. "Suck in where it must."

"Excuse you. I've never had to suck in anything in my life."

Lu snorted. "Lucky boy." She shrugged again. "Or maybe not."

I crossed my legs. "I swear, woman, if you have me out here in this desert looking like a damn fool..."

Lu did an exaggerated blink-and-eye-roll combo. "We're going to a heroes cosplay convention in the middle of the desert. I'm sure we won't look any more foolish than—" She stopped short.

"Than...what?"

"I don't know. Let's just say we'll fit right in, I'm sure." She frowned, then started to laugh. "Fit right in. How funny is that? As if we've ever done that in either of our lives."

I looked at her. "Some people are just not made for it. It's standing out or nothing at all."

CHAPTER 25

NIGHT HEAT

BETHANY LU

I wish I could bring this type of beauty to my work," I mumbled to myself.

True and I had finished eating and were walking along the winding river path that Martina had told us about. I felt it was safest to get a little distance between us and the itty-bitty camper.

The beauty here hadn't been captured by any of the photos I'd seen on Google and Pinterest. *Note to self: Maybe I should venture out a little more in real life and not rely so much on the internet for research.* There was a squawky type of sound and yet another lizard came way too close to my shoe. Yeah, this was why there was YouTube. The world was scary. And also exhausting. And really unpredictable.

Yet there was a grace in this beauty I'd never experienced in trips to the beach with my girlfriends or to Europe with my parents. It didn't feel like it had to put on a full face of makeup or nail tips or lashes. It was all natural—like those ageless women you could just tell lived their best life. The ones whose radiance would last forever.

The river was wild and free, as was the vegetation that sprung up alongside it. The trees, bushes, they all seemed to be doing exactly what they wanted and were meant to do. Even the landscaping looked so natural I had to wonder whether the buildings had been constructed around the nature. Like maybe the little prickly bush whose name I'd never know had been along this pathway with the azalea forever, and the hotel, the lane and the camper stalls were all put here in tribute to their beauty. This type of freedom would leave the tightly planned and highly maintained flowers of Central Park's Conservatory Garden staging a freedom march.

"Why can't you bring this to your work?" True asked.

I stopped walking and looked at the scene a moment. Listened to the birds. I shook my head. This was straight out of the opening scene from a Disney nature show. "Because it doesn't fit. What I'm trying to show in my work is real. What's happening in the real world. The chaos, the discontent, the pain."

True looked at me and his eyes clouded over. "So let me get this straight. Those emotions are somehow real, but what you're feeling now is not. This moment of quiet, no cars, no horns, just birds and water in peace is not real? Then what are we, not here?"

I looked at him. "Mr. Erickson."

"Ms. Carlisle."

"Of course we're here. But this moment is passing."

"And aren't those other moments passing too?" He

shrugged and continued along the path. "Why is pain the emotion we so easily make our home? It's like we sign up for the thirty-year mortgage on pain, but only do short-term leases or annual time-shares on pleasure."

I shook my head and he continued down the path. Who was this True? Mr. New York Economics talking leases and time-shares and turning them all poetic. Maybe New Mexico really was the Land of Enchantment.

I snapped a few photos as the sun was setting, vowing to get up early tomorrow and sketch before the convention. It felt good to want to sketch. It felt good to feel good. I looked at the pics I'd taken. True's shoulders, tapered waist, long legs. Even in this shot you could see the fine muscles in his behind.

I swallowed. *Nature. Focus on nature, Lu. True's ass is not the subject here.* Though as an artist, how is it I never noticed what a fine figure he'd turned into?

My little beatnik economist poet.

True turned my way. He was making quick hand gestures like he was shooing away a fly coming at his peen. I jumped. "Is it a lizard? Scorpion?"

He grabbed my shoulders and turned to push me back around the way we came.

"What are you doing? Could you not manhandle me?" I said, while thinking quite the opposite.

"Shhh!!" he hissed. "Lower your voice."

"Truman Erickson. I know you're not telling me to lower my voice. Unless there's a bear in these woods I will not lower my voice for any—" And that's when I heard it. A growl and then a splash. Followed by a sexy sound that definitely was not coming from a bear.

"Oh." I looked at True.

He tilted his head and gave an "I told you so" look.

I could hear. I could hear the water sloshing, and then Jason's voice came through the trees clearly. "You want any more kebabs, hon?"

Hon? They were so cute. I smiled. "Let's head back," I whispered.

We made it back to our little campsite and both hit the stairs of the camper door at the same time and froze. After all the years we'd known each other, it was ridiculous that the idea of a night together would make us uncomfortable, but it did. I could tell True was feeling just as awkward as I was, no matter how he tried to hide it.

"You want to have another glass of wine or something? Sit out for a bit. I mean, it's late but not that late," he said.

I stepped back down. "Sure." I nodded and swiped at a bug on my arm. It would probably be more comfortable in the camper. Safer on my bare arms and legs. But so much more intimate.

True stared at me. "You sure?"

The sounds from what we'd almost walked up on moments before and my overactive imagination suddenly went into overdrive. There was no way I was ready to go into the camper. Nope. Not right now. "Definitely," I said. "You want me to get the glasses?"

True shook his head. "No, let me." He ran inside the camper, ducking low in the doorway.

I let out a long breath. "Get a grip, Lu. You are not

twelve. When are you going to start acting anywhere close to the age on your birth certificate?"

I walked back and forth a few paces, swatting my arm, but mainly taking swings at the pesky thoughts in my head.

This would be no different from any other time that True had just so happened to fall asleep at my place. Even though here we'd be tighter, closer, more squished together.

I kicked a rock at the end of the camper and was surprised to see colored lights that I hadn't noticed before. I peered around the corner and let out a legit gasp.

Martina didn't lie when she said this place was beautiful at night. It was breathtaking.

I heard a buzz near my ear and swatted the side of my neck. "Wow. If it weren't for the nature, this really would be paradise," I said. I was looking at a private spring with a lush tree-lined canopy adorned with glowing yellow, pink, purple and green little paper lanterns throughout. They looked so delicate, as if sweet little romantic fairies had put them there to set the mood.

I suddenly felt guilty. Like we'd let the fairies down and were wasting their precious work.

"It's a real shame."

"What's a shame?" True asked, coming up behind me with a plastic cup. "Here. I figured it's kind of dark and a little rocky back here. I didn't trust bringing the glasses and having them break."

I nodded. "Very smart of you, thinking ahead about my clumsiness. Besides, we wouldn't want to be charged for them."

He gave me a slightly withering look.

"Or I wouldn't want you to trip, smash a glass and then have to take you to the emergency room because your pretty little toes got sliced."

I looked down, eyeing my toes in my sandals. I could now imagine that exact scenario being possible, given how clumsy I could be and how rotten I was when it came to night vision. "Like I said, it was very smart of you."

True twisted his lips, then looked over my shoulder, really taking in our hot spring all lit up and in its glory.

I stepped forward and turned. Moving out of his space.

"It's beautiful, huh?" I asked.

He looked at me and something in his gaze had my face immediately heating.

"It sure is," he said.

I cleared my throat. "That's what I was saying about it being a shame. It seems a waste it not going to use. It looks like Martina pulls out all the stops for her guests."

He stared at me. "It sure does. I'm sure she'll ask us what we thought when she sees us around or at checkout."

I narrowed my eyes on him and took a sip of the sweet wine. I couldn't help pulling a face, my eyes blinking rapidly and my jaw clenching, as the flavor hit the back of my throat and what felt like the top of my brain at the same time. True laughed, then cautiously sniffed his own cup before tasting.

He shook his head at me. "You are such a dramatic lightweight with your skunky wine faces."

My eyes shot up to his as I fought to school my expression. "I am not a lightweight, and I don't make skunky wine faces. Also the Bonet-Momoas would never gift skunky wine. This wine is delicious. Sweet and maybe a little peachy with a hint of cherries," I said, trying to sound like an expert. "It just took me a little by surprise is all."

True reached out, petting the top of my head. "Sometimes you crack me up, Lu."

I stepped back out of his space. Or maybe I was taking him out of mine. Either way, I took another swig of the wine. This time more of a gulp instead of a sip and I did my best to hold tightly on to my expression. *Smooth, calm and unflappable.* I forced myself to focus on the words as I let the flavors of the wine take over my senses. *Don't think of anything that might rile the serenity of this space,* I told myself, as I tried my best to not think further ahead than the second I was in.

"Truth or Consequences," True said from behind my back.

"What?" I opened my eyes and looked at him.

"Truth or Consequences." He was holding up a little index card with a road sign with the town name and waving it in front of me.

"What are you going on about? I know what town we're in. I thought we were out here relaxing and having a glass of wine. Now you want to share fun facts? Are you missing teaching so much already?"

"No, this was a game card that Martina had in our basket. I guess it's like Truth or Dare but they renamed it after the town. You want to play?"

"You can't be serious."

"What, are you scared?"

"No, but what I am is too tired to play games."

He looked at the card, then back at me and nodded. "No problem. It's been a long day and tomorrow will be too. We should turn in."

He turned to head back to the tiny camper.

"Wait," I said, with probably a little more urgency than the moment warranted. He looked back at me and I held out my hand. "Give me that card."

I'm sure in any other place and with just about anybody else, this would be perfectly relaxing. But as I sat in our private hot spring under the fairy lights in the middle of a campground in New Mexico with a shirtless True by my side, relaxing was the very last thing I could do.

True licked his lips, then raised a brow. "Truth or consequence." Oh boy, he didn't know how badly I wanted to say *consequence*.

I stared him straight in the eye. "Truth."

He grinned. "Fine. What's the most embarrassing thing you've ever done?"

I laughed. "That's easy. Most likely it's this trip."

True nodded, then drank from his cup. "You're right, that was easy. I don't know why I asked. I guess I was hoping for some long-lost salacious story."

I made a face. "Like you don't know all my long-lost stories and I don't know all yours." He just stared at me then. I frowned, feeling like there was something way deeper. Something maybe I really didn't know. I nodded. "Or maybe not," I amended, remembering his job offers and suddenly wondering about what other secrets he could have been keeping. I let out a breath, not wanting to go there.

Suddenly I was splashed. "Hey!" I splashed him back. "I shouldn't get a consequence for that."

"Well, stop holding up the game. It's my turn."

"Okay," I said. "You asked for it. Truth or consequence?"

"Truth." He said it quickly as if he were answering a roll call or something.

I shook my head. "Could you lighten up? This is not an interrogation, True."

He shrugged then and leaned back. Stretching out on the rocks behind him. Showing off his chest even more and making me regret my lighten-up request. I forced my mind to focus. I needed a question. What did I want to know?

Before I could stop myself, I asked, "What's the worst thing you've ever done?"

True's smug smile suddenly disappeared and I immediately wanted to take back my question. I held up my hand. "Forget that one. You don't have to answer it. How about this one? Did you ever have a crush on a coworker?"

He didn't hesitate. "No."

I grinned, wanting so badly to lighten our mood again. "That was too fast. I feel like I wasted that question. Can I get one more do-over?"

True shook his head. "No more do-overs and yeah, you wasted that one." He was suddenly looking at me so intently. "Or maybe not. Maybe you knew exactly what you were asking."

"You're no fun," I pouted.

"I'm tons of fun," True protested. "How about this? I'll give you a free consequence. Come at me." His grin was sexy and devilish again in the moonlight as he dared me.

I splashed him and he splashed me back. Hard. Suddenly we were acting like two kids having a water fight. Our thighs touched, and our legs were suddenly intertwined as were our hands. True pulled me in close. So close that his face was right on top of mine, the steam rising between us, our breaths mingling as one.

"Fine," I groaned out.

"Fine?" he asked me.

"You win." I took a breath. "The game. You win." I swallowed and pushed at his chest, enjoying the slide of his long legs against mine as I pulled myself off his lap and went back to a relatively safer space.

I leaned against the warm rock and looked up at the pretty lanterns, not daring to look over at True in my current state. The lights and colors above me began to swirl, and I felt something nip at my neck. I slapped down on it. "Darned pests," I said, then looked back over at True. Just as I knew he would be, he was staring at me. Those same eyes that always found me all those years ago remained unchanged.

I sighed. "Though this is beautiful," I said, gesturing toward the spring, "I'm afraid I've fed enough bugs and pruned up enough for one night. I'd better get out. Do you mind letting me go first and then you can change after?"

"No problem." His voice was even. I pushed up on the ledge to find my footing to get out.

I slipped back, but True was there. Fast with his reflexes and already up to catch me. His arms went around my middle, strong bands of security as I landed back against his chest.

"Don't worry. I've got you."

I reached back and stroked his curls. "My True. You always do."

True helped me up and out then as a breeze caught us, hitting us with the reality of being out of the steamy water. He shuffled back a few steps.

I almost moaned, hating this awkward space between us.

He coughed. "Sorry, I wasn't thinking. Take your time. I'm fine out here." He walked over to one of the lounge chairs and stretched out his long legs. "You get yourself"— he did a little hand wave—"together and don't worry about me. Out here all alone, in the dark. With the bugs." I knew he was trying to lighten the mood, for the both of us. For the night to come.

I'd do my part too.

"Boy, please. Finish your drink and think about dialing it down. Also think about putting your shirt back on if you want to hold on to that lovely smooth brown skin of yours."

He grinned and tipped his cup my way. "So, you noticed?"

I raised a brow. "Barely."

As the camper door closed behind me, I leaned against it then quickly pushed myself back up, worried about leaning against the walls and tipping the camper or something. "Barely indeed."

Looking around the space, I tried to admire its beauty and appreciate the lack of bugs and not focus on the very tiny size and the fact that we'd be sharing it after all the sexual tension of the day and night.

I did a quick scan for alternate sleeping arrangements

to the shared bed. There really weren't any. Even the little dining bench was too small for either of us to sleep on. The floor was an option, but I couldn't ask True to do that. Not after he'd done all the driving and planning for this trip. I sighed as I pulled out a tank and sleep shorts for the night. I guess I could do it. I looked across the bed, which suddenly looked a hundred times more comfy. Then I remembered our fall and True sprawled on top of me from earlier. I shuddered. Or maybe it was a shiver. The floor it would be.

In the shower box, I did my business and flushed, trying my best not to think about where everything went or didn't as the little Jiffy popper took it all away. After a quick shower and rinse of my hair I dried it as best as I could, then was grateful for my microfiber towel. "Ha! Light packing as if," I muttered to myself. What natural girl could?

I stared at the door, wondering how True was doing out there and if he was having any of the same apprehension that I was. Probably not, but if so, he sure was hiding it well.

This cool True I could take, but the carefree one, not so much. And the too-sexy-for-his-own-good one was just too freaking much. I wondered if he hid this side of himself all the time back in New York or had hid it just in front of me. Was this something his other friends, students and colleagues, like Aimee, saw all the time?

I finished with my hair, adding some leave-in conditioner to my ends, and it was almost dry, thanks to my little magic towel. After a final shake, I was looking for a place to hang the towel when there was a knock on the camper door. I practically jumped out of my skin.

Shit. Coolness, where are you? Why have you forsaken me?

But damn. Those few minutes went really quick. I stared at the door, not quite ready to let True in but also not understanding why I was being so foolish suddenly when it came to True. I opened my mouth, looking for the right casual voice, the "come in" still on the come out when there was another more insistent knock.

True opened the door a crack. "Hey, are you okay in here?"

Cool. Act cool. "I'm fine. Why would I not be?"

"Why would you not be answering?" he asked, not peeking his head in the doorway.

I felt the wave of heat from outside and thought of the bugs. "Come in and close the door, True. You're letting out the cool air and letting in the bugs."

He hopped in and immediately made the space feel about three-quarters of the size smaller. "Are you done? You were right about the bugs out there. You should put on long pants and a sweater while I get ready for bed."

"So you expect me to go outside now? I just got clean."

He stared at me. I stared back. He once again took off his shirt and I lost the damn game of chicken, blinking like a tornado was swirling through my house.

"You can go or you can stay, but I'm taking a shower now."

True rummaged through his backpack and pulled out cutoff gray sweats that I guess he'd be sleeping in and, I noticed, nothing else. I blinked. "You got a topper for those?"

He chuckled. "A topper? I don't normally sleep in this much."

I swallowed.

"Besides," he started, "I noticed you're not wearing all that much, so I just assumed it would get warm with the two of us sharing this space."

I sucked in a short breath of air. Goose pimples suddenly pricked up on my arms, and my nipples had the nerve to harden. Fuck. Here I was, thinking about what he was wearing, and I didn't even consider my own self. Shorts, tank, NIPS! I reached up and scratched at my hair in an attempt to appear cool and purposely not cover my chest. I wouldn't give him the satisfaction.

"Wear what you want, True. Just hurry up in the bathroom." I sat back on the bed and reached over for the curtain pulls, drawing one of the sheers closed and then the other. "Problem solved. I'll just sit behind here and check out my messages and on Morphie, and you do you."

He looked at me. "Why didn't we do that when you were showering and I was out there getting bit?"

"Because *you* weren't smart enough to think of it."

True turned away, grabbing a towel from the counter and heading to the little bathroom/shower stall. A moment later the Jiffy Pop toilet flushed and the door reopened, only for him to throw his shorts outside and onto the floor.

I crossed my legs and groaned.

"I thought you weren't looking," he yelled.

Jerk. "Who says I'm looking?"

He laughed from behind the door. "Sorry. My mistake. I was just testing you."

I gave one last look to his discarded shorts, wet and soggy on the floor. Why didn't he leave them to dry with my swimsuit? Oh well, I was sure he'd hang them up later. It was True. Of course he would. I lay back in the plush bedding, surprised at how comfortable it was for a bed that was essentially in a box on wheels. I was about to reach for my phone when I looked up and caught a glimpse of deep blue of the night sky through the window so cleverly cut out in the top of the camper. I'd never seen a skylight with a more perfect view.

I suddenly felt so small but at the same time larger than I'd felt in a really long time as I looked out and saw the tiny stars, twinkling through my squared-off frame. It was perfect. And strangely, though nothing had gone perfectly I'd been catching a lot of glimpses of perfect since starting this little quest with True.

I felt my brows start to knit. That was ridiculous. Perfect had nothing to do with him. Perfect was thanks to Keanu and, well, fate.

"It's perfect, isn't it?" True's voice in that moment made it just that much more so.

I swung my head from the view toward something else entirely, though no less perfect to me.

I didn't answer for a moment but instead stared at True freely since he was still looking up at the stars through the skylight. His eyes were bright as the brightest star on the top left. I could stare at them all night.

"Are you going to move over and let me in, Lu?"

I blinked, embarrassed at being caught staring like Dawn at a K-pop idol. Shit. I was in way too deep.

CHAPTER 26

INFLUENCE

TRUE

If Lu kept looking at me with those big eyes of hers, all sparkly, with that hint of smolder and a touch of possibility, well, it was more than likely that one of us wouldn't make it out of this night with their heart intact. And that one would most likely be me.

I quickly considered the viability of sleeping on one of the lawn chairs outside or the hammock strung up between the two large trees on the other side of the camper, but my back screamed in protest with just the consideration. Besides, I was neither a boy scout nor an idiot. I didn't want to sleep outside. Just this day alone had tested my Man vs. Nature limits. I didn't want to push it. And looking down at Lu now, so unlike her usual overpowering self, smaller than normal in the cloud of blankets and pillows in the fortress that was the tiny camper, there was no way I wanted to let this moment pass. Sharing the space with her would be torture, but it was the type I was willing to take.

As if I wasn't already taking hella chances. We both were. That little game in the water damn near had me bursting.

I looked back up at the skylight, out toward the vastness and beyond. This spot, this night, would be perfect if only we could keep the magic we had here and still come out as the friends we'd always been, I thought, and then immediately wanted to snatch the thought back. That was the problem right there. Our friendship that was hardly a friendship at all. I mean, how could it be when it was built on nothing but a foundation of pain?

At this point, it was time to shit or get off the pot. But should I really? Could I? Even if I hurt, kept hurting, maybe it was better to continue as I had been. Following Lu around like her other little pup. Me and Morphie duking it out for her affections till the bitter end. Only he got to sleep over.

I wanted to sleep over too. All the time. But all I had right now was now. This time. With no buffer and very little space.

Her tan skin glowed and was just slightly flushed with a hint of rose. It wasn't all from the wine or even from the hot spring. There was something else there, maybe because she wanted me too.

But in her eyes was that hesitance, that fear. I hated that it was the same hesitance I saw every time I looked in the mirror and thought of her. How could I go there now, after not going there for so long? How could I risk screwing it all up and losing her?

I could take her teasing me, friending me, as long as she kept me near. In all Lu's years of teasing, she never once made me feel inferior. Never did she make me feel anything less than handsome, brilliant and like someone to be cherished—even with her ridiculous worry and nagging. It was in her radiant smile. She looked at me like no one else had. With her, I never felt like I was taking up space where I wasn't wanted. With her, I always felt wanted and needed, and because of that I needed her.

Screw it. This was getting sappy as hell, and tomorrow was another day of this push-and-pull torture. Some people might consider it foreplay, but it left me with blue balls and a blue heart bordering on stone black.

"So are you gonna move over and let me in, Lu?" I ground out.

Lu let out a sigh, then kicked her feet back and forth, sending the blankets scattering. She really was half a child. I looked at her pretty foot attached to her shapely-as-hell calf. Maybe just a quarter of a child. The maturity part. The rest of her was all woman even with the way she was pouting up at me now.

"Come on, True. You know how wild I sleep. Don't you think you'd be more comfortable on the floor? There are enough pillows and blankets, and the space looks long enough for you. That way you won't be cramped."

I looked down at the camper floor then back at the pillowed nest she was snuggled in. "Aren't you just the sweetest, thinking of me, but I'm sure I can tough it out with you. This is a double bed and we're two people."

"But you're so big you're practically one and a half people by yourself."

I grinned. "Flattery won't get you anywhere, woman. Now scoot unless *you* want the floor."

Lu gave me a sharp look but knew she was beat. The leg tucked back in and she shimmied back over to her side. I moved to get into the bed and she reached a hand up to stop me.

"What now?"

"Is the door locked?"

"Of course."

"Well, can you do a double check?"

"What do you take me for? Don't you think I did? The worst someone could do is hitch this thing up and ride off with the two of us."

Lu leaned back again and gave me a softer look this time, then shrugged. "Oh well, it would be the two of us. At least we'd be taken together."

She said it jokingly, but I caught her vulnerability and wanted to kick myself for being so hard on her and so into my own feelings. So fucking horny and just thinking about my dick.

All of this was a lot for Lu, getting her to come this far and letting me come with her, even if the whole K-90 plan was hers to begin with. I knew as soon as I saw her manic whiteboard that, for all her talk about Keanu and her list, she'd take the project only so far.

That was part of her panic. She would never go full out on this quest alone. Lu didn't leave her safe zones—her spaces with her people, where she knew they were safe. It was her form of control, and though I hated coming on this quest with her—what man wanted to be with the woman he loved while she chased after the dream of something he could never be?—I knew she had to chase that dream since her other one had been snatched from her so coldly.

After Cole's death, Lu had kept her circle small in hopes of having less to lose. Not that I blamed her. Once you got the rug snatched out from under you, you held on to the remnants pretty tight.

Fuck. Now I deserved another kick. The potential job in LA? Of course she'd be pissed at the idea. The fact that I didn't tell her about it must have terrified her. By keeping it from her, even if it was to protect her, I was a shithead, since there was the potential of her finding out. Which she did. The anger she'd had at that silly party and the pain in her eyes came back to me again.

"I've moved over, True. Are you getting in?"

Great. Now I was the hesitant one. I stepped back, rethinking the floor. Decided to delay.

"You want another drink? There's enough wine left for about a glass for each of us, and it would be a shame to let it go bad."

"I thought you were tired," she said.

"I am, but I can't just conk out that easy."

"Why? I've seen you do it plenty of times before. And you're the one who was so tired."

I shrugged. "Suit yourself. I'm having one."

She shook her head. "Fine, but just get one cup. We'll share. No need in dirtying up two."

I sighed. She was playing me now. With these words, she

had to be. I willed my dick to stay still and got the wine, then handed the bottle to her.

Her side-eye was strong. "So, because we're in the woods we've devolved to our base animal instincts?"

"Suck it up, Ms. Fancy," I said, finally coming to get into the bed beside her. "No need to dirty a cup at all." I leaned back. It was still warm in the spot she'd vacated and warmer where the side of my leg just grazed hers.

Lu looked me straight in the eye and took a long pull from the bottle before handing it back with a tilt of her head.

I smiled and was grateful for the covering in front of me as I caught the way her lips now glistened. Did they taste more like peaches or cherries? She licked at her top lip and I gulped at the wine way too fast, coming up with a choke and a cough.

"What are you trying to do?" Lu said, slapping at my back. "I thought we were sharing."

I turned her way, taking in the concern even when she was admonishing me—and she always was. Would I never be more to her than someone to take care of? In her heart did she really just think of me as her dead brother's all-grown-up little friend?

She swiped at my chin, and then her thumb moved to my lip. "Look at you. It's going all over. You'll end up spilling it on the bed."

Lu went to pull her thumb away, but before I could think, my tongue tipped out and licked at the pad. That tiny taste of her skin was worth the momentary look of shocked horror.

I let out a sigh and went to put the bottle down. "I guess that's enough of that."

Lu reached out. Her hand at the top of my arm was hot enough to brand my skin. She took the bottle and finished the rest before handing it back to me. "No need to waste good wine on such a beautiful night."

I felt young and dumb and happy as I looked at her looking up at the sky.

Her eyes suddenly shifted and hit me square on. "True, either lay down and go to sleep or just kiss me already."

Finding my voice past the lump suddenly lodged in my throat was hard, but I did. "I think I have to let you make that decision."

"I wouldn't have given you an option if I didn't already make my decision."

I looked up at the skylight as if the stars could tell me the answer or at least tell me if I'd fallen asleep and this was all a dream.

"It's okay. I get it," she said, then chuckled softly, trying to cover up her embarrassment. "You don't have to feel awkward. Come on, I was just joking. Like you said, it's getting late and we have a big day tomorrow. Costumes to get into. We have to look fabulous. Now relax, it's already bad enough that I've embarrassed myself in front of A-list Hollywood stars. I don't need to have you looking at me like that. I feel like I'm laying next to the panic emoji. Pretend I didn't just say what I said. Okay?"

She gave my chest a quick nudge and then started to turn away from me, toward the wall of the camper.

What kind of idiot was I? Also, what man in the history of cool ever gave off panic emoji face when the offer of a lifetime was finally presented to him? I bet Keanu didn't.

Jason Momoa sure as hell didn't. But me? This jackass? I was the total fucking package, for sure.

If you don't like it, then stop doing it, dummy. I heard the voice, and it sounded like mine but not quite. It was me but remade with Hollywood confidence. *You two know each other well enough by now to let the pretense go.*

I reached out and touched her bare shoulder. Her skin was smooth and warm under my hand. And before I could stop myself, I leaned forward and kissed her silky brown flesh. The first brush of her against my lips had my tongue pressing forward. Heaven. I pulled myself back and turned her toward me.

Lu's eyes met mine and emotion rocketed through me. I caught a glimpse of unshed tears on the tips of her lashes.

"Dammit," I muttered. "Please don't let those tears be for me."

"Tears?" She sniffled. "Getouttahere!" She blinked and grinned, though the grin was half-assed at best. "My, Mr. Erickson. Aren't we full of ourselves today? Have it out with one sex symbol and you think you're all that. Got the women in tears, do you? Hell, that must just be the drink talking." She frowned and looked at me then. No, not at me but just slightly past me. Up at the skylight with the moon shining bright making her eyes practically beam back my way. She had the nerve then to nibble at her bottom lip a moment before turning back to me with a frown. "Where did you see a tear anyway? It's just my allergies." I could hear her trying to make her voice steady. "All this nature can't be good for anybody, though I will admit the spring did soften my skin."

I practically groaned then, thinking about her skin and just how and where it had softened. Lu stared at me a moment before speaking again. "So can we now just forget about what I said a few minutes ago?" She gave my chest three quick pats. "Let's go to sleep."

Three pats. I really was Morphie. Did she think of me as no better? I think it was that exact thought that sent all rational thinking out of my head. That and the fact that with those pats she was essentially brushing the potential of us aside, of what we could have.

She was just about to pat me once more when I stopped her. I took her wrist and brought her hand up, interlacing our fingers.

"Let's not," I said.

"Not what?" she asked. As she faced me, I could feel her heart beating against my chest. Or was that mine still?

"Let's not go to sleep. Let's, um, let's not go to sleep," I said.

Lu grinned as her eyes took on a different kind of glow. "Fine then, what do you want to do? Talk, watch a movie on YouTube, play a game? Or we—"

I took her mouth under mine. Finally tasting her lips and all their delicious fullness.

"Cherries," I murmured.

"Huh," she moaned against my lips as her tongue started to tangle with mine. I was gone. Where to? A place far better than the world I'd ever imagined, and I never wanted to come back. I pulled her to me as I sank into her. Kissing, sucking, inhaling.

"You taste like cherries. I wonder if that's the wine or if it's you."

Lu pulled back and looked at me. For a moment fear hit me, and my immediate reaction was to hold tight to her. But I loosened my grip slightly.

She smiled. "I think it's the wine. You taste like cherries too."

My heart sped up over her smile at the same time as relief washed over me. She wasn't backing away.

"Well then, I guess that further exploration is needed on both our sides to find out the truth. Get to the bottom of things as they say."

She pulled a face. "Really? You gonna use that joke now?"

I closed my eyes tight. "It's all I've got."

Her mouth was on mine again, her tongue grazing across my lips, and I opened my mouth to let her in. "You're so cute, it's all you need, my darling True."

I pulled her closer. Bringing my hands down her sides now, to her waist and pulling her in snug against me. I stroked at her velvet tongue as I breathed deep, wanting to savor her. Become one with her breath.

I looked at her. Lush lips, bright eyes, flush skin. "That's not all I need, Bethany Lu. Not by a long shot."

I reached forward, going for the hem of her tank as she lifted her arms. Her breasts were perfect in their fullness, and I was on them in an instant. Hungry and wanting. She rocked her hips against my cock and once again the almost uncontrollable fear along with a need for release reared its head, just about literally. I gritted my teeth, telling myself to hold on. I had to at least get inside her first. At least satisfy her first. I moaned while she ran her tongue over my neck, down my chest. I shivered, almost clutching for the wall behind me as she got below my belly button.

In my head I started to chant: *Don't let go, don't let go, don't let go*... Were the words to her or were they for me? It didn't matter. I was about to explode, and I wasn't inside her yet. She'd barely even touched me. Her hand went to my waistband and my stomach muscles contracted. She touched my tip. Silky. Her hands, her tongue. I would not last. I forced myself up and pulled her up, over me and onto the bed. I was on my knees quickly. Where I should be. Where I wanted to be.

Catching my breath, I looked down at her delicate feet. Kissed their tops. Her ankles. Kissed those too. Up her calves, behind her knees, lifting her legs, I licked at the sweet delicate skin right under her buttocks. I stopped to catch my breath before looking back up at her.

My queen. My everything.

I reached for the waistband of her shorts and looked to her for permission once more.

She gave me a look that took me back to years I know we both wanted to forget, to a time when she put all her trust in me. I silently vowed I'd never let her down.

She touched my cheek softly and went to pull her shorts off. I stopped her. "No, lean back."

Lu nodded and did as she was told. I went to my duffel and got a condom. Came back and eased down her shorts. Between her thighs she was all cherries and peaches, just like the wine but infinitely better. Infinitely sweeter, and with my first taste of her I was gone drunk, so very high that I was immediately addicted.

My tongue delved deep, wanting to pleasure her like she never had been and never would be until the next time she'd be with me. Her moans were all the assurance I needed. Her whimpers were like extra little bonus prizes and when she finally came, it was as if I'd won the ultimate prize. But little did I know that was just the beginning.

With shaky hands, I attempted to slide on the condom. I would have been embarrassed by it all, but I was too excited and turned on to care that she had to take it from my hands and help me. Her hands shook too, but we both let out breaths of exquisite relief when it was finally on. She wrapped her legs around me, and I sank inside her. She cried out my name while I repeated hers over and over in a quick rush. Strange, though, how to me both words sounded like *forever* to my ears.

I wonder what she heard.

CHAPTER 27

YOU'RE MAGNIFICENT

BETHANY LU

Dreams were the best. In dreams you could lose yourself in what might have been and the possibilities of forever. You could let all your inhibitions go without any remorse or consequences. I was currently losing myself against a solid, delicious bit of a dream that smelled and tasted and felt like my own life-size True. All sweetly musky and slightly woodsy. I rubbed against my dream man and felt his erection thickening against me.

I nuzzled at his neck and he brought his large hand up to caress my breast. I felt my back arch as I pushed farther into his palm.

His other hand reached around, and long assured fingers parted between my legs from behind. Hmm. Dreams like this were rare. I'd savor this one. Make it last as long as possible before real life threatened to—

I slapped at my ear when something buzzed a little too close. *Wait, what?*

My heart rate sped up, as the solid form under my chest, between my legs, the fingers between my thighs became a lot less fuzzy and got a lot more real.

"Fuck," I moaned.

"Absolutely!"

"True?" I asked.

"Were you expecting someone else?"

"Ohhh!" I scooted off the top of him and onto my side of the bed, pulling the sheet up. When I slid open one eye, True was looking at me. Not with curiosity or annoyance, but with a smile.

"Don't smile at me like that. You're looking way too happy and I don't think I can take that much happiness this early in the morning."

True tightened his lips and it brought out his dimples. Against my will, my body shivered with the memory of all the magical things he could do and the way he could make me feel.

Shit. I was completely screwed. Had been completely screwed. In the best and worst way.

I flopped back onto the pillows, wishing my body could sink deeper—through the bed, to the ground, and to the center of the earth would have been perfect. But no such luck. I was stuck with the sun beaming and True staring.

Don't cry. Don't you dare cry, woman! You brought this shit on yourself. I covered my eyes and still felt True's smiling stare bearing down on me.

Crying is for babies and something you should have thought about last night before you were all up in this man's pants. Time to think on your feet and make decisions. Who are you going to be? Come on, Lu, are you going to be your usual mistress of the dark who hates mornings or because you've shown one of your oldest friends your orgasm face a few times, are you going to now pretend to be a fucking smiling ray of sunshine and light?

Either way, you can't fucking cry!

Ugh. It was shit like this, that was the reason I'd resisted for so long. Why I knew we'd never work. Why I didn't work. Our friendship was worth more than great sex. There was no way I could put on a convincing, happy morning-after persona for True. True knew I wasn't worth shit in the morning. He'd know I was faking it. I was screwed!

Why did I have to go and ruin it?

I flopped my hands down and shut my eyes tighter. A few seconds later I felt True's lips at the corners of my lashes, kissing away the tears that had gathered. "Stop it now," he said, his voice dark and gravelly with morning misuse. "You are going to give yourself a headache with all that overthinking, and you haven't even had your coffee yet."

I let out a breath.

"Lu." He said my name firmly and my body reacted. Wow. That was new.

I forced myself to breathe slower.

"Don't let your mind take you places it has no business going," True said. "That is not our road. It's not our journey."

I shut my eyes tighter then. As if it would shut out his words. Silly man. What would he know of a journey?

It was better if any journey we had ended here, if we were going to salvage any bit of our friendship.

My eyes shot open, and I gave True a smile. His eyes narrowed as his nostrils flared.

"You're right. It's not our road. Our road is this one that leads to the hero convention and finding Keanu. This was fun. The wine was great but it's not our real life." I laughed, my voice light. "I mean look at this place. Can you imagine your colleagues at the college seeing you in all these pillows?"

He shrugged. "I imagine I'd have even more students on the waitlist for the next semester."

I rolled my eyes. "Really, True, I don't have time for this and neither do you. We're both busy people with busy lives and careers. This wasn't a big deal. It's not a big deal. It was one night, we can blame it on the wine and move on. You never would have acted that way toward me without it."

He looked at me with deadly seriousness. "Wouldn't I?" He leaned down and nuzzled at my neck, going up to nip at my earlobe.

I sighed and gently pushed him away, against my body wanting to pull him back. "True, this is not real life," I started. "This all is a dream. A really beautiful, sweet and sexy dream. But we can't take it home with us."

He brought his thigh over mine, then bent down, cupped my breast and lifted my nipple into his mouth. He sucked and I forgot my words and when he went lower still, spreading my thighs and pulling me to the edge of the bed to make room for his legs to dangle over the edge while he feasted between my legs, I damn near lost my breath.

Later, when True came up and looked me in the eye again, I was smiling for real.

"See, that's better," he said, grinning before getting more serious than I'd seen him in a long while. He pulled me into his chest once more and talked in almost a low whisper. "This may not be the real world, Lu, but it doesn't mean you still can't be real with me. I don't want you putting less importance on what's going on here just because we're not at home. Just relax and stop thinking this is not real life."

I was quiet. Not knowing how to react. Hating that he'd seen right through me again.

He tapped my thigh. "Did you hear me? Or did you pass out from orgasmic bliss?"

I groaned. "Okay, I heard you. Fine." I pushed up and looked at him. "Now, Mr. Erickson, can we please get a move on and at least get some coffee in me. Before we have to face the real world today in our fake superhero costumes. My imaginary boyfriend could be out there waiting on me as we speak."

He laughed. "There is so much wrong with that sentence, and yet you said it without the least bit of irony."

I stared at him. "I did. Aren't I fancy?"

We were all dressed up. Well, I was all dressed up—full-on Trinity: latex bodysuit, hair stuffed within an inch of life into a bob wig and me walking in boots that squeaked with every step. I sounded like my great granny's old couch, but at least I looked hot. True was as minimally dressed as he could be. I'd ordered him a cool purple Morpheus suit, and the damn shop sent it in a size too small. He could hardly get a leg in.

Credit to him for going low-key on the I-told-you-so's.

So instead of Trinity and Morpheus, we were now more like Trinity and old Neo or Mr. Anderson before he turned. True looked like some guy in jeans and a tee with a jacket going to a thing. I couldn't be nearly as disappointed about that as I was behind the fact that when we arrived at the venue we were met with the news of having missed out on Keanu. Again.

"Gone?" I asked another kick-ass Trinity.

"Yeah, about fifteen minutes ago."

"But he wasn't supposed to be here for an hour," I said. "The schedule says so."

"Oh, we really go by our own times out here," she said with an easygoing, un-Trinity-like smile. The least the woman could have done was stay in character. "Besides, it's Keanu. You know how he is. He just goes with the flow."

I looked at her. Go with the flow? She might as well have done one of those Trinity, Matrixy suspend-in-air-a-moment things and then flicked her foot out and kicked me in the chin.

"The flow, huh?" I wanted to hurl.

Seeing my expression, the woman leaned in and hugged me.

True separated us and looked at the other Trinity with an awkward smile. "Thank you."

"No problem," she said. "You watch out for her."

"Don't worry, I will."

He led me toward the exit, and I let him, shuffling much

like a person in shock, squeaking with each step. "You and your multiple orgasms," I seethed.

"You gonna sue me?"

"I just might," I growled. "Or Martina might." I felt my cheeks heat. At one point I thought the little camper was going to tip over backward and we'd end up in the hot spring.

True leaned in and whispered close to my ear, "Don't worry. I read the contracts carefully on the stay. They have plenty of liability insurance."

Heat ran down my neck to my breasts to my thighs. I shook my head. Only he could make liability insurance sound sexy.

"I picked a fine time to wear latex."

"True, Lu!" There was a loud voice from our right. We turned and there was Martina, walking our way dressed as a female Mandalorian. There was a woman with her who came up to her shoulders, cosplaying as The Child, aka Baby Yoda, complete with a little broth cup.

She introduced her friend as Mindy, and like The Child, Mindy did little more than give us wide eyes.

"Well, you two look great," Martina said.

"Thank you," I responded, trying to regain my composure. "And thanks for the food and wine. It was all wonderful."

"Well, we just like to do our best for our guests, make you all feel comfortable enough to unwind and just let go." She looked closely at True and me then, and for a moment it felt like she was summoning her witchy powers to see into our heads. "And did you enjoy the springs?"

"We did, thanks," I said quickly. This little minx. This whole setup was a sex trap. It wasn't right, and yet I was all ready to rebook for the same time next year.

"Well, Mindy and I have to be off. There is a light saber seminar coming up in the east hall. But I hope you got to meet Keanu before he left," she said casually.

I felt like I'd been sliced with a saber and this was the added salt.

"So he really is gone?" I asked. "Do you think he's still somewhere in the hall or maybe still in town?"

She sighed. "I don't know, he might be, but I doubt it. Usually with these things a lot of the stars are in and out unless they're vacationing." She leaned forward. "But it's Keanu, so you never know. I did hear about a place in the mountains where he likes to go either skydiving or para-gliding. I don't know which one. He's such a thrill seeker, and when he's on that bike . . . Well, who knows?"

I let out a breath. The disappointment was painful but at this point not surprising. "Well, thank you. You don't want to be late for your class."

I started down the exhibition hall again.

True was quiet as we passed character after character. Finally, at a Lord of the Rings and Black Panther junction, there was a bottleneck and we got stuck behind a team of elves who appeared to be jockeying for fan space with the people of Wakanda. True spoke up. "I'm really sorry we missed him again."

I let out a breath and whirled on True. "Did we really have to have that third round of sex?" I yelled.

He looked at me. "Um, I believe that was your request."

I turned away from him, only to see two elves and three hobbits looking at me rather leeringly. I jutted my chin their way and gave them my best "you got somethin' to say to me? I didn't think so" look before going past.

I just wanted out.

My costume was tight as hell and my wig was hot and itchy and these stupid shoes were announcing me with every step I took. I felt like an idiot. And *oww!* Someone had stepped on my damn toe. Even from the back I could tell this someone was from Wakanda. Going for total Killmonger realness: tight pants, chestplate, tapered fade and dreads. But still, my toe was throbbing. I was just about to say something when True's voice rang out from behind me. "Yo, you think you can say excuse me. You stepped on her toe."

"Oh, damn. Are you all right, sis?" The guy turned toward me. "I'm sorry. That was my bad. It's a real crush in here."

He smiled and Kill-mothereffing-monger indeed. Mother of all that was gorgeous, it was Michael B. Jordan. And if True hadn't come up behind me I would have been dead on the floor at Michael B's feet.

As it was, I wasn't dead on the floor, but I felt more like a Walking Dead on my feet—zombielike and without words.

"Is your foot okay? I wouldn't want your boyfriend to get all up in arms." He grinned, and I thought I may have been looking at a TV screen it was so perfect.

"Huh? Wha?" Great. Language, where art thou? I looked down, then back at Michael B. "It's fine. Thank you." Then it registered what he said, and I felt True at my back, his breath coming out in an angry *whoosh*. What was True so mad about? I was the one who should have been mad. I straightened and brought my hand up to smooth my messy wig. "Thanks, I'm good." I smiled. "Both my friend and my foot are fine. No worries."

Michael B. nodded, then was whisked through the crowd of fans and behind a screened area. I turned to True. "First Captain America and now you're yelling at Killmonger? You're making quite a name for yourself, Mr. Erickson."

He let out a long breath, as if he couldn't quite believe it either. "So it would seem, Lu. So it would seem."

CHAPTER 28

THE WHOLE TRUTH

BETHANY LU

L u, we can still do this," True said. "I know you're pissed, and I know it's all my fault you didn't get to finally see Keanu today."

Okay, so it wasn't all his fault, but the way he was throwing himself on his sword was kind of chivalrous. Except it did absolutely nothing for my mood and the fact that I was feeling like a complete and utter fool baking in the New Mexico heat while wearing black latex and a cheap wig.

"Can we just go home?" I asked.

True started up the car and put the air-conditioning on full blast, then screeched out of the parking lot and onto the highway. "Don't worry, we'll be back to the camper soon and you can get out of that costume."

I turned toward him. "No, I meant home-home. Back to New York. This is cute and all, but even I can admit when

I'm defeated. It's time to get back to New York. I have work to do. A dog to care for. A show that's coming up. I have to face reality sometime, and I think I'm ready to face it now. I have to."

I turned forward, not even taking solace in the beauty of the barren landscape, the colors of the glorious mountains. All I could see was the tightening of True's grip on the steering wheel.

"Tell me why you're in such a hurry to leave so fast. What do you have to rush home to?" True asked, not looking at me but looking straight ahead.

There was Morphie to rush home to and then there was my work that was still waiting on me. Not that my work couldn't wait an extra few days. I knew I had to do it but also knew I'd factored in time to do this. To get better and fill my creative well.

Even with Dawn still visiting her parents and my other best friend right next to me, I just needed to get home. To get back to what I knew. To safety. I hated that True knew it.

He drove faster now. Our exit was coming up ahead but before that a sign read SKYVIEW PARAGLIDING.

True blew right past our exit and kept on going. "You know that was our exit back there, right?"

"I know."

"And didn't I say I wanted to get back?"

"I heard you."

"Why are we heading there?"

He turned and looked at me for a moment. His eyes filled with a twinge of hurt I hadn't seen in a long while.

"When did you stop trusting me?" he said. "*Why* did you stop trusting me?"

I was stunned. And there I was thinking that Trinity had knocked the crap out of me when she said Keanu was gone, but here came True. I thought he would say more but he just kept driving, hitting the button to make the top go down on the car. He flipped the radio on and cranked it up to a high volume. Erykah Badu and "Next Lifetime" blasted through the speakers. Her soulful voice vibrated hauntingly through my body, talking of love missed because of hesitation and poor timing.

~

TRUE

"Okay, so now what? You have me out here in the middle of the desert and up on some rocky-assed cliff. You can forget any thoughts you have about me parasailing. That's not happening. And if you think you're bumping me off and leaving me for dead, there are a few too many witnesses. What are we doing here, True?"

Lu was really going all out with the anger today. I thought I knew just about every facet of her with our long history, but this side? This woman struggling with her feelings of possibly being in love, this was a whole other level. And for half a second I wondered if I was even up for her drama.

But of course I was. Lu's drama was my everything.

I loved that she was so fierce, and the fact that she would

even consider going on this Keanu quest, despite her fears, gave me the ridiculous hope that she'd one day be that intense, love just as hard, for an economics nerd like me.

She was cute and passionate and hot as hell—probably literally right now in that plastic suit—and I'm sure that made her even angrier. Lu had shed her boots for a pair of more sensible Vans. She'd taken off the jacket and her curls were wild and free-flowing. She looked like even more of an action hero than she had when she was all dressed up for the Hero Fest earlier.

Yeah, I was all in for her. No matter what venom she sent my way, I'd either dodge it or take the poison and spit it back out onto the ground. Hell, I was practically immune at this point anyway. Lu was worth it. Somehow I'd let her know that it was safe to be all those things—sweet, dangerous, even poisonous—with me. She needed to know she was safe.

She made an impatient gesture with her hands. "Well? What are we doing? You've got me out here and out of the car. Now what? If you say paragliding, I swear I will hitch a ride back with a trucker. Because that's a hard no."

"Well, you hitching a ride is a hard no for me, so we're in agreement there. Now look over there in the middle of the bridge. They have bungee jumping. Do it with me."

She gave me a shocked look before responding. "I think I've done enough unexpected things with you for one trip."

Snake venom, snake venom, snake venom. I put the words on repeat like a slow mantra, then let out a long breath. "Come on," I said. "Why don't we give it a try? The jump looks fine, and it's something we can't do in the city, at least not with this view. And this way, the day won't be completely lost. Besides, you'd look fantastic doing it in your outfit." I tried my best to muster up a small smile with that one.

There was a loud scream then. We turned quickly toward the sound as a couple went over the edge of the bridge holding tight to each other, the woman shrieking as a bungee cord took them clear down to the edge of the water, then ripped them back up in a quick jerking motion and up and down again, dangling them in the air before they were cranked back up.

Lu looked at me wide-eyed and shook her head. "First of all, jumping into the abyss with the only thing between you and death being an elastic cord secured by a person who doesn't know you and doesn't give a shit about you is not a thing you just *try*. And two, who are you right now? Where is the Truman I used to know so well?"

I walked toward her, put her hand on the left side of my chest. "Who do you think I am? And who would know me if not you? Now I'm gonna ask you one more time: When did you stop trusting me?"

Lu threw up her hands. "That's it, I'm hitchhiking." She frowned at me, shoving a finger into my chest. Her curls tickled the tip of my nose before she shot me with a hard glare. "No," she said. "Better yet, give me the keys. I'll leave your ass out here. Let you find a way back to the hotel and the camper. I'm due for a good soak and maybe you need to walk off whatever it is you got fogging up your brain."

I took her by the wrist and gently pushed her hand down

from my chest. "I'm perfectly clear in my brain, body, heart. All fine and normal."

"So what, you're saying I'm not?"

"I'm saying you're not acting like yourself. You are being all jumpy and skittish and strange around me."

She stepped back out of my reach and turned away for a moment before turning back to me, looking at me head-on. "What do you expect? We had sex last night. And you went and said you were my boyfriend."

"What? Is that what's getting to you? The boyfriend comment? If it's bothering you so much, let it go. Call me whatever the hell you want. Besides, that was Michael B. assuming. And what did you expect me to do in that instance, come out and say 'No, I'm not her boyfriend but the guy who's just her friend who she treats like a boy who loves her and she finally let him make love to her after twenty years last night'? Because that would have been a really long-assed explanation for the convention floor."

Lu stared at me in silence. I knew I had said too much and still, I felt like I hadn't said nearly enough.

I pointed at her. "And even if we hadn't made love, Lu, you've been weird anyway, even before that. What do you want me to call us? Tell me please and I'll be whatever you want. Just as long as whatever label you give me is still by your side. I can't just be nothing to you."

She turned away then and looked out over the edge of the cliff down to the river below.

I reached around behind her, put my arms around her waist and whispered in her ear, "Can you honestly, honestly say there isn't any love between us? Come on, Lu, I thought for a minute that maybe I could pretend this is all for play. Just a road trip dream, but that's bull. I mean shit, you and me say I love you even when we say goodbye."

"And we will again," she said softly, and somehow I knew her words to be true even though they broke my heart.

I nudged at her, then forced myself to smile. Somehow it felt like she needed it. I turned around. "Okay then. How about this? You take my hand, trust me, jump with me. And continue this journey, and I'll make sure that we get back to a place that feels right and like normal for us." I fought to make my smile brighter.

It was amazing the way the two of us could turn our safety masks on and off at will. I saw the moment that she did it and wondered if she saw the moments that I did it too. How long would we continue this little game? Would it go on indefinitely, or was there an ending to this play? And who was the real author of it anyway?

Lu took my hand and led me toward the car. "Okay, Truman Erickson, I'm doing this. But just so you know, if I die today, I will haunt you like you've never been haunted before."

I couldn't help but laugh at that. "You call that a threat, Bethany Lu Carlisle? You gonna have to come a lot stronger than that, ma'am. You haunting me is my regular nine-to-five."

~

BETHANY LU

Between the latex of my costume, the harness that was giving me a wedgie of epic proportions plus the feeling of potential impending death, I would have rather been stuck on the subway in the middle of August with no air-conditioning or cell service between tunnels for an extra hour.

But then the bungee operator said *Go* and I tucked my face into True's chest and he squeezed me extra tight and whispered, "I've got you. I'm never letting go." into my ear, and dammit if I didn't want to ante up immediately for another go-round.

CHAPTER 29

THE NIGHT BEFORE

BETHANY LU

So yeah, things kind of went a little haywire, and we both ended up oversleeping."

"Wait," Dawn said. "True overslept? And you did what? Jumped where? I must be talking to someone else. Where are my friends? Admit it, you're aliens who took over their bodies in Area 51. I knew letting the two of them go out there alone was a bad idea."

"You're hilarious," I said, deadpan. "But listen, we got this great tip that Keanu is heading west on a motorcycle, and True decided that we should extend our trip. Do you mind still watching Morphie for me? We're going to try to catch up with Keanu in Las Vegas. I know I should get back to my work, but I feel like I need this time."

"Hey, you do you. I think what we have so far for the show is great. I told you that already. If you want to add another piece or two, sketch it out on the road. We'll make it work. The most important thing is you being happy," she said. "I really can't believe you got True into a costume..." She trailed off.

I listened to the quiet on the other end of the phone as I looked out over the beauty of our campsite and wondered what Dawn was thinking. I'd probably said too much. I'm sure I said too much. Dawn was no fool. Maybe it was me telling her about the bungee jump or maybe waking up late for the heroes festival, but I was sure she knew True and I slept together. Not to mention I was now asking her to watch Morphie even longer. I'd never been gone this long from him! Crazy what good sex and an over-rush of adrenaline could do to a person.

True was pacing and gave me a rather unconvincing thumbs-up. We'd just finished having dinner, and I finally mustered up the courage to call Dawn to ask if she could continue watching Morphie for a little longer.

I was still listening for Dawn's reaction, wondering if it could help my swirling feelings. Though I'd already asked her to watch Morphie, I was torn. Sure, my original mission of getting Keanu to stop his wedding was still my goal. Only, I was feeling, ugh, squishy about it. Or perplexed, at least. I mean, it wasn't like True and I were going anywhere after we got back to New York, but it was different out here. And I wasn't ready to give up this new version of us quite yet. Back in New York it would be different. I knew it, and I had a feeling he knew it too.

I was totally tempting fate enough with the bungee jump, but hopefully the rest of the trip would be less thrill and more chill. No Ferris wheel rides or silly parties. I had to admit I was surprised at myself and True after the bungee jump. This new daredevil side of him was impressive but scary as all get-out.

Finally, there was a loud shriek on the other end of the phone.

"You two totally did it!"

Oh, dammit. She knew. "Did what?" I said, way too innocently. "I just told you we bungee jumped."

"Oh, you were jumping all right. I bet you were, ma'am. All over that bungee. *Boing. Boing. Boing.* Probably all night long too. Weren't you? Weren't you? Jumping those bonzzz."

I think she may have actually been cackling.

"Are you twelve? Come on, this is True we're talking about."

"If you don't tell me, I'm calling him right now," Dawn said.

"Don't you dare," I hissed.

"Well, spill it then? Keeping this big a secret is not fair. It goes against code."

"I didn't know we had a code."

Dawn squealed again. "I knew you did it! You all but just admitted it right now."

True came up behind me and slipped the phone out of my hand. "All right, Columbo," he told Dawn. "I see we're not getting anything past you. So we did it. And I'm not giving you any details. Let's just leave it at I was magnificent. So magnificent that your very best friend now wants to get in a tiny little car and follow me across the country like a bona fide groupie. Yes, it's true I've got the magic stick. I've taken her all the way to the candy shop and now she just can't get enough."

I heard Dawn's scream of *eww* through the phone and True handed it back to me. "Sorry," he said. "But she deserved it."

"Are you back?" she asked.

"Yes, I'm back."

"Truman's smart ass is gonna pay for that one when he gets back home."

"I'm sure he knows that he will. Now, do you mind watching Morphie a little longer for me?"

"For your Mr. Magic Stick. Girl, you eat your fill and don't come back here with fewer than four cavities."

CHAPTER 30

RIVER'S EDGE

BETHANY LU

I looked down at Dawn's text and smiled, getting a little choked up at the same time.

> **Dawn:** I'm happy for you, woman. Be happy for yourself for a change. ♡ ♡ ♡

She'd attached a picture of Morphie looking quite annoyed with a little bow tie around his neck.

I swiped at my eyes, blinking quickly, and turned back toward True.

"Are you okay?" he asked. He looked so concerned, and because it was him, I knew that there was no pretense, that he wasn't faking it.

I nodded, though I was faking the smile I gave him in return. "I'm fine, perfectly fine. Dawn, probably not so much. And if you don't have life insurance, you may want to think about it, or at least check your medical coverage. She's out for blood. Yours, not mine of course."

He grinned. "I'm sure I'll be fine. As long as I keep you happy. Also, what do you mean, just mine? Don't you have any responsibility to keep me happy? Dawn has to have some allegiance to me too, right?"

I gave him a skeptical look.

"Ho—"

"Don't you dare say it," I warned. "But pretty much. Yes, though I will say she does care for you a bit. So I'll be careful."

I tapped on my cell phone and pulled up the picture of Morphie that Dawn had sent. "Here, take a look. She's got my poor dog all decked out in bow ties and crap. The poor thing looks miserable. I can only take solace in the fact that she's probably at least spoiling him like mad." I swiped my screen. There was Morphie giving me sad eyes in a bowler hat. "Look at what she's done!"

True laughed, and I fought against the lump in my throat and found it hard to get the last words out as he wrapped his arms around me. I buried my face into his chest, torn between this little spot of fantasy and my mind telling me that this wouldn't make it back home. That True was doing this to once again just take care of me like he'd always done.

I thought of Cole then. Crap. Just when I wanted to not think of him, there he was. A silent presence, always there over the shoulder of either me or True. Watching over us, so to speak. I was never sure if it was kindly.

I knew in my heart that if he still lived, none of this

would've ever happened. I'd be who knows where in New York. Maybe an artist, maybe married, maybe having kids who might be eight or nine by now and he'd be an uncle. I wondered whether he'd still be friends with True. Probably. True was solid like that and so was Cole.

Me, not as much. It was with Cole's passing that I'd glommed onto True and Dawn, needing familiarity and safety. If Cole had lived, I'd probably see True at the occasional gathering of friends and family. But let's face it, how often would I really even show up? I was more likely to be the eccentric auntie if I'd stayed single. I pictured myself dropping off inappropriate presents that Cole's wife would probably hate and toss out.

This man who was holding me so solidly now in his arms, like he truly loved me, wouldn't have been saddled with my baggage all these years, protecting me and caring for me like some fragile thing that might fall apart any moment. No, True would've had the life he deserved, a life where he could date freely, live freely and not be worried about his best friend's sister.

I hated myself for it. Not always but sometimes. And the secret worst part of me wondered if he resented a part of me too. If not me, then at least the obligation I'd become to him. How many jobs had he turned down over the years? Overseas teaching positions? Hell, out-of-town sex dates? Just to babysit me?

Would he be working at some fancy firm in LA right now, rolling in cars and cash, if it weren't for me?

I was scared to ask. The answer felt too devastating to face.

True rubbed at my back, then kissed the top of my head

like he'd done so many times before. I stepped back and looked up at him. "So, you ready to give that hot spring another go? I don't think we got to see the true medicinal benefits of the waters last night."

True's eyes lit up and his smile went wide as he lifted me up. I wrapped my legs around his waist. He carried me toward the back side of the camper where the spring was. "Wait, I need to go inside and get my suit," I said, slapping at his shoulders.

"Ms. Carlisle. Sometimes you really say the silliest things," he said. "Now hurry out of those clothes and let's give those fairies of the forest something to really talk about once we're gone."

CHAPTER 31

RELOADED

BETHANY LU

Welcome to the Bazooka Blaze Rio Grande," the receptionist said as we hit the check-in desk at our destination hotel on the outskirts of Las Vegas.

I looked around at the out-of-control Western décor. "You sure this is the place that your Gary said?" I asked True.

He gave me a long side look. "Unfortunately, that's what my text said: The Bazooka Blaze Rio Grande."

The receptionist looked up at us and blinked, obviously insulted over her hotel being dissed. I chose to keep my comments on her eye makeup to myself. Not wanting a whole standoff.

She smiled, and I thought her heavily caked lipstick was going to crack.

I looked around cow prints and cowhides and antlers, at the non-PC totem poles and wondered what in the world we were doing there. What could Keanu be doing here?

"I don't know," I whispered to True as we got on an elevator that looked like something straight out of a '70s Hollywood Western. "Doesn't this feel strange?"

The door opened on our floor with a loud ping and he grabbed my hand. "Everything about this trip has felt strange from the beginning, but we're going all the way now."

I stopped in the hallway and pointed at him. "See that right there. Since when do you say things like 'we're going all the way'? If I wake up tomorrow and you've turned into some character out of a sixties spy movie, I'm kicking your ass."

He laughed. "Come on, this looks fun. Stop being such a stick-in-the-mud and go with it."

I rolled my eyes and let this alter of True lead me down the hall to continue our trip into *The Twilight Zone*.

For the next few days, we had more nights of great sex and absolutely no Keanu sightings.

The messed-up thing was that I wasn't feeling all that bad about it. Or maybe it wasn't all that messed up. I didn't know at this point. It felt strange, but I was having actual fun. Sex and True and fun.

The thing is, now it seemed like True was having just as much if not more fun than I was. He wasn't looking at his phone as frequently. Wasn't talking about school. Though he'd once in a while spout off something all economics-like and really smart and make a note of it on his phone. I only understood some of what he said, but I loved the way his eyes lit while he talked about it and could listen to him go on and on forever.

He was already mapping out the next and next leg, ready to ditch the car in Vegas and fly on to the next stop, some watering hole where Keanu was known to surf.

We just finished dining at the River Grand, which was the hotel's signature steakhouse. I was full and happy. For all its quirks, the hotel was pretty jumping. Gary knew his stuff and there was definitely some kind of filming happening. There were tents and trailers around the property, and people who looked like LA or NY movie types clustered in groups.

But for all our searching in between dining and sex, we never saw Keanu.

We found out the movie was an indie with a high budget, and the most we were able to get out of anyone was that it was being directed by a Brit. No one would cop to Keanu having anything to do with it, so we were coming up empty. Again.

"So should we head back to our room now?" True said after dinner.

"Sure." It was early, but there was nothing else out here but the hotel, the restaurant and the small connecting casino.

We walked through the casino on the way to the elevators just to pass the time. A bunch of locals were playing slots. There were a couple of truckers and a few couples at the bar. In the darkened lounge area a band was covering Maroon 5.

We walked past the craps table, and there seemed to be some action. A few film people and town guys were cheering. I pulled True's hand when a cheer went up.

"You want to play?" he asked.

I shook my head. "No. I'm good."

"Come on."

"Are you kidding me?" I protested. "You don't gamble. You absolutely hate to waste money. And you don't know how to play."

"How do you know?" he shot back.

Well hell, he was right there. How did I know? What I knew about True was really only what I wanted to know. But what I realized now was that there was still so much to learn. Even after all these years. For so long I kept True in the safe little box, one that felt good to me. Anything slightly on the edge of being edgy, I preferred to keep out of my view.

True squeezed my hand, I guess noticing my hesitancy. "You're right," he said and grinned. "I'm no big gambler, only having done it on a few occasions on work trips. But it's just a little fun, and I've got my own Lady Luck with me tonight." He pulled my hand up toward his lips and grazed them across my knuckles, then looked into my eyes. "You've got to at least indulge me over here."

I nodded, suddenly feeling very Bond girlish, or as Bond girlish as I could be in my jeans and cork heels and one-shoulder top. True was in a semi-upscale knit tee shirt and jeans. But hitting the Bond mark? Yeah, no. But we might as well have some fun.

I was shocked further still when True reached into his pocket and peeled off a few hundred-dollar bills and casually handed them to the dealer. Look at the professional. I nudged him with my elbow as he got his chips and stacked them in front of him.

I blinked. This was either sexy or an indication of a potential problem. I didn't know which, but I was in Vegas. We were going with it.

But then True casually picked up the dice and asked me to blow on them. My eyes went wide. "Who are you and what have you done with my friend?"

"Just blow, Lu. Whatever I win tonight we'll use to buy you a gift at the jewelry store. How about that?" He raised an eyebrow.

I knew I probably should have been offended by the blatant chauvinism of the whole act, but dammit I wasn't. I got swept up in the whole fantasy and blew on the dice for all I was worth and started to cheer. Mama wanted a new necklace or maybe a sparkly bracelet. "No whammies! No whammies, no whammies aaaand STOP!"

True rolled the dice and came up with a seven on the first go. The crowd cheered, and True gave me a surprise kiss, which I felt all the way down to my toes as my body warmed. When he held the dice to me again, I blew on them eagerly and without hesitation.

The next roll was a nine. The middle-aged man across from me with a receding hairline and seriously deep-set eyes broke out into a huge grin. "That's my number, that's my number," he said. "I like this roller." He looked at me. "Keep doing like you do, little lady. Just keep doing like you do." He gave me a wink that in any other atmosphere might cause me to call the cops.

But I couldn't help but agree with the man. I liked the

roller too; he was pretty cute, and his Lady Luck was kind of fine. Besides, I wanted True to win. I'd seen this lovely little moon-and-stars necklace in the jewelry store window on the way to the casino when we left the restaurant. I'd only glanced at it quickly because it was really not my usual style. But seeing it here with True reminded me of our nights in the camper making love with the stars and the moon as a night-light.

I blew on the dice again. This time when True rolled he got double twos. The table cheered again. We were freaking on fire!

Oh yeah. We kept this up and in no time that necklace would be mine. But the best part was seeing True win. He looked so cool and full of joy, like he was having the time of his life. My man was on a hot streak! The thought pulled me up short, and I blinked. But it wasn't a lie. At that moment, True was my man and he was hot and on a streak.

His stack of chips had nearly tripled when I heard it.

The cover band that had been playing a lot of 2000s-era music made a switch to '90s pop and did a little '70s and some '80s punk and rock. I was grooving to the music and vibing off the energy of True and this wild bunch of silly craps players when I heard the big familiar bass of the Clash. But the voice. It was the voice I'd been searching all across the country for. Keanu. It was him playing the bass and leading the cover band.

True was holding the dice in front of my face, staring at me. "I need you to blow. Everybody's waiting, Lu."

Keanu's deep voice was calling me. "Should I stay or—" I looked at True, wide-eyed, and blew on the dice, then bit my bottom lip. Keanu's voice was pulling me away from this table, away from True. Once again everyone cheered.

Dammit.

This time when True won, I felt like I lost. The dice were handed back to him and he lifted them and held them in front of me. I looked at him again. He pulled them away, gave me a little nod, telling me to go.

I didn't budge. Instead, I pulled at his shirt sleeve before he was able to roll.

True looked back at me. "I thought you had said you had to go," he said. "Or at least your face said it."

I pursed my lips and held up the dice and blew on them once more.

This time True threw them without looking, and I could practically feel his annoyance in the flick of his wrist. "Seven craps!"

Everyone moaned.

"Can't be mad at that!" the guy across from me said. "It was a good-ass roll." He looked at True, then threw him a black chip. True caught it.

"For your lady," the man said. True's eyes slid toward me, and it felt like he was expecting me to correct the guy and tell him I wasn't True's anything. Instead I took the chip and said thank you to the man. True whispered in my ear: "Go, go before you miss him."

I took off practically at a sprint and I was surprised security wasn't on my tail. I made it to the bar area when the song was ending. Just in time to see Keanu's profile and a flash of his smile as he headed offstage.

That was it.

I suppose I could've run faster. I know I would have made it for most of the performance if I'd left True sooner. But the fact was, I did stay with him. I'd stayed with him throughout the whole game and missed yet another opportunity to see my idol. Still, it didn't stop the look of regret in his eyes when he saw that I wanted to leave in the first place. The inevitable was coming toward us and it was coming fast.

After catching the fleeting glimpse of Keanu, True and I rode up to our room in silence. It wasn't like we could chitchat or anything with a tour crowd from Norway and a couple with two kids crowded into the large elevator. But still, everyone else was chatting with each other, and it was weird that we weren't. Even heading down the quiet hall toward the room, I didn't know what to say to him.

Our lovemaking that night was intense. Even more intense than normal, which seemed ridiculous since we didn't even have a normal.

I couldn't tell if he was saying goodbye to me or me to him, but it was definitely a goodbye of sorts. It made me want to hold on to him just that much tighter.

CHAPTER 32

TUNE IN TOMORROW

BETHANY LU

True and I held hands on the flight back to New York from Vegas. I'd always hated flying. The whole idea of being hurled through the sky on a jet never appealed to me the way it had others. Maybe it was the lack of leg-room or the tiny, horribly lit bathrooms that, come to think of it, bore a striking similarity to the one in our camper.

Our camper. Look at how fast that transition to *our* and *us* had happened. I knew already, even if we never went back, that I'd think of that place as our camper, our river, our spring. This would be our adventure. But it was now done, and we each needed to get back to our lives.

As much as I hated flying, I could have stood this flight for an extra hour or three, my leg rubbing against

True's while he traced lazy circles into my palm. I was transfixed watching his thumb as it made those tiny circles, and at times he'd move up and massage my wrist. He'd only let go once to turn off his phone early in the flight. My one distraction from my relaxation was seeing his long email list. There were a lot of urgents and contact immediatelys. But still, he'd always had time for me.

In all these years, he'd always had time for me.

I sighed.

"Are you tired?"

I looked over at him. "A little."

"I picked you up some magazines at the newsstand. Art ones and the entertainment ones you like so much." True pushed the Hudson News bag my way.

I shook my head. "No thanks. I'm fine just relaxing here."

He nodded, and I put my head on his shoulder.

He was my comfort space. But would he still be when he showed up on my doorstep with coffee in the next day or two, or would he want to share more than just coffee and I would have to bring reality back to our world?

When we finally landed, the unspoken words between us spoke volumes. We stayed silent all the way in the Uber back home to our building.

"You want me to come inside?" True asked after dropping my bags by my door. He placed the Hudson News bag to the side of my luggage.

I shook my head. "No thanks," I said. "I know you have to be tired. It's been a long couple of days. I'm sure you need to get some rest. Besides, it's late."

He shook his head and didn't move. "I don't know if I can get some rest," he said. "I've kinda gotten used to you, stealing the covers and kicking my legs."

"Yeah, about as much as I've gotten used to you hogging the covers."

He laughed. "That's a ridiculous and malicious rumor. Everyone knows I'm extremely caring, gentle and sharing in bed."

Now it was my turn to laugh, though laughing was the last thing I wanted to do. "Go check on your place, and we'll talk later. We both need some sleep."

I was about to turn and go into my apartment, but True stopped me. He turned me back toward him, leaned down and gave me a gentle kiss on the lips. It was sweet. Sweeter and softer than any kisses we'd shared in the past weeks. I let it linger, wondering if it was a promise and if so, for what?

I walked back into my place, surprised to find Morphie and Dawn both fast asleep like Goldilocks and her one little bear on my bed. At least they were getting along. Morphie looked up at me, and like the low traitor I knew him to be, snuggled into Dawn's breasts where he was comfortable and went back to sleep. "I didn't think I was rushing home for you," I mumbled as I quietly toed off my shoes and lay down on the other side of him.

Despite all the thoughts racing through my brain, I was asleep in no time.

"I don't get it," Dawn said. "How can you be so lucky but still so unlucky at the same time? It's like your own tragic comedy and fairy tale rolled into one. To miss out on one star while still running into other ones that many times, it's like some sort of bumbling game of Whac-A-Mole."

I shook my head as I stirred another teaspoon of sugar into my coffee and finished recounting all the stories of my trip to Dawn. "I know. I know it's ridiculous when you really think about it. Something like this would only happen to me."

"No, something like this would only happen to *you and True*. I mean, you two see each other practically every day, but you have to go clear across the country to finally hook up. I swear you're about as exhausting as Kim and Kanye."

"And you see how well that went."

Dawn made a face. "Okay, terrible analogy. Sorry. But still, you both are disturbingly tedious. You don't know how mad I was to wake up and see you on the other side of dear old Morphie this morning. He looked annoyed with it too. We've been so patient. We deserve to see the full payoff! Imagine this: If you'd started screwing each other when you should have, I could be well on my way to being almost a grandauntie now."

I grimaced. "What you're on the way to is a punch in the nose. And I thought *my* imagination was wild. Your talent is wasted. You should be a writer with the stories you come up with."

I took a long sip of my coffee and leaned back. "But seriously, don't hold your breath. You won't be seeing any sort of payoff anytime soon. As a matter of fact, it's best if True and I just cool it. At least until we can just be our usual selves. There's no way that kind of whirlwind could work with us. I'd like us to go back to what we had and get back to normal as quickly as we can."

Dawn was quiet as she stared at me. Finally, she let out a moan. "That's what you really want?"

I was silent for a moment. Then I smiled at her. "Yeah."

Dawn's expression grew serious. "And is True okay with that?"

I gave Morphie a smooch, not meeting Dawn's eyes. "Of course."

"Liar."

"What? I'm not a liar."

"You so are. And frankly I'm insulted that you'd choose to lie to me, your best friend."

"Dawn, come on. Don't be so dramatic."

"Me? Look at you. Number one, you two are never going back to normal. Not after that man has given you sex that has turned your face to this." She pointed at my face now.

I frowned. "My face to what? I'm the same old me."

"Yeah right. The same old you, just more in love with him than ever. And yes, I said 'than ever' because you've been heavy in love with him forever. Or at least ten years, but I was staying silent because I don't like to get in people's business and I also believe a woman should have as much sex as she wants before settling down with one man and I reckon you've had your fair share now."

I stared at her, not even sure what part of her declaration to address or how to rebut any part.

"Now, back to my last statement. You, my friend, are a liar," she summed up.

My face crumbled as I choked out a sob. "Okay fine, maybe a little bit, but really it is for the best."

Dawn took me in her arms. "Oh, honey. I don't know if I agree, but I'm here for you. Whatever you need."

CHAPTER 33

SOMETHING'S GOTTA GIVE

TRUE

I was frustrated.

Okay. *Frustrated* was too light a word, and anyone who saw me in my current state—panting, sweaty and sprinting up the side of the West Side Highway like a bat out of hell—would hardly use such a tame word.

It had been days since I'd seen Lu. Sure, I'd texted. I tried to keep the messages light, give her some space, knowing that was what she wanted. The frustrating part was that my fearless chatterbox was suddenly reduced to noncommittal, one-word answers.

How are you doing? I'd ask, opening the door for her usual dissertation on her work and a possible invite.

Her response: Fine.

Me: Thinking of you. Okay, maybe that wasn't giving her space, but it was truthful and she could at least pick up the phone and give me shit about it if it was a problem.

Her: ☺ Hope you're well.

WTF? She hoped I was well? If she really wanted me to be well she could call me or come over to remedy the situation.

She knew I was going out of my damn mind. After the taste—no, the sip—I'd had of her, I was craving a full-on drink. And the fact that she wasn't craving me, calling for me, was frustrating, angering, demoralizing and heart-breakingly hurtful.

Was I just a momentary fantasy for her? A curiosity? Someone niggling in the back of her brain and now that she'd gotten her fill, she didn't need a refill?

I stopped short and shook my head. Something about that just didn't sit right. Not when it came to Lu. She was deeper than that. We were deeper. We'd had over twenty years of history that came down to more than just sex. We'd had a connection. And I knew deep in my bones, it wasn't just one-sided.

I ran faster, as though trying to run away from my thoughts. But it seemed the farther I got from our apartment building, the closer I moved to her in my own mind. I was past the Columbia Medical Center now and almost under the George Washington Bridge. It felt like I was running out of road. I looked up at the massive bridge and suddenly all I could think of was how I wanted to cross it. To go west. Toward New Jersey and farther still. Go back to where our adventure started and just stay there.

But how far could I run? Wherever I went, I couldn't escape my head or my heart. It was like I could feel Lu everywhere I went, and I knew wherever I ended up, all I'd want was for her to be there.

My phone dinged with a text. Idiot that I was, I immediately paused my run to see if it was from Lu. But no.

Dawn: What the hell? Why aren't you sealing the deal?

As if Lu was a deal that could be sealed. If that were the case, she would have been claimed long before—by me or one of at least a dozen other guys.

Still, Dawn's words about deals had me thinking of Daniel Lim and how he'd looked at Lu at that party. How he'd claimed to want to work with her. I'd heard rumors about his working relationships with women. Now that I'd seen that look and knew his history, the whole thing burned me up.

A guy like him was the total opposite of a guy like me. Lim had zero hesitance in his bones. He'd go all in and all out for a woman like Lu.

I glanced at the Hudson River below as I continued my jog across the bridge. The sunlight glinted off the water and the sun heated the back of my neck. And suddenly, I had an idea...

CHAPTER 34

SMACK IN THE MIDDLE

BETHANY LU

This frustration was beyond frustrating. But I had to soldier on.

Dawn and I had just finished lunch at a new bistro around the corner from my apartment. The food was pretty good, though terribly overpriced for what they were calling a French-Jamaican fusion. It didn't matter, though, because we'd bill this to Daniel Lim.

Though my ninety-one days weren't up, he'd asked to meet with me. I decided to bring Dawn to this meeting, and she picked the restaurant. I wanted her to hear his pitch. Get some objectivity.

Daniel was a lot more professional this time. I don't know if it was the venue or our relationship or the fact that he and Dawn hit it off right out of the gate. I could tell he was stunned both by her looks and her no-bullshit, all-cards-on-the-table, take-it-or-leave-it attitude.

I had to give him credit for being open to modifying his terms. I was not one for all-or-nothing when it didn't suit my needs, and Daniel's idea of using my name in a way that seemed to imply ownership on their part just didn't sit right with me. Even if it fell under the terms of so-called licensing.

"Listen. My art and my name are all I have. It's all I can control. If I give it to you, then what do I have left? Sure, I can create something else under a new name, and sure, I can make money with it, but it wouldn't feel the same. It wouldn't have the same ancestral connection as what I'm trying to do with my original work. If you're going to work with a Black artist, or any person of color whose culture has been oppressed, things like names, titles and ownership mean everything."

Daniel nodded, then did little else for a long while. He ate, he listened and he seemed to really get what we were saying.

"I hear you, Lu," he said. "I really do. And though it's not my final call, I'll take everything you're saying back to my company. We really do want to work with you. But in a way that you're happy with."

I smiled. "That's a better start."

He frowned. "What are you talking about?"

"Well, for one you said, 'we want to work with you' instead of 'we want you.' That wasn't cool."

He made a face. "Eww, sorry. Thank you for telling me. That was shitty as hell. Also, you're cool people. I was a jerk. I'll admit it, and my pinky paid the price. I didn't mean what I meant with the pass. I apologize."

I could practically see the wheels in Dawn's head turning while her hormones were firing on all cylinders. She could tell there was not a bit of chemistry between me and Daniel, our only connection being my work.

Gotta love my BFF. She chimed in then, taking over more of the business part of the meeting. "If this deal happens, Lu would have full creative control over what designs carry her name. Also, we'd have to talk about production, your factories and labor practices." I was glad to let her take over that part of the conversation.

In the last week, I'd gotten quite a bit of work done. Call it deprivation work. Or maybe it was inspiration work. But either way, something had changed. My work felt easier than it had been in months, a year maybe. And I think it was due to having a different kind of excitement in my life. The Keanu Chase seemed to be just what I needed. And I guess I was okay with that.

When True asked me how I felt about not ever getting a chance to talk to Keanu, I told him it was fine. I didn't know whether it was true at the time, but looking at my work now, I knew I really was fine. Or at least close to getting there.

I no longer feared venturing beyond my comfort zone. Morphie and I went for more walks. I got up a little earlier. Worked a little later. And was better and better about not constantly checking my messages to see if there was another from True.

I'd decided not to pursue him. True. Not Keanu. It got a little murky there even in my own mind. I didn't want to consume him or let him make me his project. He had to make decisions for himself. I couldn't dictate his life or his choices, and if that meant I'd lose him, no matter how it hurt—and it hurt—then so be it. I used my therapy app to book a full consultation and knew this was for the best. Or at least I thought so. The therapist was annoyingly less talkative than Dawn when it came to concrete advice.

But still, I was a little annoyed at Dawn. She was pushing my boundaries to the limit—especially when she let slip to Daniel that I had a few new pieces in my latest collection. He practically begged to see them, and before I could protest, Dawn had agreed and the three of us were on our way to my place so I could show him what I had.

We were just making our way into the building when we ran smack into True.

He barely glanced at me, his eyes going straight to Daniel. "What are you doing here?"

I frowned. I know he was mad about me not responding to his texts, but that was no reason to be a dick. Well, maybe it was, but still. I was just about to say something when Dawn hopped in front of his field of vision. "What, you don't see anybody else standing here?" Dawn said, hitting True on his arm.

"Hey, Dawn. How you doing?" he asked tonelessly.

"I'm doing good. Miss seeing you. You owe me a coffee."

He nodded. "I'm on it." Then he looked right back at Daniel as if awaiting his answer.

"I've got business," Daniel said. I knew that was the most cryptic and frustrating thing for True to hear.

With that, True turned my way and looked me in the eye. His expression was all glowering, and for that I should've given him stormy right back. Instead, I looked down, ready to be done with this encounter. And then I noticed his rolling suitcase.

"Where you going?" I blurted, trying not to sound as desperate as I felt and completely failing. What if he took the job in California after all and didn't tell me because I was being a shit?

He looked at Daniel, then back at me. "I've got business," he said, mimicking Daniel's answer.

I narrowed my eyes at him while he just returned his usual unaffected stare.

Fuck you, Truman Erickson. "Well, you have a safe trip," I finally blurted. *Why the hell did I say that?* The words I really wanted were *I'm sorry. I've missed you. I don't want to be the anchor holding you back.* But for once, the words I was thinking couldn't get past my lips.

I got a short and expressionless nod as he turned and headed out toward the door. I wanted to follow him. To tell him not to go. That I was full of shit and only acting like I was okay. I was not okay. There was a huge hole in my life where he was supposed to be. A hole in my heart that he'd always filled.

But in the end, I didn't move. And True didn't say another word. He left me with the view of his back as he headed down the corridor. He and his roller. Gone.

As the elevator door closed on the three of us, the quiet seemed so much bigger than the small space. Dawn filled the void with her chatter, going on about how Daniel was in for such a treat when he saw my work.

Yeah, huge treat. Come look at some art made by an emotionally stunted fraud.

I got a poke in my side just then. I turned and looked sharply at Dawn. "I was just telling Daniel how amazing your work is. How amazing you've always been." Her expression and tone dared me to argue.

I blew out a low breath and shook my head before turning my attention to Daniel. I'd missed my chance with True, so the least I could do was focus on my work.

I smiled and did my best to sound professional, as if the whole awkwardness downstairs hadn't happened. Better to ignore than acknowledge. I felt myself slipping backward.

"She has to say that," I said. "As my best friend and agent, she's double invested." At least that was true. I did love Dawn and not just because she stuck around. I loved her faith in me, how she pushed for me even when I didn't push for myself.

Once inside my loft, I got myself together well enough to explain my latest two pieces in a semi-coherent way. Daniel surprised me by gushing over the desert hues, saying he loved the surprising new direction. Frankly I thought he'd be a little put off by the lighter tone to the pieces. It was quite different from the darker edge of my work from just a few months ago.

"These are great, Lu." He stared at the start of my Truth series. I didn't say the name out loud, but that's what I called these works in my head. They were my truths in the moment. I had to force myself to keep my attention on Daniel. My mind was darting off. Going into space. Losing focus. All I could see was True. His dark, un-readable eyes, firm lips, determined jaw. Then it hit me. I didn't even see his dimples when he said goodbye. He hadn't been moved enough to give me a real smile. He just wasn't moved.

I looked back at my pieces as Daniel went on. "Hey, I don't want to be too greedy and say I want both of these. I'll save that for your show. How about you put them on hold for me?" he asked.

Dawn was about to speak, but I interrupted her. "I can put one on hold for you," I said.

In the end, I promised him my mountain scene, the one with the river running through and the mysterious couple on a walkway with paparazzi shots as cutouts for their faces. The other work, of a little camper in the woods whose source of light came from the wand of a magical fairy, I already knew I'd never part with. Even if it ended up on the floor in the corner of this loft just watching me as I watched it as it was now.

I considered it my Consequences. Since there was always a flip side to everything.

With Daniel gone, I lay out on my bed while Dawn stretched out on my sofa and leaned back, putting her feet up.

"So that was a lot," she said.

"What?" I said. As if I didn't know where this was already headed. "You mean with Daniel? It was. I'm still a little leery, but I'm glad he was so much more"—I paused—"I don't know, less of a dick on this meeting."

She gave me a look. "He wasn't too much of a dick at all. As a matter of fact he was kinda charming."

"Charming, huh?"

"Shut up. As if you didn't see it. Also, I don't know why

we're talking about this. You're clearly trying to deflect. You know the 'a lot' I am referring to here, and it's not Daniel. The whole True thing was so weird."

I leaned back and stretched. "Was it?"

"Heffa! Now you're pushing it. Don't make me fight you." She picked up one of my end pillows and threw it across the loft at me, hitting right over my head.

I jumped up. "Hey, you could injure a person! Watch it."

"Oh, please, if I wanted to injure you, you would be. Now cut the shit." Dawn suddenly shifted, then reached down toward the side of the couch. She pulled out the bag from Hudson News that True had gotten me at the airport.

"What's this?"

"Oh, I wondered what happened to that," I said. "Those are some magazines True picked up for me on our flight back. I thought I lost the bag, but I guess it slipped down there."

Dawn pulled out a copy of *People* magazine and held it up so I could see Regé-Jean Page on the cover. "What a freaking hottie! I'm surprised you didn't see him on your Keanu trek." She fanned herself with the magazine. "Shit, his fine ass makes me almost wish I was born in the Regency period, as if I'd have a chance with a duke and not end up stuck as somebody's damned house slave."

"As if you ever would," I said.

She looked up at me, shrugged, then smiled. "You're so right. I'd be some sort of badass freedom fighter, or more likely than not running the most exclusive brothel in town."

She pulled the magazine closer to her face and gave it a pretend smooch. "Come and ruin me, Duke," she said in a horrible British accent. "Ruin me good and hard."

I snorted.

Dawn reached into the bag, bringing out the other magazines, and then she shocked me by pulling out a small black box. Dawn being Dawn, she didn't hesitate to open it, and her eyes immediately sparkled.

"Excuse me," I yelled from the bed as I stuck out my hand. "So I'm guessing that must say FOR DAWN on it the way you're just opening my couch merch over there."

She looked up at me, a hint of guilt in her eyes. "You mean your forgotten couch merch? Like, when do you clean behind your pillows or at least fluff things out? Do you ever even sit over here?"

"Not really all that much unless there are people over." Then I waved my hands impatiently. "Just gimme my stuff already."

She looked down at the open box, smirked, then snapped it back shut. "Fine. This must be for you." She shrugged. "I guess. Definitely not my style."

I scooted up off the bed, snatched the box and bag from her and flopped down on the other end of the couch. Not merciless, I left her with the *People* with Regé-Jean.

I stared at the little mystery box for a few moments. "What the hell is this, True? You said it was just magazines in here," I mumbled.

"You know True and his taste. Don't go getting your hopes up. Typical touristy gift shop stuff." But something in her voice had me curious.

"Hey, don't be such a snob," I snapped. "At least he tried, and his taste is charming."

She rolled her eyes. "Sure, honey. Charming."

I let out a breath. Not knowing why I was taking so long to just get on with it and open the damn box. What could it be anyway? I flipped the lid and was stunned, transported to another world.

I was looking down at the beautiful necklace but at the same time it felt like I was looking up. At the night sky and stars beyond. My heart raced with the excitement of anticipation of the potential bliss to come. I was scared but so excited. Because he was with me. Because he was a part of me.

I swallowed and looked back over at Dawn, coming back to my senses and back to reality. "He gave me the necklace," I said through stifled tears.

She nodded. "I see. It's pretty. And I was just teasing you. Our boy came through with the taste."

"But how did he know this was the one I wanted? How would he know this was the one?"

Dawn looked at me and let out a long sigh. "You are too much, you know that?"

"Of course I know that, but you're not answering my question. I saw this in passing at a casino we were in. It reminded me of the skylight in the camper and how we were both looking up at the stars that night before we'd made love." I stopped and felt my cheeks flush and my body get all tingly. "Still," I said, "I didn't say a thing to True about it. I didn't point it out or linger on it. So how would he know?"

My friend shook her head, seemingly done with me. "First of all, you two are still infuriating but sickeningly cute. So cute you make me want to gag. And second, you idiot, how would he not know?"

"What are you talking about?"

She shook her head. "You can never keep your true feelings from him. He must've seen you looking at this necklace or felt you thinking about it through that weird telepathy thing you have going. Which for some dumbass reason has a block when it's time to finally get your shit together and commit. But either way, that man notices everything about you. Just like you notice everything about him. You probably know more about him than his damn mother."

"I'm not his mother," I jumped in.

"You sure as hell are not," Dawn countered. "Which is why I say you know more about him than his mother. You know every one of his likes and dislikes, his tastes. You even keep his favorite soda and beer in your house and you don't even like either of those."

"No fair. I'm just being friendly. I like to keep my friends happy."

Dawn crossed her arms. "Really?"

"Of course."

"I could use a glass of wine," she said. "You got any pinot grigio?"

I stared at her. She stared at me, knowing she had me. I knew pinot was her favorite wine, and no, I didn't have it on hand.

"Shut up."

"Case closed, Your Honor. Lock her up until she's ready to handle the truth."

I let out a breath and looked back at the necklace. "Shit, I can't believe this was in my couch. I didn't even say thank you."

"Nope, you didn't."

"I didn't answer his calls."

"Yep, that was you."

I stared at the little circle that seemed like a shield for the star in the center. "I really fucked up this time," I said. "I wouldn't blame him at all now for flying off to take that job in California. Hell, my dumb ass practically pushed him out the door."

Dawn was flipping through the magazine when she zinged me further still with her next words. "He's not going to California for a job. He's going surfing."

"He's going where?!"

She put the magazine down with a huff. Dawn looked me in the eye and for just a second I caught a glint of mischievousness. "Well, if you must know, he's gone surfing. Off to where..." She paused, looking up at my recessed lighting before coming back to me. "Oh yeah, it was Malibu. Or that's what I think. Some quickie learn-to-surf course." She leveled me with a look of *I told you so* and continued. "It all has to do with that Keanu quest of yours. I told him it was fine and that you said you were settled with the way things had turned out, but you know True. He thought you wouldn't be settled until you were good and settled. You want Keanu, he's gonna do whatever he can to get you Keanu."

"That idiot!" I blurted.

"Who?" Dawn countered. "Him or you? Seems like a toss-up to me."

I challenged her with a look. "Do not fucking start with me. I mean he could have just told me when I asked where he was going."

Of course, Dawn had a comeback. "And you could have just answered some of your fifty-eleven messages and texts from him over these past few weeks instead of avoiding him like you're starring in your own high school rom-com." She waved a hand. "Besides, what did you expect after all your drama? Plus, after all that, he sees you coming into your building with Mr. Just Doing Business. I swear I don't know what's with the two of you. I guess he's trying to prove something. Poor thing, competing with a dream of a man and scenarios of a life you made up in your head." She picked up the magazine again and started to flip through it. "Our dear nutty professor never had a chance."

I sat stock-still as the world seemed to get small and tight around me, then expand once again. I imagined True leaning casually back on my kitchen counter, coffee in hand. I looked toward my couch, where he'd be watching TV and fall asleep, traitorous Morphie snuggled up against his chest, before I'd wake him to go back to his own place. What a fool I was, I thought, blinking and seeing only empty spaces now where True should be.

"But surfing?" I said to Dawn, though it was more to myself. "That makes no damn sense! He doesn't know how to surf! Hell, he's hardly the most graceful at standing. How in the hell does he think he'd be able to surf? Do you know how dangerous surfing is? Not to mention how he hates the sand. The possibility of cleaning little grains out makes him practically break out into hives."

Dawn shrugged then and looked at me. "Yeah, but at this point he's also got this crazy wild love for you, so I guess that tops it all. I don't know. It's like the man's gone full Johnny Utah on us."

I let out a heavy huff. "So if he's Johnny Utah, then who does that make me?"

Dawn grinned. "Why Bodhi, of course. Always looking for that perfect wave."

CHAPTER 35

RUSH RUSH

BETHANY LU

Truman Erickson. Get your ass out of that water before you break your neck! And don't make me have to come in there after you, because if I do, you're going to wish you did break something!"

I couldn't believe that True actually had me out on Zuma Beach, yelling at the top of my lungs like somebody's old grandmother from the top-floor window of a New York City tenement. But here I was. After pressing Dawn only the tiniest bit more, she spilled it all on where True was going and why. It was nuts, and my guilt had me Googling cheap flights as fast as my fingers could take me.

What had pushed him to do such a thing? How could I have been so selfish to take him so off course and out of his norm that he would do something so nutty. Part of me was ridiculously flattered that he would do this for me, continue the quest to get to Keanu. But the bigger part of me was just plain mad. The question was, was I mad at him or myself? Honestly I didn't know. But I was pissed off and scared and right now I wanted True out of what looked like some really choppy and dangerous water.

Yet even in my anger, I noted the way the beach looked like Hollywood perfection. It was late afternoon, the sun was lowering in the sky and giving everything and everyone a rosy glow that could make a person believe in things like wonderland and magic and happily ever afters.

I stared out at the water, my eyes searching for True once again.

I found him easily, even though he was not much more than a faraway dot, dipping above and below the water on his board. Just another of the crowd. That part surprised me, made me look twice and wonder if I was focusing on the wrong dot. But this was True. Paddling. And then paddling some more, out toward the sun, and then paddling out some more. Away from me and farther from the safety of the shore.

I watched as the waves began to dip higher, then low and higher, then low and then scarily higher still. They swelled more and more, swelling the tension in my chest along with them.

All right, True, this was enough. *You've gone far enough!*

There was suddenly a strong shift in the wind, and the air around me got thick with the fragrance of cotton candy and tacos mixed with a light saltiness from the ocean. I looked out at True again and dammit if he wasn't coming in toward me, but the newfound madman was standing on top of his board like some sort of California surfer dude and not

Truman Erickson, professor of economics at NYU. I felt instant heat radiate from the sand up my legs and stop dead center between my thighs as I stared at him. I shivered. How could a person be so hot and so cold at the same time?

I didn't know if the question was for me or him as I took in his lean, muscular figure balanced between the water and sky under the setting sun.

A wave came up then, over his left side, and his hips tilted. I saw a flash in his eyes and the brightness of his smile before he went under the water. I gasped, holding my breath until I finally saw him bob back up.

Finally, I could talk some sense into him and we could go home and back to normal, whatever that was. But before I could even take a second easy breath, he was once again paddling away from me.

"Dammit, True!" I yelled.

It was starting to get dark...well, soon! I wanted to run in after him as if I was some super swimmer and could catch up.

The wind blew harder and my heart moved up about five inches, only to settle somewhere in the middle of my throat. This man was out of his mind. Who was he pretending to be all of a sudden? What was he trying to prove?

I continued to watch True and fight with my conflicted feelings. I hated this, hated being angry with him and with myself. What was I doing out here anyway?

"True!" I yelled, knowing there was no way he could hear me. And yet I yelled his name again, walking forward until my own bare feet hit the frigid water. "Truman Erickson, turn around and come in before you get hurt."

I shook my head at my own ridiculous desperation. Then I watched him pull himself up on the board again, tall, strong, happy and confident as he let go. It was like he surrendered control and became one with the water. His smile was so pure and magical that I felt it pierce my heart.

Oh, fuck it. Let him have his fun.

But then something happened. A heaviness seemed to come over the beach as a rolling wave started to pitch up. And further up, there came another. More and more began to advance faster than my mind could process.

I looked at the waves, then back at True. *Come back in. Come back to me where it's safe.*

But he looked like he had no intention of coming back. He looked too happy. Happier than I'd seen him in a long time. And so very free. Like there was a weight being lifted and he was doing exactly what he wanted. I stared at the beauty of seeing that emotion on his face.

"Whoo-hoo!! Go, True! You got this!"

He grinned wider and looked my way. The little shit. He'd known I was there the whole time. I couldn't help but laugh, and it was in that moment, the one of complete contented bliss, that I saw it all hit him. The water shifted and his face took on an immediate look of terror.

In less than a second, it seemed like everything shifted to black as True fought with his balance, the world above and below the water, and then he was gone.

Under.

The world below had won.

I held my breath, not wanting to believe what I saw had been real, even when I knew it was. So I waited. Waited for him to pop back up with that gorgeous smile or a grimace with that determined look in his eyes, ready to take on the challenge once again. I just needed him to come back up. And to be True.

But what came up and out of the water instead was a half-lifeless being, dragged along by another two surfers. True's head hung low, his mouth gaping open as he gasped for breath. Blood—oh my God, the blood!—dripped down the side of his beautiful head.

I was an asshole. No, I was an idiot and an asshole. Why did I follow him here? Distract him? Fuck, why did I start this quest and lead him here? Why did I even fall for him in the first place?

TRUE

Dammit! Over the past two days I'd wiped out dozens of times. But why did I have to do it so majorly in front of Lu?

After getting looked over by medics, I gathered my courage and peeked at Lu out of the corner of my eye. I could see she was still scared to death. Totally gorgeous and completely terrified. Sure, it was kind of scary for me too and hurt like a motherfucker, but seeing the look of pain in her eyes was much more painful than the knock on my head.

I hated that my wipeout had come right after getting a

glimpse of pure joy on her face, and then a peace like I hadn't seen on her in a long time. I didn't want to delude myself, but I couldn't help thinking I might have also caught a hint of love. Thinking that way would lead to too much heartbreak. Her peace and contentment was good enough for me. But any peace I thought I'd seen was gone now as I lifted my head.

I thanked my rescuers for hauling me out, for the beach's medics for checking me over and giving me a Band-Aid for the cut on the side of my forehead. Then I reached for Lu. "I'm fine, Lu. I'm fine." But she didn't respond. "Beth. Are you listening? I said I'm okay."

I pulled her to me, holding the tops of both of her arms, and kissed her. Urgently and sloppily. I was getting sand on her cheeks and in her hair, but I had to reassure her and let her know that everything was all right.

Suddenly she was pushing back at me. "You little asshole," she finally said, giving me a hard smack in my arm. Her eyes filled with tears and fading sunlight. "I hate you so much right now."

"No, you don't."

"I do," she snapped back. "And I'm going to hate you even more once you get properly checked out and they tell me you're okay. You could have died doing something as reckless as this."

"I'm not reckless, and besides, how is this any more reckless than what your Keanu does all the time?"

She smacked me again.

"Oww! Other side next time, please."

"Reckless is you saying stupid shit like that and thinking

that I'll let it pass or let this pass without you getting a full brain scan. You're acting as if I don't know that's all stunt doubles and movie magic shit."

Another lifeguard came over just then. "Why don't you guys call an ambulance and get him to a hospital?" Lu ordered. "He obviously has a serious concussion."

I shook the guy off and leaned down to kiss her again, pulling her in tight, loving the way she softened against me this time, like she'd been drained of fight. She opened her mouth, and her tongue danced with mine. Once again, I felt like I was going underwater. Drowning, but this time in the most delicious way.

Lu pushed me back again hard, and I stumbled. "Shit, Lu, aren't you the one who said I was hurt?"

"So do you need me to call an ambulance or the cops or both?" the lifeguard asked, his expression one of mild amusement and confusion.

Lu turned toward him. "Neither," she answered begrudgingly. "I guess he's fine."

"Exactly!" I said to her back as she started stomping her way down the beach.

I caught up with Lu only a short walk away.

She gave me a wobbly smile as I took her hand. "I hoped you'd come find me," I admitted even before my mind could warn me not to say the words.

"Then why didn't you invite me?" She reached up to touch the Band-Aid on my forehead but stopped short, shaking her head. "Forget it. I know why."

"You think you know a lot, huh?"

Her stare was sharp. "I know enough."

"Enough for what? To keep hiding away and running from your life?"

Lu whirled on me with anger sparking in her eyes. "And what about you? What are you suddenly running to? Why are you doing all of this when we were doing just fine?"

I snorted. God, she was exasperating. "Yeah sure. Whatever you say, Lu." I pulled her along.

"Where are we going?" she said, pulling her hand from mine.

I took her hand again. "We're going to get something to eat. All that surfing, kissing and arguing has me starving."

Now it was Lu's turn to snort. "The way you casually say it, as if you didn't just almost get killed."

I pulled her in close, taking in the impatient rigidness of her body and enjoying the tickle of her wild curls as they grazed my nose. She smelled delicious. Like the sea and sun mixed with jasmine and the comfort of home.

I caught a sparkle at her throat and realized she was wearing the necklace from Vegas. I touched it gently.

"Thank you for that," she said softly.

"I was wondering when you were going to get around to thanking me," I teased. "It's terribly rude of you not to at least have sent a card."

"Oh, hush. In my defense, I just found it. The whole bag fell between my couch cushions. You could have given it to me straight out and gotten your thank-you in person."

"Oh, really? And what sort of thanks would you have given me?" The fact that she wore it today, all the way out here, was more than thanks enough for me, but I didn't tell her that. Instead, I just looked at her as she looked up at me. The sun danced in her eyes and played tricks with my heart.

Lu bit her bottom lip as she thought of her response. Finally, she shook her head. "Feed me first and then I'll show you." She pulled my arm to lead me along the beach, but instinctively I pulled her back. I captured her mouth again and kissed her long and slow, wanting to hold on to this moment until the sun set and pray tomorrow never came.

"I love you like crazy, Bethany Lu Carlisle. Have loved you forever," I murmured into her mouth.

She let out a long breath. Becoming one with me as the waves crashed and the world moved around us.

I told myself then that the sounds I heard around me were her telling me she loved me too.

That night we ate, made love, ate and made love again. I knew as the night turned to morning and I couldn't fight sleep any longer that our last time was her last goodbye.

The one we'd both been avoiding for the past twenty years.

"You are going to leave me, aren't you?" I asked her after she came out of the bathroom and snuggled against me.

She didn't move or look up at me. Only snuggled in further and wrapped her leg over the top of mine. "I don't know what you're getting at," she finally said. "You'll leave me one day. Maybe soon. Hell, you're in California already. Your dream job is within your reach."

I grabbed hold of her thigh and pulled her in closer. "I'm already doing my dream job right now. Why are you trying to demote me? If anything, it's you who's constantly on the run. Is it fun for you, making me chase after you?"

Lu looked up at me, and in the dim light I could see the worry etched on her face. "When have I ever asked you to make me your job?"

Oh, fuck.

I pushed up. "Lu, come on. You know I didn't mean it like that. I'd never think of you that way. I never have. Now what is it? Why are you fighting so damn hard to push me away when we can go back to New York and have this and more? We can have us."

She shook her head. "We and us is not for the real world back home. What we have, this thing right now, is for here or New Mexico or Vegas, but not for every day."

I let out a breath. "Why? Why would it be any different from what we already have except we won't be walking on eggshells all the time?"

Lu stared at me. "Because of that. I never walked on eggshells with you, True, and now all of a sudden, I find out that's what you've been doing with me? You talk of loving me forever, but how can you even know if that will last? I can't take the chance that it won't and lose both this and what we had. If I had to choose, it would be what we had. What I've always known. At least there I felt secure. Hell, you could have died today!"

To that, I had no answers. All I could do was wrap my arms around her, sink down with her deeper into the pillows and hold her tight while I could. She wanted what she'd always known. And what was that? Only sadness brought on by me. She was right. I was living in a fantasy. We both had been.

We were silent for a long time. But I finally found my

voice and the confidence to ask her what I needed to. "Lu." I paused and took a deep breath, already feeling out of air. "Beth, I need to know this and I need you to be honest. Don't think about my feelings but only think of yours when you answer: Are you mad at me? Have you always been a little bit mad that it was Cole and not me? Is that why you can't love me? Because I took away your happiness?"

Fuck all, I was crying and now I couldn't stop. If I was naked, I might as well go all the way. Be naked and true. If I couldn't finally do that, then I might as well change my stupid name.

She pushed away from my chest again and looked at me as if she didn't believe what I'd asked. "So now you just want to be ridiculous on top of crazy? Did you really get a concussion out there in the surf?" she asked. "How could you possibly take away my happiness? And why would I be mad at you?"

A lump had formed in my throat and it was hard to talk, but I did. "Before you left for school you asked me to look out for him. I promised you I would," I whispered. "I'm sorry I failed you."

The words I'd been wanting to say for so long were finally out. I thought I'd have some relief but all I felt was small. "Sure," I continued, "I know, rationally it was not my fault. I didn't give Cole keys to the car or make the decision for him to race, but I could have been there. I could have seen the signs of his recklessness. I should have warned him against something like that. Those kids. Partying. Wanting to do dumb shit to fit in.

"But after you'd left I got selfish. Selfish and stupid and I took my eye off what I should have been focusing on. Seeing Cole felt like too much of a reminder of you, and I retreated. Like a lovesick turtle, I hid in my shell while my friend, my silly reckless friend, pushed himself to fit in. I didn't stop to think that he may have needed me too. That he was missing you just as much as I was. I'm sorry, Lu. So sorry. To you. To your parents. To Cole. Please forgive me for not looking after him like you asked me to when you left and stealing your happiness. I'll hate myself forever for it."

Lu let out a long sigh, then lay back down and closed her eyes.

I reached down and pulled her back up to look at me. "Did you hear me? I'm sorry for stealing your happiness."

She pulled her hands free and pushed at my chest. "Okay, so now is when you get over yourself, Truman Erickson, and bring it down a notch or three. Nobody can steal my happiness except me. And I turned that into my other full-time job. If anything, I stole yours. How long are you going to take on the burden of a problem that isn't yours? You were just a kid back then and still you pulled me back from the brink all those years ago. And the worst part is I've let you keep pulling me back ever since."

She shook her head and sighed. "How many opportunities have I kept you from? How much of your life have I stolen?" She pointed a pretty long finger at me now, almost touching the tip of my nose.

"You're so wrong," I said. But I don't know if she heard me or was pretending to be brave and purposefully not hearing me.

Lu shook her head. "Now I'm sure you and I both have

enough regret to throw out into the sea and surf back in on, but neither of us is responsible for Cole's death and we both need to leave that regret out there. Let it wash away. It's between God, the universe and Cole now. Between taking on the guilt of going away to school and leaving him…" Her voice started to crack, and I could almost physically feel her pain.

"I'm sorry. I really am," I said. "Just stop. We don't have to talk about it. I shouldn't have brought it up."

"It's okay," she replied, meeting my gaze with more determination now. "You did bring it up and that's good. For too long we only danced around his memory and never talked about what it did to us. I think it's something we both need to work on. I know I do."

She let out a long breath before continuing. "I also know that for too long I've lived with the pain of losing him in a blink. I questioned myself time and again with what-ifs and if-onlys. But the fact is, Cole died. Died without our permission because it wasn't ours to give. His life was not our responsibility."

Her voice broke on a hard sob then, and it nearly ripped me apart. I tried to pull her in close, but she resisted and looked at me, continuing. "Just like it wasn't for me to tell you to watch over him. Now, will you please forgive me for that? All I can say to that is I was stupid and I'm sorry. For all I've put on you, I'm most sorry for that."

I reached out to wipe away the tears sliding down her cheeks. "But if only I'd told him not to do it or been there to see he was struggling. I should have been the one to stop it."

"No buts, True. We all suffered here. I lost my brother and my parents their son. It's time we all stopped beating ourselves up and let Cole rest. Let ourselves live and stop tying each other up in those awful memories."

I nodded to let her know that I'd heard her. "I'm still sorry," I said, and I was. Though I know she was right in all that she said. She opened her mouth to argue with me again, but I shook my head. "Please just let me say this, Lu. I am sorry. Sorry we lost him and so sorry for the pain I saw in you for so long. If I could take it all away I would."

She nodded then. "I know."

I looked out the window and toward the changing light. I patted her thigh and pulled her in by her waist, turning her around to snuggle against me, spooned tight, back to front. I breathed in the sweet smell of her. "I'm not sorry for this, though. This is perfect."

There was silence, too long a silence as I waited for her answer.

"Neither am I," she finally whispered. "Now go to sleep. Tomorrow is a long day if we're going to head up the coast to Santa Barbara. I'm tired and D-Day is here. I might as well put closure on this quest and be done. Over twenty years is long enough for an unrequited love, don't you think?"

Closure. I hated the finalization in her words. I know she was talking about Keanu and tomorrow being the big day, but why did it feel like she was talking about us?

CHAPTER 36

MAYBE MY ALWAYS

BETHANY LU

I'd made it. Finally. Here I was at a beautiful hotel on a hilltop overlooking a gorgeous vineyard in Santa Barbara, California, with Keanu possibly on the other side of the door, and I was hesitating.

All I could think about was how pissed True was going to be that I snuck out early, took the car and left him sleeping. I also really wished he were with me to share this moment, this view and maybe have some wine with me.

I shook my head. It was nuts. I was nuts. Keanu was in my reach, and I just needed to finish this. Sure, True would be mad, but I had to do this on my own. I had to show him that I could make a fool of myself, take the rejection and still stand. Stand and get on with my life, by myself, and move on. Just as he should too.

Everything went shaky inside of me with that thought, though I knew it was right. Even after our talk last night, even after our lovemaking, even though I still wanted True. We couldn't let our youth and past pain control us. Not anymore.

Oddly, getting past security in the hotel and to this point felt easyish, almost too easy. Using my CIU method and using it with authority got me past all security and check-points. I just acted like I belonged and just didn't know quite where I was going. I took a breath and tried to shrug off my feeling of unease.

Maybe it was easy because it was meant to be. The voice in my head sounded so much like Keanu that I almost thought he'd said it through the door. Yeah, I was losing it. But if I had calculated correctly, Keanu was just past this door, and either my ending or my next chapter would be on the other side.

"It's now or after the 'I dos,' Lu," I told myself as I let out a breath and opened the door.

In the span of that opening it was as if the past ninety days flashed before my eyes. True chasing that bus, the Wonder Wheel, the festival party, Aquaman and loving True under the stars. I could see him in my mind's eye as he was when I silently shut our hotel room door. Naked and lovely and thankfully breathing well and evenly after the surfing accident. I was thankful. Grateful that he was okay but so afraid he wouldn't be the next time he did something ridiculous for me.

True didn't hear me as I'd said my final goodbye, since I'd only said it to myself. But I hoped when he read the note I left he'd understand. When he got the breakfast I sent and the first-class ticket back to New York. I hoped he'd forgive me and not be too mad. I had to believe he wouldn't be, that he'd understand and in that way remain my True.

Oh well, this was it. Time to face Keanu. I cleared my throat and smiled, only to face two bodyguards when I opened the door.

Well shit. I looked at one and blinked because he seemed so familiar, like Dave Chappelle or maybe a cousin of his? And to his side was that intern from the Wonder Wheel.

Before I could form what to say, a voice rang out: "Let her through, Gary."

Keanu.

I knew it was him. Just as I'd imagined in every dream I'd had when the world closed in tight, or worse, got too big. And here he was standing in front of an altar that faced an open window that looked out on nothing but sky. He could've been posing for another movie.

"Breathtaking," I whispered.

And as he turned, I got a head-on, face-to-face look at my dream for the first time.

"No, you are," he said and smiled.

I blinked as my mind stuttered and Keanu laughed. "Sorry, that was too easy. It's nice to meet you, Lu. Or is it Beth?"

His smile was beautiful, he was beautiful, but still I couldn't help but prickle when he called me Beth. "Um, Lu is fine, thanks. That's what all my friends call me."

He came toward me and stopped about ten feet away. "I'm glad you consider me a friend."

"And I'm glad that you consider not having me immediately kicked out of here." My eyes darted around quickly. "Unless the police are already on their way and if that's the case, let me start with an apology and then I can leave. You'll never again see this highly suspect but in no way stalkerazzi face again." I took a step back.

He frowned and cocked his head to the side. "Is that what you came for? All this way to say we're 'friends' and then leave?"

The air was heavy as he waited for an answer to what should have been a simple question, but the problem was I still had no answer. I lived having no answers.

"I don't know," I said, then leaned on one of the spindly chairs and almost fell over. Keanu stepped forward, but I held up a hand to stop him as I righted myself. "I'm fine. I will be fine," I said, looking into his beautiful brown eyes.

"Are you sure?"

I nodded. "I am. Or I will be. The truth is, I came to say don't get married. Don't get married and please don't quit acting. You and your movies are a wonderful escape from…I don't know if you know, but it's a lifeline for some. And if you need a rest, I get it. But maybe not announce retirement and just continue to give people hope that there will be something coming next." I cleared my throat. "It's the hope that's the important part."

His brows rose and I laughed. "Annnnd now you're probably rethinking the cops thing. I get it. I might as well end with a bang. I also was going to make a plea for you to marry me. Me, a person you don't even know, the same as I don't know you." I smirked at myself then. "Ugh. I'm sorry, I should go. Yes, it was crazy and I apologize once again for taking up your time." I turned and took two steps back toward the door.

"But why would you want to marry someone you don't know?"

Dammit, Keanu! Can't you just let me and my mortification go?

I turned back and looked at him. "Just for that reason. I don't know you and you don't know me. The idea of not having a past to pull pain from. Doesn't that sound amazing?" I laughed then, trying my best to find someplace within myself to fall back on. "And hey, I'm not the worst catch."

Keanu chuckled and nodded. I took it as a good sign. "No past pain," he said. "Now that is interesting."

"Yep, no past. Only future. The possibilities are endless. No attachments, no engagements, no boyfriends. No—"

He cut me off. "True love?"

I frowned, for the first time the whole situation really sinking in. How had he known it was me coming in? How did he even know my name?

"Wait. What are you talking about true loves?"

"I'm just wondering what past you're running from to bring up marriage to a stranger and if there was a regret you were leaving behind."

"We all have those. But maybe I'm just trying to right some wrongs. Let someone in to let someone go. Let him know he doesn't have to take up my empty spaces anymore, bring me coffee, walk my dog. Sit with me in a dark movie theater. That I'll still be just fine."

"I don't know. Sounds like you're leaving a lot to chance." He took a step closer and looked me in the eye. "I mean, what if we're not compatible?"

I shook my head. "We? Now you're just screwing with me, Keanu. Of course we are probably not compatible. I'm not compatible with anyone right now. The quicker I get that into my head, the quicker I can let True go and be over him."

There was silence as we stared at each other. I narrowed my eyes. *True love*, he'd said. I looked over at the Ferris Guy and the woman. "Yo, Gary," I said quickly, and he turned. I raised a brow.

Keanu laughed. "I guess it's coming together. How you got in here so easily."

"I think it's starting to," I said.

"And I think you've been regretting everything that's transpired this morning since you left your hotel room."

"You really know everything, don't you?"

He raised his shoulders and shrugged. "I don't know everything. But you can rest assured, I'm not getting married." I opened my mouth, but he continued. "At least not today. This is all for a shoot and I really need to get on the studio about their social media postings. And no, I'm not retiring. I'm having too much fun on this adventure. I also know that for you, I'm not the one. You already know that in your heart."

I sighed. "That is literally something The One would say. And of course I know it. But I ruined my One, or if I stay with him I will. I can't take that risk."

"But isn't that what love is? A risk."

I frowned. "Who knew you could be so infuriating, Keanu?"

He laughed. "Believe me, plenty of people know."

I stared at him. "So you spoke to True?"

He nodded and I lowered my head. "Shit, he must really be pissed to have found a way to get in touch with you. I guess I should say goodbye and call him."

"Or you could head out that side door and try and catch him. He was just here. Do you really think you could have gotten through security as easily as you did?"

"Here, as in here-here?!"

He nodded. "About ten minutes ago. I have to say your whole plan, though flawed, made for one hell of an adventure... When he told me about the Hero Con, what a near miss."

Keanu was still talking, but all I could think of was True and where he was now. The fact that he'd gotten up, rented a car and beat me here was amazing. Maybe I shouldn't have stopped for those souvenirs or for coffee, but there was no way I was making the trip without it.

"Thanks, I have to go," I blurted, and Keanu went silent and wide-eyed. I didn't think many women voluntarily leave his presence, but hey. Then he nodded and pointed to the side door again.

"He went that way," he said.

"Do you think I can catch him?"

"If anybody can, I bet it would be you," he said.

I stood and looked at him for a moment more, fully taking in my dream and then silently letting it go.

"Are you going to go, or are you going to stand here staring at me while the man you really want is out there wandering the vineyard hoping you'll appear?" Keanu broke in.

I shook my head and smiled. "You're right. And thank you. Wish me luck, Mr. Anderson." I headed through the chairs, toppling and righting a few.

"I would, but I have a feeling you won't need it, Ms. Carlisle."

CHAPTER 37

MAGNIFICENT

TRUE

Why was I even here? I paced the pathway outside Keanu's dream wedding suite and waited for Lu. Would I spend my entire life either chasing, racing or waiting for Bethany Lu Carlisle? Shit, I was tired and my head hurt.

I pulled her note out of my pocket and read it again.

Dearest True,

I'm giving you your wings. Thank you for giving me mine. Fly, darling. Fly.

Lovingly,
Lu

Melodramatic much? *Fly?* Then she had the nerve to draw a bird. After the way we both came, multiple times practically flying around the room, I get a sketch of a little bird. The fuck?

I crumpled the letter in my hands. I could head to the airport. Trade my first-class ticket in for a flight anywhere but New York and just get home whenever. Maybe I'd go to a different airport. Better to not run into Lu there. She wanted me to fly, well then why shouldn't I?

I turned down the little lane to head to the parking lot. But what if Lu was in trouble? What if she was in there and Keanu was breaking her heart? What if he didn't stick to script and called security on her?

Shit! No, I told myself, she's fine. Of course she's fine. I had almost convinced myself of it when I heard the sound of rushed footsteps on the gravel behind me.

I turned and there she was, looking incredibly beautiful. She also looked seriously mad. Not happy or in love, but mad. Dammit, Keanu!

"What happened in there? Was Keanu mean to you? What did he say? Are you all right?" I placed my hands on her shoulders and studied her closely.

She pushed my arms down. "I'm fine. And it should be me with the questions. Starting with have you always been this deceptive or is this a new thing you picked up?"

"What are you talking about?"

"I'm talking about how I feel like an idiot and you obviously set all this up from the beginning. It's a straight-up Keanu ruse and what for? Was it to continue to keep tabs on me or was it just to get me to fall in love with you and make it harder to let you go?"

"I didn't set all this up for that," I said. "I wanted you

to get what you wanted. To be happy to find Keanu, get happy again and—"

I stopped as the words she'd said finally caught up with my brain, heart and soul and clicked. "Wait, did you just say you love me, or did you say you fell in love with me?"

She sighed and tapped her foot. "Is there a difference?"

I nodded. "Yes, to you, there surely is. But either way, what did you say? Would you care to repeat it?"

"I'm in love with you! There, are you satisfied? I said it. So now what?" She threw up her hands, then flopped them back down. I could see the exhaustion coming over her when she next looked up at me. She spoke hesitantly. "Now, do you love me?"

I sagged against the car and reached for her hand. I needed to feel some part of her skin make contact with mine. "Oh, Lu, why are you asking a question when you already know the answer? You've known the answer for years. Yes, of course I'm in love with you. Can you still doubt it?"

She sighed. "I know. And yes, I've always known."

"Then why do you doubt it? Why are you scared of my love for you?"

She pulled her hand away. "It's not your love I'm afraid of. It's me loving you that terrifies the hell out of me."

I pulled her in close, not able to be apart from her a moment longer. "Oh, honey, like I told you before: Just hold tight. You may be afraid, but I've got enough courage for both of us to make this thing work. I've got you, and I'm not letting go. Not ever."

She pushed back from my chest and gave me a crooked

smile as she touched my bandage and looked into my eyes. "Either that wave hit you harder than we thought or this mad quest has finally gotten to you. You look like my True, but you're sounding strangely like some B-movie action hero."

I grinned. "It's A-list for me all the way. Didn't you know I won a door-shoving match with the Captain?"

Lu tilted her head and made a face. "Captain who? Crunch?"

I pulled her in tighter, cupping her ass and pressing her against me. "Oh, just shut it and kiss me. I swear, everyone's a critic."

EPILOGUE

A WALK IN THE CLOUDS

BETHANY LU

I couldn't believe it.

One year to the day since I had confessed to Keanu, and now here we were, having a wedding and this time it was a wedding for real.

"And they say dreams can't come true," I murmured as I looked at myself and made one final adjustment to my earrings before my father came to walk me from the Board-walk down toward the beach.

When dreaming of fantasy wedding spots, I never thought of the beach at Coney Island, but once True proposed on the moonlight Wonder Wheel ride six months ago I couldn't dream of anyplace else.

Our affair was smallish with about 150 guests. I would've gone for less, but my mother and Dawn wanted our big day to have as much coverage as possible.

"You may be taking on a new name, but Lu Carlisle is

still a brand," she said. "And we're selling that." I admired her determination and the masterful way she navigated the tightrope between BFF and best agent ever.

True had an agent now too, after a tweet dubbing him The Sexy Economist had gone viral. With a new book deal and more TV appearances, my man was in high demand. So high that he had no problem securing a year off from his teaching job.

Dad had gone for one last bathroom run, and I was waiting in the side vestibule for our perfect moment between sunset and darkness. Dawn came up behind me with her escort, Morphie, who looked like he was barely tolerating the crystal-studded bow tie Dawn had made for him to match the crystals that accented the neckline of her dress.

She was giving him a stern talking-to. "Now Morph, you be a good boy and don't piss on the runner and Auntie Dawn will buy you all the treats you want and a pretty new hat."

"My dog doesn't need any more outfits from you, woman."

She scratched Morphie under his chin. "Aww, he loves it and has *the* best taste. When I had him choose between the cheap satin and the custom bow tie I had made for him for today, he picked mine right away."

"That proves nothing."

She huffed. "It proves that he at least knows how to dress the part when standing by my side."

I looked at her, confused, and then down at Morphie. "You know, I never thought I'd say this, but you may be getting too attached to my dog."

"Hush, you. Don't rain on my parade just because you're about to go off into your bliss."

I grinned. "I am, aren't I?"

Dawn grinned even wider than me. "Hon, I think you always have been."

Just then my father walked in. He looked like he was about to burst into tears at any moment. "Hey there, mister, don't you start. I'm too old for you to be at the tearful 'giving away my little baby' stage."

He blinked at the tears really fast now. "As long as I'm breathing, you will always be my baby and don't you forget it," he told me.

One of the wedding planner's attendants nodded our way, indicating it was time. The sun would be setting soon, and we were trying to catch the light perfectly. "So you're ready for this?" I asked my dad.

He chuckled. "Shouldn't I be asking you that question?"

I laughed. "Oh, Dad, I'm so ready."

The sound of the violinist's wedding march began, and then was joined by a bass guitar.

He was here!

My heart did a little flip and I looked up from my start down the aisle and there was Keanu, playing for me and my sexy economist. He gave me that smile that always hit me right in the heart, then put his guitar down and sauntered toward me to take my other elbow.

"A little eager, aren't you?" my dad said.

"Sorry about that, Mr. Carlisle, but I think it's best given her penchant for the unexpected if we just go on and get her married."

"I think you're right about that."

I looked down the aisle just as True stepped from behind the arch and came into view.

After that moment I wasn't aware of anything. Not my dad, mom, Morphie, who got loose and started barking around True, or even Keanu by my side. All I saw was True.

All I ever saw was True.

At the end of the runner, Dad kissed me on the cheek and went to join Mom in the audience. Keanu put my hand inside of True's, and it felt just like home.

"I thought you guys were going to take all night to get down here," True said. "You had me nervous for a minute, Lu. I was afraid you and our officiant here might make a run for it."

I shook my head. "The only place I'm running from now on is home to you, Mister Er-ick-son."

He leaned in and kissed me, and our guests all laughed, gasped and cheered in unison. "That's Mister Husband to you from now on, my dear wife."

ACKNOWLEDGMENTS

The time in the outside world leading up to the publication of this book has been more than a challenge for so many of us, and because of that, I'm overflowing with even more gratefulness than usual as I write the acknowledgments for what I've come to know and love as Keanu90. Writing this rom-com has given me many moments of unexpected joy in a year when joyful moments were in short supply. I mean, how often can you have full-on Keanu movie marathons and count them as research? So there is something to be grateful for and pause to acknowledge right there.

Now with that said, I'd like to start by giving all thanks to God for (1) keeping me safe and (2) keeping me going throughout this year. This one little uninspired line of thanks is not enough, but it's all I've got.

I'd also like to thank my extraordinary editor at Forever, Leah Hultenschmidt, for her amazing insight, patience and believing in my wild idea right from the start.

And I must take a moment to thank the outstanding Beth de Guzman for also believing in the joy of Keanu90. Thank you so much, Beth!

A huge thanks to Estelle Hallick, Sabrina Flemming,

Mari Okuda, and the rest of the team at Forever for championing Keanu90 all the way. I couldn't have done it without you all. Books coming together seriously take villages and mine rocks!

I'd like to give a special thanks to Sabrina again and Daniela Medina in the art department for my gorgeous cover. This cover is a rom-com lover's dream come true. Thank you so much!

Now a big thanks and tackle hug to my incredible agent, Evan Marshall. Thank you for never thinking any idea I send you is too farfetched, or at least not saying those words out loud so I can hear them.

As ever, thanks to my family: Ma, James, Ash and Semaj for always having my back. And to my Destin Divas for being a safe space in the not always safe world, not to mention the best and most talented group of writer women ever.

Synithia, Farrah and Pris. Thanks for being the most stable of sounding boards when I was feeling wobbly.

To Wendy for being my Gemini ride or die. I can't thank you enough, but I'll keep trying.

Karli, our rooftop summers were the best of times.

To my Dear Twins, Kayla and Will, for being my reason for it all...always. And to Willie for being my forever.

And finally, to you, dear readers, for joining me on this road trip, I thank you. I hope you enjoy taking the ride as much as I enjoyed being the driver.

As always, I'm wishing you all joyful reading.

KMJ

ABOUT THE AUTHOR

A native New Yorker, K.M. Jackson, who also writes as Kwana Jackson, spent her formative years on the A train, where she had two dreams: (1) to be a fashion designer and (2) to be a writer. After spending over ten years designing women's sportswear for various fashion houses, this self-proclaimed former fashionista took a leap of faith and decided to pursue her other dream of being a writer.

A longtime advocate for diversity and equality, she is a mother of twins and currently lives in a suburb of New York with her husband.

You can learn more at:
KMJackson.com
Twitter @KwanaWrites
Instagram @KwanaWrites
Facebook.com/KMJackson